For Trish—

The Wren

Wings of the West
Book One

by

Kristy McCaffrey

I hope you enjoy the series!

My Very Best—
Kristy McCaffrey
xoxo

Books and Additional Works by Kristy McCaffrey

Wings of the West Series
The Wren
The Dove
The Sparrow
The Blackbird
The Bluebird

Echo of the Plains (Short Novella)

Stand-Alone Novels
Into The Land Of Shadows

Anthologies
Lassoing A Groom
Cowboy Cravings
Cowboys, Creatures, and Calico Vol. 2
Cowboy Kisses

Short Novellas
Canyon Crossing
Lily and Mesquite Joe
A Westward Adventure
The Crow and the Coyote
The Crow and the Bear

Long Novellas
Alice: Bride of Rhode Island

"I...commend McCaffrey for the historical accuracy of her stories...a phenomenal read that I'd recommend to anyone who enjoys historical romance, with a hint of the other."

~ Jonel Boyko, Reviewer

"Ancient Hopi and Havasupai legends have a new voice in McCaffrey. Her inspired writing made her main character's mystical journey into another realm entirely believable and kept the pages turning long into the night."

~ City Sun Times

THE BLACKBIRD

"With dastardly villains, plenty of action, a strong heroine, surprising twists and turns, and a sexy cowboy, all underlined by a sensual love story, this historical western romance has something for everyone."

~ Janna Shay, InD'tale Magazine

Dedication

For Kevin,
with love

Chapter One

North Texas
May 1877

"Are you lost, miss?"

Startled, the woman turned in her saddle and glared wide-eyed at him. Beneath the brim of her dark hat, vibrant blue eyes watched him.

In this isolated corner of the Texan plains, the last thing Matthew Ryan expected to find was a lone woman atop a horse, staring at the three gravesites nestled into the hillside. A vision of a girl from long ago, her blue eyes just as vivid, flashed in his head. A lifetime had passed since that August night when he last saw Molly Hart on this earth. The loss, only a dull ache now, never fully seemed to leave him.

"No, I'm not lost," she answered. Her voice was rich and layered, and slid around him like a warm fire after a cold spell.

"You're a long way from nowhere," he said, shifting in his saddle and adjusting his hat as a gust of wind blasted them. A storm brewed, teasing the land with its ever-increasing presence. Dark clouds pressed low on the horizon, and Matt suspected that soon neither he nor the woman would be riding far. He ought to leave now.

"So are you," she replied.

1

"Did you know the Hart family?" He inclined his head toward the graves.

The woman turned away from him and nodded almost imperceptibly. Strands of dark hair escaped the confines of her hat.

"My name is Matt Ryan." He scanned the small, enclosed valley and the dilapidated house about a quarter-mile away, the remnants of the Hart Ranch. A corral, stables, and bunkhouse also still stood, overrun by tumbleweeds and dust, ghostly sentinels of a once-vibrant place. "My family has a ranch about thirty miles east of here."

When his gaze settled back on the woman from nowhere, he found her staring at him in genuine shock. "What's wrong?" he asked immediately.

Her horse, a fine-looking chestnut mare—the hue almost the same shade as the mystery woman's hair—pranced nervously in response to her rider's agitation.

"Matthew Ryan?"

"Have we met before?" he asked.

Instead of answering, the woman questioned him again. "How did the Hart family die? How did *Molly Hart* die?"

Matt paused. It had been ten years since he'd been to this place, ten years since the funeral when the three graves had been dug and the murdered bodies laid to rest. Was he a coward for not visiting sooner? He wasn't sure. All he knew was Molly Hart's death weighed on him still, like a vice around his guilty conscience for not staying with her that night.

"About ten years ago, the ranch was raided during a party. Mr. and Mrs. Hart were killed. Molly disappeared." His tone was even, a mannerism

2

honed during his years in the army and the Texas Rangers. Hiding his emotions had become second nature, a useful trait in his line of work. But at what cost, he sometimes wondered.

"And that made you think she was dead?" Distress played across the woman's face.

"We didn't. Not at first. Not until we found her."

"*What* exactly did you find?"

Wind whistled through the valley and black thunderclouds formed quickly overhead. It was said if you didn't like the weather in this part of Texas then just wait five minutes. It often changed that swiftly. He and the woman needed to find shelter.

Reluctantly, he pushed his mind to answering her. "A badly burned body."

The woman struggled to rein in her horse when a lightning bolt shot out of the sky. "How could you be certain it was her?" she demanded.

"A small gold cross she always wore was found near the body. And the remains…were the right size."

She turned back to the graves, giving Matt a view of her profile. Though she was dressed like a man in dark trousers and an oversized pale shirt, it was still obvious she was a young woman. Slender hands grasped her horse's reins and a pleasing feminine arc graced her posture. Despite the animal's uneasiness, it was apparent she had a natural instinct in the saddle.

"What's your name?" he asked loudly, to be heard over the howling wind.

She nailed him with a look of distrust, disbelief and…abandonment? The thought baffled him.

Rain began to pour down in sheets.

"Let's get down to the house," he yelled, immediately guiding his horse down the slight slope they currently occupied. Over his shoulder he saw the woman hesitate, glancing at the broken-down remains of the ranch house with fear in her eyes.

But when he arrived at the deserted dwelling, she was right behind him. "I'll take the horses to the stables and see if I can find a dry spot for them." He pulled his saddlebags, then hers, from the animals and handed them to her. "Why don't you go inside and see if there's a place where we can wait this storm out."

She nodded apprehensively.

While he tended to the horses—the stable was in better shape than he would've thought—he wondered about the woman and how she could have known the Hart family. Ten years ago she would have been just a child, probably not much older than Molly herself, and Matt was certain he would've remembered her. The summer the Harts were killed he had worked at their ranch, helping out Robert Hart at his pa's request.

It was during that time Matt's friendship with nine-year-old Molly had blossomed. On the surface they'd appeared mismatched—he was eight years her senior—but their easy camaraderie put him in mind of a sister he'd never had. The little sprite had worked her way into his heart in no amount of time, and he became her friend and protector. But it was in that last role that he failed, and even today the cost was almost more than he could bear.

Running through the rain, he nearly barreled into the woman in the front entryway. He wondered if she'd moved since entering the house. Immediately he pulled his six-shooter, scanning for a wild animal that might've taken refuge from the storm as well.

Reaching out, he touched her arm.

She jumped.

"Easy," he murmured, gently moving her aside. Walking through the house, he inspected every room. Water leaked in several places, but luckily there was no sign of anyone, or anything, else. "The back bedroom seems dry."

Instead of following him, the woman with the penetrating blue eyes and intriguing voice paused at the threshold of a different bedroom.

Matt frowned. When did he begin thinking of her as intriguing?

From the end of the hallway where he stood, a flash of lightning suddenly illuminated the almost-darkened house. The rain had plastered the woman's pale shirt to her, clearly outlining her very feminine curves. Matt forced himself to look away. He wasn't of a mind to take advantage of a lone female in the middle of nowhere.

She disappeared into the bedroom. He removed his hat and ran fingers through damp hair. Attraction or not, there was something strange about this woman. He followed behind her.

"Do you know what happened to Mary and Emma?" she asked softly, her back to him.

So, she knew of Molly's two sisters. "They went to San Francisco to live with their Aunt Catherine."

A quick exhalation, and her shoulders relaxed slightly. Bending down, she retrieved an old, filthy doll. "This was Emma's," she whispered.

"How is it you know so much about the family who lived here?" Matt asked, suddenly frustrated with this woman he hardly knew. "Who are you?"

As she turned to face him, a bright flash of light revealed tears running down her face. "I could tell you, but I think now you won't believe me. I've been such a fool, thinking I could come back, that everything would be the same." Staring at the doll in her hands, she said quietly, "A lifetime lost, for all of us."

"*What* is your name?" Matt demanded, feeling an uneasy sensation in his gut. It couldn't be, it really couldn't. It wasn't possible.

Even as she spoke, his mind and heart railed against it.

Her richly textured voice floated through the clash of rain and distant thunder.

"Molly Hart."

Chapter Two

Molly watched Matt's reaction in the fading light. His tall frame dominated the room as he stood utterly still, staring at her as if he were a hunter going for the kill. Disbelief and shock easily showed on his angular features, and water dripped from dark hair onto a drenched shirt. The anger she sensed lent him a feral expression—or was it his taut muscles, tensed as if ready to attack?

"What is your name?" he demanded again. "Your *real* name."

"I just told you."

"And I just told you that Molly's dead. I don't find your little joke amusing."

"I wish all of this could be a joke," she said past the constriction in her throat. "But it's just a nightmare that never seems to end."

An endless, ten-year nightmare. She hadn't even known until two weeks ago that her parents were dead. A trader en route through the New Mexico Territory had told her—evidence of how little contact she'd had with white men over the years.

It had devastated her.

Her one hope had always been to return home to her family. Now that she had, the irretrievable loss of her childhood was a pain so sharp she almost couldn't breathe.

She would never see her folks again. Even during the past week, she'd found the knowledge difficult to grasp completely. At least her sisters had survived. It was something; a tenuous link to grasp within the shaky foundation of her life.

Her own death, however, was the final blow, dropping any semblance of security she might have felt. For ten years, she'd hoped and dreamed for a rescue from her captors. For ten years, she'd wondered how and when she might escape and return home. But everyone had thought she was dead. No one had ever searched for her. Matthew Ryan, her childhood friend, had never looked for her.

Matt, who stood across from her now, a virtual stranger, a man she would almost fear if she hadn't known him so well years ago.

"Mind explaining how the hell you could be Molly Hart?" His voice brimmed with contempt.

"I was taken that night by the men who attacked the ranch."

"Comanche?"

She shook her head. "No. A group of Comanche attacked us much later, after we'd ridden a while. Most of the men were killed, and nearly all were scalped. The Indians took me then."

A flash of lightning illuminated the room and lit the broken frame of a bed still sitting in the corner. Her little sister's bed. She and Emma had shared this room as children.

"And how do you explain the girl's body we found? And the gold cross?"

"After I rode with the Comanche for a time, another band joined up with us. There were several white captives with them. One was a girl near my age." Molly paused, then continued quietly, "She was quite hysterical, and the Comanche were impatient. One of them shot her with an arrow, nailing her to a tree. Some of the others seemed upset at the one who had done this, but by then it was too late. She was already dead. So they burned her. I threw my cross at her feet—it was all I could do for her. It was all I could manage because I was trying so hard not to scream myself."

Molly swallowed past the lump in her throat, remembering the terror she had lived with in those early days. On the edge of her mind, the thought had loomed time and again that her own gruesome end was imminent.

Matt appeared pushed to the edge, uncertainty clouding his features.

"If what you're saying is true," he ground out, "then where've you been for the last ten years? It wasn't unheard of for Comanches to barter their prisoners to the army in exchange for goods. I handled such exchanges myself several times."

"You did?" Had he been nearby during her captivity? Could he have somehow helped her? "Were you in the army?"

"For a time."

"I don't remember much contact with other white men. I wasn't really kept prisoner. I was adopted into the lodge of a Comanche called Bull Runner and raised with his two daughters."

"How'd you get away?"

"I was with them for eight winters before they left me with a trader in New Mexico."

"Which tribe were you with?"

"The Kwahadi," she answered.

"They were always fairly remote. I never dealt directly with them."

So he wasn't as close to her as she initially thought.

"Why did they trade you after eight years?" he asked.

"There was some confusion about an offer of marriage for me. Bull Runner's eldest daughter was angry. He chose to return me to my people as a gesture of goodwill."

"Goodwill, my ass," Matt said scornfully. "He held you hostage for eight years."

"Then, you believe me?"

Her words hung in the air, unanswered. Rain pelted the roof, thunder boomed in the distance, and darkness wrapped around her like an old friend. Countless times she had huddled beneath the flap of a teepee with her Comanche sisters while a sudden storm caught the tribe off-guard.

"Why didn't you show up here two years ago?" he asked, apparently still doubting her.

"The trader beat me," she replied, her voice suddenly hoarse. "An old miner named Elijah took pity on me. He bought me and took me deep into Mexico."

A flash of lightning showed Matt's jaw flexing. His hands rested indifferently on his hips, but there was nothing casual about his mood. She never remembered him like this.

"Who was the trader?" he asked.

"A comancheros named Jose Torres."

Matt swore fiercely under his breath.

"Do you know him?" she asked, surprised.

"Yeah. He's a worthless piece of — ," he stopped, and took a deep breath. "Many captives, unfortunately, passed through his hands."

"When Elijah died a few months ago, I had no choice but to find my way back," she added. "I didn't do it before because I had no idea where I was."

"It took you two months to return to Texas?"

"I stopped for a few weeks outside Albuquerque to help a friend. She accompanied me here."

"Where's your friend now?"

"We plan to meet tomorrow. Her name is Claire Waters. She was in bad shape when I found her." It surprised Molly that she had found Claire at all, bruised and bloodied as she had been, lying at the bottom of one of a thousand arroyos in and around the foothills of the Sandia Mountains.

Fatigue washed over Molly. The events of the day, of the last few weeks, were finally catching up with her. "We should make a fire." She moved toward Matt to leave the room. He didn't move. She could feel his eyes on her.

Pausing beside him, she said, "Do you remember when I stumbled onto a rattlesnake hiding under a mesquite bush?" She kept her eyes forward. "I was ready to pop the thing with my slingshot, but you grabbed me before I could. You looked out for me that summer, more than anyone ever had."

Lifting her chin, she looked at him, wondering what the years had done to him. He appeared rough, angry, and jaded. He walked with a slight limp. Was he married? Did he have a house full of children? He'd been so good with her ten years ago — patient, tolerant, and amused by her antics. She knew he would be a good father.

11

"I never thought I'd see you again, Matt." An uncertain smile reached her lips.

He simply watched her.

Brushing past him, she left him alone to sort it all out in his own mind.

Chapter Three

Matt stood in the darkened room, heavy rainfall echoing around him, his own thoughts ricocheting in his head.

Molly. *Alive.*

It was incomprehensible. The woman was simply a very good liar. Perhaps she'd heard the story of Molly Hart and had taken it upon herself to swindle those closest to Molly's family. But that made no sense. What motive could this woman possibly have? She couldn't have known he would be here at the Hart's abandoned ranch, today.

He only came after a two-month long recovery under his mother's tenacious care had left him discontent and in need of fresh air. Never mind that his soul was restless as well.

For four months, he had been the prisoner of Augusto Cerillo—a Mexican bandito with a reputation for torture. Matt and the other Rangers in his band had tracked the man for two years, and Matt nearly had him. Almost. If his old army buddy, Nathan Blackmore, hadn't gotten him out, he was certain he would've died in the hellhole Cerillo had created just for him. His body had healed, with only a slight limp from the damage to his right leg, but his spirit was taking more time to recover.

Maybe that was why, after ten years, he'd finally decided to pay his respects to Molly's gravesite.

What if the woman really *was* Molly?

Matt couldn't even fathom what that would mean. Scratching his roughened cheeks, he noticed his hand shook.

From the moment Molly Hart had died, Matt's life had changed. Angry, he'd vowed to avenge her, somehow. He'd joined the U.S. Army, fighting during the relentless campaigns to eradicate the Comanche from Texas. When the Kwahadi—the last and most lethal of the Comanche tribes—had finally surrendered, going to the reservation in '75, he'd resigned from the army and joined the Rangers. The work was grittier, the pay less, the conditions often worse, but it fulfilled his objective—to remove those who sought to terrorize the innocent, those who thought nothing of killing defenseless men, women, and children.

If Molly truly was alive, did that mean he'd fought the wrong battle all these years?

He was nothing if not cynical, having seen far too much butchering to bring back the innocence of his youth. He would demand more proof from this woman. If she wasn't Molly—and he had to believe she wasn't—he would break her until she confessed.

Matt moved through the house to find her. He paused at the threshold of a different bedroom. The woman—the imposter Molly—knelt before a fireplace. The flickering flames cast a glow of light that engulfed the room. As she swiveled on her booted heel and reached for something more to burn, Matt was struck by how young and vulnerable she appeared. At the same time, the firelight illuminated the outline of her breasts. High, round, nicely shaped. For a mere second, his mind dwelt on the sight, then he ruthlessly pushed it aside.

Hell of a time to be attracted to a woman.

Her hat was gone, revealing dark brown hair tied at the nape of her neck. Molly had dark hair. So did hundreds of other women, he reminded himself.

"Since I doubt there's anything dry to be found outside, I'm burning parts of a chair," she said when she noticed him.

"What name did you call your slingshot?"

Sitting back against a nearby wall, she blew a tendril of hair from her face. "The wren."

Could be just a lucky guess. "Why?"

She didn't appear worried, just tired. "Because I always believed all of the rocks I used were actually left by wrens." Reaching behind her head, she pulled the cord that held her hair in place. She ran her fingers through the surprisingly short, wet mass and fixed him with an intent gaze.

"Once," she continued quietly, "I told you that you'd be able to find me by following a trail I'd leave only for you, much the way a wren leaves a trail of rocks to its nest."

She certainly had intimate knowledge of his childhood conversations with Molly. Perhaps Molly hadn't died immediately. Perhaps this woman had been with her, had spoken to her. Maybe *she* was the child she claimed was actually killed by the Comanche. She had lived and Molly had died.

The lack of reasoning and logic didn't escape him. He was trying his damnedest to deny this woman's claim, but he could find nothing to contradict her. Embracing it, however, would shatter his world.

15

"Why is your hair so short?" he asked.

She touched the shoulder-length locks, a bit self-consciously. "When Elijah found me with the trader, I was in pretty bad shape. Wanting to keep any more trouble away, he told me to cut my hair and pretend I was a boy."

"And Elijah kept his hands off you?" For some reason the image bothered him.

She smiled. "He was an old man. And while he wasn't completely sane, he also had a goodness in his heart. He was more of a grandfather to me."

"Apparently not that much goodness if he kept you for two years."

"Well, his mind was ruled by the gold and the silver. It really is a sickness for some. I owed him for saving me from Torres, but once I was strong enough to leave him we were lost deep in the Sierra Madres. Before he died, though, he told me he'd help me return to Texas once his latest mining obsession played out. In the end, he intended to do right by me."

"So he up and died, and you headed here?"

"Yes. Why is it so hard to believe it's me?"

The rush of emotion surprised him. He glanced down at his well-worn boots while clearing his throat. "I looked for Molly," he said, "until I was so tired I couldn't sit my horse." Still standing in the doorway, he faced her across the room. "I won't smear her memory just because you ride in from the south and proclaim yourself Molly risen from the dead."

With resignation she shook her head. "Then I think I'll get some sleep. I'm too tired to continue, especially if you won't believe anything I say."

Throwing a wet blanket on the hard floor, she lay down near the wall. Matt took up a post on the other side of the fireplace from her, to keep her in his sights. In case of what? He wasn't sure. His instincts were in knots.

She cushioned her head with her arm and focused her very blue eyes on him again. "Are you married, Matt?"

"No."

"You don't have any children?"

"No."

"How're your folks, and your brother, Logan?"

"Well enough, I suppose."

"That's good." She closed her eyes. "I thought of you so many times," she added sleepily, then smiled, cracking an eye open. "I remember you said you were gonna marry yourself a fine society lady, all gussied-up and as smart as any man. It's nice to know you got over it."

She shut her eyes again, and in no time her steady breathing signaled she slept.

Matt noticed the light sprinkling of freckles across her nose. *Molly had freckles.* He noticed, too, the shape of her fingers where one hand lay nestled near her face. They were similar to Molly's, not in any specific way, just familiar to him.

He could see it now — the shadow of the child in the woman.

Molly lived, right there before him, a miracle from out of the past, against the odds.

Matt wasn't a religious man. Nevertheless, he couldn't help but feel God played a hidden hand in His deck of destiny, and probably laughed while He did it.

The woman across the room was a message—Matt's life was not what it seemed. Everything he thought he believed about the world, and about his own world, was wrong.

Molly lived.

And with that revelation a breath of life swept through Matt's soul. A nurturing, hopeful breath.

Maybe life *was* worth living after all.

Chapter Four

Matt awoke with a start. Bright sunlight broke through two grimy windows, illuminating an empty room. Dust floated in the slanting rays, the air still heavy from misuse despite his presence with the woman during the night.

Not just any woman.

Molly.

Standing, he shook off his grogginess and determinedly went outside. He saw her immediately, walking on a hillside not far from the house. He took a deep breath, relieved. A part of him thought she might have left.

If she had departed, then it would have been obvious she was a fraud. Did that mean, since she stayed, she was who she claimed to be? Matt had no idea how to proceed. But his gut told him his life would never be the same from this moment forward.

He positioned his hat to shield the sun from his eyes, then joined her on the hill. It was the very place where he'd left her that night ten years ago, the last time he'd seen her alive.

"Is something wrong?" he asked.

She paced around, staring at the ground. "No, not really." Resting hands on hips, she sighed. "You don't happen to remember where I buried it, do you?"

"What would that be?" he responded, still refusing to give her an inch.

"My survival kit." Squinting at him, she made a box with her hands.

He stared at those hands, fascinated by the slender, feminine fingers, darkened from the sun.

"Do you remember? I was burying it that night, the night of the attack. It was a metal box with, gosh, I don't even remember everything I put in it now."

"Yeah," he heard himself say, "I'm sure you don't." Was he really such an ass? He'd have to ask Nathan. He was the only one who'd give it to him straight.

Waving him off, she turned away in disgust. "Go away, Matt. You're really not much use here."

He blew out a breath, trying to summon some of the manners his mother had tried for years to instill in him and his brother. "Why don't you try near the oak shrub?"

She stared at him, then walked over to the scraggly bush. Grabbing a large rock, she began digging in the dirt. It was an eerie replay of the same night ten years ago.

He had found her out here, having sneaked away from the party to bury her survival kit. Her pretty yellow dress had been smudged with dirt and her chestnut curls had hung loose from a matching ribbon as she'd hunched over the hole, digging away with a rock as she was now. She'd told him she was burying it in case of an Indian attack—the Comanche had always been an ever-present threat. But Molly's mother had also feared the Kiowa to the north and even the Tonkawa to the south, and had instilled a bit of paranoia in her daughters.

Matt knew, even then, that his pa and the other ranchers had gone to great lengths to co-exist peacefully with the Indians in the area, but he was never quite able to convince Molly she was safe. And in the end, she wasn't.

The knowledge twisted like a knife in his gut.

The rock hit something solid.

"I really didn't think it would still be here." She pulled the box free of its dirt home. Dusting the top clean, she carefully unhinged the lid and opened it.

He knew what was inside, for she had shown him that night before burying it, but curiously he looked over her shoulder. A compass, an empty bottle for water, a knife, matches, and swatches of cloth in the event of an injury. She removed the old tattered slingshot resting on the bottom. "The wren," she murmured. Pushing the remaining contents around, she pulled out a folded slip of paper, then replaced the slingshot.

"What's that?" he asked.

She closed the box, tucking it under her arm, but kept the faded parchment in hand as she stood. "Just a letter I thought I should hide at the time." She unfolded the missive and began reading as she walked back to the ranch house.

He followed and she slammed into him when she suddenly turned back.

With a serious expression on her face, she asked, "Did you ever find out who killed my folks?"

"No." It had been a hell of a time, for him, his ma, his pa, the ranch hands, as well as the surrounding landowners who all came to help search for Molly and the killers of Robert and Rosemary Hart. The suspects had somehow eluded them.

"No clues at all?" she asked expectantly.

"We trailed the men who attacked and took you," he said, "but at the end, we found nothing."

"But when the Indians attacked, I know some of those men were killed."

"No bodies were ever found. Did you recognize who took you?"

She shook her head, then hesitated.

"What is it?" he asked.

"You don't even believe who I am. Why should I share my suspicions with you?"

His gaze locked with her vibrantly blue eyes, and he knew, beyond a shadow of doubt, she was Molly Hart. The how or why of it he couldn't reconcile, but as he looked at her now, under the bright azure Texan sky, he heard the whispers of the past—not just theirs, but thousands of years of lives struggling in this barren land—echoing through his heart and his mind, reminding him how he felt the day he thought he'd lost her.

Molly's body had been recovered and draped with a blanket where it lay on the ground before the group of men and boys who had searched for her. The remains had been brutally abused. Stunned, Matt had walked out of the valley where the Hart ranch stood, finally stopping at the crest of a hill to stare at the setting sun. The open Texas plains stretched as far as the eye could see; the sunset brought dark shadows and a high wind over the land.

It was as if the blast of air blew right through him. His mind, his heart, his dreams—they were all encompassed in what was left of Molly.

He opened his hand and stared at the gold cross resting on his callused fingers. The grief he struggled to ignore rushed over him, and the tension in his gut uncoiled so swiftly his legs gave out beneath him.

He fell to his knees, his body wracked with uncontrollable sobs. He cursed God, he cursed the

Comanche, he cursed Robert Hart for bringing three
young daughters to such a God-forsaken place, but mostly,
he cursed himself. If only he'd stayed with her that night
then she might be alive today.

She *was* alive.

"I do believe you," he said raggedly, "and it
scares the hell out of me."

"Why?"

"Because I should've found you. Because if I
had stayed with you that night you never would've
been kidnapped in the first place."

Surprise registered on her face. "It wasn't your
fault what happened."

"Maybe not, but my own actions were my fault.
I can't imagine what the last ten years were like for
you. It's a miracle you survived at all."

"I stopped believing in miracles a long time
ago," she replied softly. "It's hard enough just
surviving day to day."

"I'll help you in any way I can."

Another bewildered look from her. "I don't
expect your help."

"What do you plan to do? Where do you plan to
go?"

Resignation crossed her features, and she sat on
a nearby rock. "I don't know. I haven't planned that
far."

"My ma can help you get in touch with your
sisters."

She nodded. "Yes, I'd like that." She fiddled
with the faded paper in her hand.

"What's in the letter?"

Chewing on her lower lip, she didn't answer. "Is
Davis Walker still alive?"

"Yes. He still runs a ranch in these parts."

She handed the letter to him.

Dear Rosemary,
You can't put me off forever. I know you told me to
stay away, but I can't. I need to see you. I need to know
why you won't see me. What are you hiding?
Davis

Matt looked at Molly, stunned. "Davis? And your ma?"

"It would seem so."

"How did you get this?"

"One afternoon Davis came here. I was playing outside, but hid when I saw him. He pounded and pounded on the door—he was so angry—but my mama had taken Mary and Emma to visit with Sarah and her husband. Do you remember Sarah? She used to help Mama look after us. Finally, Davis left but before he did, he slipped this under the door." She folded the paper carefully. "I know I shouldn't have, but I sneaked back and read it. I was young, but not that young. I knew this letter meant trouble. I decided to bury it so no one, least of all Papa, would ever find out."

"You don't think they actually carried on, do you?" he asked.

Molly shrugged. "I don't know. There's more. When the men took me that night, I clearly remember them mentioning Davis Walker's name."

"How so?"

"I don't really recall the context, it was all so confusing. But…"

When she didn't continue, he finished for her. "You think Davis was behind the attack on your family? Because he was angry your mother wouldn't see him?"

"Since I learned of my folks' deaths a few weeks ago, images from my childhood have been running over and over through my head. So, yes, the thought has crossed my mind."

Matt didn't like it. Davis Walker was his pa's friend. He had also been a friend to Robert Hart. It disheartened him to think the man could be responsible for ripping apart all of their lives ten years ago.

"I need to find Claire," she said, rising from the rock. "She went to check out the Walker Ranch for me yesterday."

"And then what do you plan to do?"

"Find out if Walker was really behind all of this," she said resolutely.

"And if he is?"

"Make sure he pays."

Chapter Five

Matt didn't see Claire Waters until they were almost upon her, hidden as she was in a slight depression in the flat terrain, approximately five miles to the south of what was left of the Hart ranch. She was hunkered down near a cluster of oak shrubs, her horse picketed in a concealing drop-off.

Molly dismounted and approached Claire without preamble.

Two women alone, doing their best to hide and stay out-of-sight.

The thought didn't improve Matt's already churlish disposition, caused in part by what Molly had told him of Davis Walker. But the basis of his dark mood began and ended with Molly herself. Her presence reminded him of the last ten years without her, of his failure to protect her.

When Claire rose, hesitant, from where she crouched, and Matt saw green eyes gazing at him from a young and pretty face, he swore under his breath. Claire couldn't be much older than Molly. The revelation surprised him. He'd assumed her to be a more mature woman.

Instead, Molly had made her way to Texas with a girl who could've been her sister. Unprotected and vulnerable, they were obviously unaware of the many mishaps that could've happened to them. And that was just from the land itself — the weather and the creatures of the desert. He didn't even want to contemplate their fates at the hands of men, especially in a land where women were scarce.

"Claire," Molly acknowledged, smiling. "Are you all right?"

The woman nodded from beneath a broad-brimmed hat, a blonde braid trailing over a shoulder. Her look of distrust was hard to miss.

"This is Matt Ryan. It's all right, he knows everything. Matt, this is Claire Waters."

He swung down from his horse. "Miss." He tipped his hat slightly.

"He was at the ranch," Molly continued. "They all thought I was dead."

"They did?" Claire asked, her voice level. "Is that why no one ever came looking for you?"

Matt sensed Claire's anger on Molly's behalf, despite the young woman's features revealing nothing but a calm exterior. Her sense of loyalty toward Molly caused him to reassess his opinion of her.

"Yes," Molly answered. "There was some confusion ten years ago, and another girl's body was thought to be mine." She smiled slightly, glancing at him over her shoulder. "He didn't quite believe me when I told him who I was. Matt was a friend of my family when I was a child."

"I remember you mentioning him," Claire responded.

Matt recalled Molly's statement about finding Claire bruised and bloody. She appeared recovered, although he did notice a jagged redness along her neck.

27

Molly and Claire possessed unmistakable shadows in their eyes, and Matt suspected life had aged them quickly and efficiently beyond their years—not an unusual occurrence in these parts. Still, it bothered him.

"I've told him about Walker, and he's offered to help," Molly said.

Claire gave Molly an *are-you-certain-about-this* look, to which Molly nodded.

"Davis Walker is still alive," Claire said, "although he wasn't at his ranch. An elderly woman, Mrs. Owens, said he was in Fort Worth for a few weeks. She let me stay the night because of the storm. Of his three sons, only T.J. was there. I didn't get too much out of him except that he wanted me to share his bed."

"T.J. was never known for being subtle," Matt replied. "He didn't hassle you, did he?"

"No," Claire answered. "Joey Walker was due back today, but I missed seeing him because I didn't want to be late meeting you. The oldest, Cale, hasn't been at the ranch in quite some time. He would probably remember more than the other two about what happened ten years ago."

"Cale was the one who found the body," Matt said to Molly. "He never mentioned anything about his father back then, but he left shortly after that."

"Did you leave, too?" Molly asked.

"Yes." He'd departed with a heavy heart and a determination to get away from the stark reminders of Molly's fate that had been everywhere at the time.

He watched Molly. Despite everything she'd been through, she stood tall and confident, her hair tucked into her hat once again. He was reminded of her knack for mischief, an extension of her curious nature, and he wondered if any remnant of that child still existed. She was strong, she'd survived, but at what cost?

Looking off to the east, trying to clear his thoughts, Matt said, "Cale joined the army around the same time I did, but after a few years he went out on his own."

"Doing what?" Molly asked.

"I've come across him from time to time. Sometimes he's a hired gun, sometimes a bounty hunter. He's around somewhere. I'm sure I can find him."

"Didn't any of the Ryan or Walker boys stay put?"

"Not much to hold a man here." Except endless days filled with memories best left forgotten. "Cale turned out all right. He's got a sharp eye, a level head, and a better trigger finger than anyone I've met. Joey's a crack shot, too. He joined the army eventually, but a few years back returned to help his pa manage the ranch. But T.J.'s been a burden, as far as I can tell. Drinks too much, gambles frequently. Davis has bailed him out several times."

"What about Logan?"

"Who's that?" Claire questioned.

"My younger brother," Matt replied. He smiled. "Believe it or not, Logan meandered into the life of a deputy. But he returned last year to help out with the ranch. My pa's been having some health problems."

"Is that why you've stayed?" Molly asked.

Like a smooth whiskey on a cold night, her rich voice warmed him. Unbidden, visions of sharing such a cold night with Molly filled his mind.

"For the most part," he answered, uncomfortable with his train of thought, knowing how out-of-line it was. Molly had always looked to him as an older brother. Indian captives, especially women, were often branded as tainted if they managed to return to their families. Molly would have a difficult time as it was, simply trying to readjust. He doubted she would welcome an interest from him that was as far from brotherly as he could get.

What he needed to do was make certain she was well looked-after. He should find a suitable husband for her, one who wouldn't hold the last ten years against her.

"I think we should head back to my folks' ranch." He glanced at the sun sitting high in the sky. "It's still a few hours' ride from here. You'll both be safe there. You can stay as long as you like, and you'll be able to sleep in a bed."

"The ground isn't so bad," Claire remarked, gathering her horse's reins then settling herself into the saddle.

"There's better ways to live," Matt said.

"A better life." Molly shook her head. "Sometimes the best life is simply being alive."

Matt could see the simple truth in her words. By all accounts, Molly and Claire should be dead.

"You don't have to worry about us, Matt," Molly said more firmly. "We can take care of ourselves." She climbed atop her horse.

Matt took the lead with Molly close behind, then Claire. He'd already made up his mind. He *would* take care of Molly. It was the least he could do. With her pa dead, she needed someone to look out for her welfare, to guard her reputation, to make certain the man she married did right by her. She needed someone looking out for her if she truly planned to chase down the men who killed her folks. That Molly might not want this from him was beside the point.

Matt hadn't been able to save her ten years ago, but perhaps if he helped her forge a new life it would lessen his guilt while at the same time bringing much needed happiness into hers.

Despite the focus this new goal brought him, restlessness stirred once again, brewing just beneath the surface.

He'd simply have to ignore it.

Chapter Six

As the three riders approached the Ryan ranch, the setting sun cast a golden hue on the terrain. Riding beneath a wrought-iron archway, Molly read the lettering—SR Ranch.

"What does SR mean?" she asked Matt, who slowed his horse to match hers.

"It's for my ma, Susanna Ryan," he answered. "Our cattle are branded with the SR insignia. Haven't you ever been here before?"

Molly shook her head. "Mama never liked traveling much. I think her rule was ten miles or less, so I don't recall ever being here." After a moment, she added, "Or to the Walker Ranch."

"His place has grown in the past few years," Matt said. "Davis runs about thirty thousand head of cattle on fifty thousand acres."

"It seems hard to imagine," Claire said. "How big is this ranch?"

"We've got close to fifty thousand beeves. My pa has expanded the SR onto close to eighty thousand acres now."

"How do you manage it?" Molly asked.

Matt smiled, scanning the surroundings. "There's talk among the ranchers of fencing in their properties using a new type of enclosure called barbed wire, but my old man isn't so sure. It would protect the cattle from theft, and let squatters know they're not where they should be, but there's something about the wide open spaces. You hate to rope it off."

A large, two-story ranch house came into view, its white-washed wooden exterior contrasting brightly with the new spring grass growing around the outskirts of the main property. Tall cottonwoods surrounded the wrap-around porch, as well as the bunkhouse off to the right. A large corral, and a smaller one containing a dozen or so horses, stood near an immense barn. Farther to the south were additional holding pens and several wooden buildings.

Molly absorbed the scene, feeling slightly overwhelmed. The Ryan Ranch seemed large and busy, with men on horseback and afoot moving about. She was accustomed to being alone. She was accustomed to loneliness.

A yearning welled up inside her. She wanted roots, wanted a real home, wanted to feel safe. And somewhere, in the darkest part of her mind and the hidden desires of her heart, she wanted a family, too.

Glancing at Matt beside her, his very presence a distraction, she realized she didn't want to be alone anymore either. She wanted children. And for that she would need a husband, wouldn't she?

The thought surprised her. Had she wanted a husband she could have simply begged Bull Runner to let her stay with the Comanche and marry Snake Eater. But while she had to admit she didn't know much about what went on between a man and a woman, she had been certain of one thing — being Snake Eater's wife would have been a world smaller than the one which she had already inhabited.

Besides, there had been nothing physically appealing to her about the Comanche warrior, despite the female following his fine-looking face had generated in camp.

Matt.

As a child, Molly had entertained thoughts of marrying him. Simple, innocent longings created by her fondness for him as much as by her sister Mary's teasings. But she had been a child then and he almost a grown man. She accepted such a fate would never be.

And now? While the idea of marrying him seemed far-fetched in the extreme, she couldn't help but hope they might be friends again. But Matt had thought her dead all these years, and she wasn't sure he believed it was her yet. It was unlikely circumstances would ever be the same between them again.

Molly's eyes burned suddenly with tears. Nothing would ever be the same again. Blinking hard, she willed them to stop.

Matt dismounted, looking back towards her. "Are you all right?" he asked, walking around to lead her horse.

Molly coughed and glanced at her hands. "Yes. I just have dust in my eyes."

She came down from her horse while Claire did the same. A burly man rounded the house, his face covered with gray whiskers.

"Hey there, Matt. We was wonderin' what happened to you last night."

"I got waylaid by the storm, Dawson. Is Pa around?"

Dawson squinted at the ladies, smiling. "He's out checkin' the herd on the north plateau. Your ma's inside."

"Thanks. Molly and Claire, this is Randall Dawson, our foreman."

"Pleased to meet you, misses. Just call me Dawson."

Molly smiled, glad for the distraction.

A woman came through the front door. "Matthew? I thought I heard your voice." She stopped short. "I didn't realize you brought guests." Immediately, a delighted expression crossed her face.

Molly's recollection of Matt's mother was vague, for she had seen her only a handful of times.

She was tall, lithe, and surprisingly feminine for a woman living in such a rugged land. Mother and son shared the same facial features—a long narrow nose, eyes slanting slightly at the corners, and dark hair, although hers was sprinkled with silver and swept atop her head in a bun.

"I'll introduce you," Matt said as he indicated for Molly and Claire to precede him into the house. "But let's go inside first."

"Is something wrong?" she asked.

"No, but you might want to be sitting down."

His mother frowned slightly, and addressed Molly and Claire directly. "You're both welcome here despite Matthew's strange behavior."

"Thank you, Mrs. Ryan," Molly responded.

Matt's mother smiled at her. "You remind me of someone."

Matt led them into the house and to a large sitting area. A maroon-colored upholstered couch with spool-turned legs sat across from two similarly-colored stuffed chairs, while a large rock fireplace dominated the opposite wall. The décor was rustic and masculine, and Molly liked it.

She removed her hat, as did Claire, and suddenly became aware of how grimy and saddle-worn she must appear. It amazed her how Claire's hair still managed to shine despite her tired and dirty appearance as well. Her blonde tresses, bound in a single braid down her back, glistened in the muted light of two oil lamps shining from the mantel above the fireplace. The quickly darkening sky could be seen just outside a large window overlooking the porch.

Matt threw his hat on a side table then gestured for Claire to sit on the long couch. "This is Claire Waters."

"Pleased to meet you, ma'am," Claire said, a certain amount of discomfort apparent.

"Please, call me Susanna. How do you both know Matthew?"

Molly took a seat beside her friend as Claire looked to Matt for an answer.

"This is going to be a bit much to take in," Matt intervened.

His eyes locked on hers, and Molly was suddenly awash with nerves. After ten years everyone had changed, herself most of all. This homecoming was proving to be more awkward than she'd imagined.

"Do you remember when the Harts were killed?" Matt asked his mother.

"Of course I do." A pained expression crossed Susanna Ryan's face.

"And when Cale found Molly's body?"

"Yes. Why are you bringing this up?"

"It seems all these years we were wrong. It wasn't Molly that Cale found."

Confused, Susanna looked at her son. "I don't understand."

"She's still alive." Matt hesitated. "*This* is Molly."

Susanna's eyes came to hers, frozen in astonishment. "Good Lord," she utterly softly.

Unsure what to do, Molly didn't move either. Should she prove it? Perhaps she should tell Matt's mother something from ten years ago to convince her who she was. But nothing came to mind.

"Of course," Susanna said finally. "You look so much like your mother." Tears welled up in her eyes. Standing, she crossed the room. "Molly, my dear child."

Molly stood reflexively and Susanna's arms engulfed her.

"I can't believe this." Susanna's words were laden with emotion. "It's a miracle. We were so devastated after what happened, and of especially losing *you*."

She stepped back, and touched Molly's face gently.

Molly smiled hesitantly, uncertain how to react.

"How did this happen?" Susanna asked.

Molly glanced at Matt, whose shuttered gaze was unreadable. "It's up to you how much you want to tell," he said quietly.

Taking a deep breath, Molly said, "I was taken by the men who attacked that night. Later they were raided by a band of Comanche, who took me with them. There was another girl with us, near my age. She was the one killed, but somehow you all thought it was me."

"Oh, Molly," Susanna said helplessly, "you were with the Comanche this entire time?"

"For a while, then they sold me to a trader who then sold me to a miner. I was with him for two years. I was able to make my way back here only recently. I didn't know my folks had been killed until a few weeks ago."

"I'm so sorry," Susanna whispered. "I can't believe this. How did Matthew find you?"

"I found her yesterday, at the Hart ranch."

Susanna stared at her son. "This is amazing." Then, turning back to Molly, "I can't imagine what you've been through. You must be exhausted. Let me get both of you settled." Susanna's gaze included Claire.

"We're very grateful for your hospitality," Molly said.

"I'm heading out to look for Pa," Matt said. "Is Logan around?"

"No. He went patrolling the southern boundary. I'm not sure when he'll be back, if at all tonight."

Matt grabbed his hat and headed for the front door. "Don't hold supper. I'm sure Molly and Claire haven't had a decent meal in some time."

Molly's eyes locked with his, then he was gone. She had an irrational wish that he would stay.

Tired and hungry as she was, she found the idea of sleeping in a real bed appealing. It had been a very long time since she'd done such a thing. Ten years, to be precise.

* * *

Molly opened the bedroom door upon hearing the soft knock.

"I've brought you a nightgown and a change of clothes." Susanna handed the garments to her.

"Thank you." Molly stepped back into the room. "And thank you for letting us stay the night."

Susanna entered and began pulling the covers down on the bed. "You're welcome for as long as you like. Claire as well. In a few days the renovations in the upstairs bedrooms should be done, so you both can move up there." She fluffed the pillows. "How did you meet Claire?"

"Outside of Albuquerque a few months ago." Molly didn't say more, thinking Claire might not want her circumstances known to everyone.

"Something has happened to that poor girl," Susanna said as she finished with the bed. "I can only imagine what it was." She crossed the room and closed the tan curtains that covered the only window in the room.

A tub sat in the bedroom, steam rising from the water. Molly couldn't help looking forward to the luxury. Once again, she glanced around the very masculine bedroom. It was Matt's room. Susanna had insisted that he could sleep elsewhere, that he wouldn't mind. Claire was in Logan's room next door.

"I won't keep you," Susanna said. "You can wash up then get some rest. Claire is already asleep."

"I wondered if you knew anything about my sisters."

Although she and Claire had eaten a quick supper with Susanna, there hadn't been much conversation. Molly had been too intent on the meal—a simple stew and hot bread—to concentrate on talking. It had been so long since she'd had such a delicious, home-cooked dish—the aroma alone was one of the best scents she'd inhaled since the cinnamon cookies her mama had made when she was a child. One glance at Claire told Molly that she was in the same state of hunger also.

Molly had gorged herself and felt a little embarrassed, but Susanna never made a comment. She simply gave the two of them second helpings and several more slices of bread each, then insisted they both have a bath and a good night's rest.

"Oh my, of course I do. I'm sorry I didn't mention it sooner." Susanna clasped Molly's hands and pulled her down to the edge of the bed.

"Matt said they went to San Francisco to live with my Aunt Catherine."

"Yes. And Catherine has been kind enough to stay in touch. The truth is, I would've kept them myself. I was always quite fond of all you girls. But Catherine insisted they leave Texas. She didn't think it was a good place for them to grow up." Susanna paused. "She was right, of course. She was able to offer them so much more.

"Mary would be twenty-four now. She was married four or five years ago. I had hoped to attend the wedding—Jonathan was ready to accompany me—but it happened very quickly, so there wasn't time. Mary's husband runs a ranch near Tucson, in the Arizona Territory. She had a child shortly after their marriage. Catherine didn't mention it, but I suspect that was why the marriage was rushed."

Molly couldn't conceal her astonishment. "Mary?"

"Yes, Mary." Susanna laughed. "I'll admit I was surprised, too. Mary was always so intent on following the rules, keeping up appearances."

"Does she have a son or a daughter?"

"A son. And she also has a daughter, who must be about three now. Mary actually wrote me a few months back. She's expecting another child, and she seems to be doing well. Her husband's name is Tom Simms and it sounds as if they are quite happy together. She'll be as shocked as the rest of us that you're alive, Molly. But I know she'll want to see you as soon as she can."

Molly nodded, warmed by the news of a nephew and a niece and another on the way. "I'll have to find a way to visit her."

"We can write to her tomorrow," Susanna said. "As for Emma, she's still with your aunt. She would be eighteen, I think, by now. From Catherine's letters, Emma has been a handful. For a time, your aunt was very worried about her—she'd become extremely withdrawn. But her most recent letter mentioned she's doing better. It sounds as if she's full of determination these days, much the way I remember you were."

Molly smiled at the gleam in Susanna's eyes.

"According to your aunt, Emma is very lovely but not much interested in the young men coming around. She apparently has developed a bit of the gypsy in her, and I don't think your aunt has the temperament for it. I suggested to Catherine that she send her here for a visit. And, of course, now that you're here, I have no doubt Emma will want to return. We'll write to them as well tomorrow."

"I'm most grateful."

"You don't have to thank me. It's such a miracle you're alive—I still can't believe it." Susanna hugged her. "You should get cleaned up then get some sleep. We can talk more tomorrow."

The older woman left the room and weariness settled in Molly's bones. She quickly undressed and bathed, then put on the long nightgown Susanna had given her.

After wearing it for a short time, Molly decided it was too cumbersome and began searching through Matt's bureau for something else to wear. Upon finding a white shirt, she quickly donned it, buttoning it down the front. It smelled of him, as did the bed: a potent mix of musk, leather, and soap. As Molly drifted off, it was as if she slept right beside him.

The thought was as comforting as it was unsettling.

Chapter Seven

The scream awoke Molly with a start. For a moment she lay still, staring into the darkened room—Matt's room, she recalled. Then she remembered the woman's scream. Claire.

Molly threw the covers back, jumped out of bed, and ran into the hallway. She stopped short when she saw a tall, muscular, and half-naked man. Then she noticed Claire standing in the doorway to Logan's room, wearing one of Susanna's long white nightgowns and clutching a blanket to her chest. Her blonde hair tumbled around her shoulders, framing a flushed face. She stared at the man next to her.

Molly suddenly recognized him—it was Logan, Matt's younger brother. He didn't appear to be quite as tall as Matt, but his dark hair and strongly etched facial features certainly pegged him as a Ryan.

"Mind telling me why there's a girl in my bed, Matt?" Logan asked in a hushed and irritated voice.

Molly jumped when she realized Matt stood behind her. Her breath caught in her throat when she turned to look at him, her racing pulse pounding even more. Half-naked as well, he wore a pair of trousers pulled on quickly, obviously too quickly since the top button was still undone. But while Logan's nakedness merely surprised her, Matt's completely flustered her.

There wasn't an ounce of fat on him anywhere, the sleek muscles in his shoulders subtly flexing from where he stood. The dark mat of hair on his chest tapered down to a vee, then disappeared beneath the open button, his stomach flat and taut. Towering over her, he stood close enough that his arm brushed hers as he lowered the gun he had drawn in obvious haste. Molly shivered from the brief contact.

"Ma didn't think you'd be back tonight," Matt said, the timbre of his voice setting Molly's nerves on edge. "This is Claire Waters. Claire, this is my brother, Logan."

Molly finally found her voice. "Are you all right, Claire?"

"Yes," she replied. "He just startled me." Claire glanced in Logan's direction.

"It seems you've got one in your bed as well. Is this Ma's version of matchmaking?" Logan asked, but his voice had softened as he looked at Claire again.

"It's a long story," Matt replied. "Grab your bedroll. You're on the floor with me."

Molly was acutely aware of Matt's nearness. He stood too close to her, much too close. She discerned in the darkness of the hallway that Logan was at least four feet from Claire. Matt couldn't be more than four inches from her. She found herself suddenly self-conscious of her nakedness beneath the thin shirt she wore.

"Sorry, Claire," Matt said. "You'd better go back to bed, Molly. I'll explain everything to Logan." Finally, he stepped back and she dared another glance at his face.

The darkness couldn't mask the speculative gleam in his eyes. At the same time, however, there was also a grim determination on his face and in his stance. Molly could sense the powerful restraint he exerted.

He appeared dangerous in the intimate blackness of the hallway, his broad shoulders tightening as he shifted his weight slightly. Molly's shivered and her lower body felt heavy.

If Logan and Claire hadn't been standing there, Molly knew she would have touched him. It still took all of her willpower not to run her fingertips lightly across his chest. She couldn't explain it, but she was certain she could release the tension in his body.

With an effort, Molly nodded. "Goodnight," she whispered as she walked back into Matt's bedroom and shut the door. The last thing she saw was his gaze fixed solely on her. It left her trembling.

Behind the closed door, Molly's breathing was fragmented. The entire incident rattled her. Had she imagined the way Matt looked at her? She had no idea how this had happened, how strongly attracted to Matt she'd become. He was no longer the young man of seventeen she once knew. He was older, more distant, but infinitely more compelling to her.

His awareness of her in the hallway hadn't been something she imagined—it had been palpable, hard to miss, filling the small space between them like a storm brewing, ready to flood the land. It stirred in her something she never knew existed, a longing that was almost painful.

All things womanly and feminine had eluded her for the past few years. Elijah had hardly been a good role model. It definitely left her confused over how to handle the situation with Matt.

Returning to bed, it was hardly surprising that sleep eluded her.

* * *

Matt walked back into the spacious parlor where he'd been trying to sleep. He put his gun back in its holster, then fell onto the couch while rubbing his eyes with the palm of his right hand. Brief contact with his cheek reminded him he needed to shave, but what he really needed was a sound dunking in a very cold creek. Too bad the Red River was ten miles to the north.

He knew, however, that a long ride and a cold swim would never erase the image from his mind of Molly rushing from his bedroom wearing nothing but one of his shirts, her disheveled hair a dark mess that framed her strikingly feminine face.

Her smoky eyes and husky voice had nearly undone him, but he had definitely been on the verge of throwing all his willpower to the wind when she had turned and her body's response to him had been readily apparent beneath the thin fabric of the shirt. He could still see in his mind the dark outline of her breasts through the whiteness of the cloth. Only the fact they had an audience had stopped him from touching her...barely.

Matt tried to conjure up an image of a nine-year-old Molly — sweet, innocent, and playful — evoking nothing but brotherly feelings. It didn't work. All he kept seeing were long, shapely legs leading to the rest of a not-very-nine-year-old body, concealed by nothing but thin white cloth.

"I don't see why you get the couch." Logan entered the room and tossed a bedroll onto the floor.

"I got here first. So make friends with the floor. I'll fill you in on the rest tomorrow."

"Like hell. You've got me curious now. Besides, it's going to take me a few minutes to recover from Claire."

Matt frowned at his brother. "You didn't offend her, did you?"

Logan laughed. "Not if she didn't mind seeing me in all my glory."

"Christ," Matt said wearily. "You didn't have any clothes on."

"Not a stitch." Logan's grin made him look much younger than his twenty-five years. "I don't think Claire is terribly experienced with men, but she didn't cower or faint on me, I'll give her that. I've never seen a woman move so fast. She twisted her legs up and slammed me in the chest with the soles of her delicate little feet. A little lower and I probably wouldn't be walking right now."

Logan settled into one of the chairs, wincing a little as he gingerly touched his upper torso.

"Go easy on her," Matt said. "I think she's had a rough go of it."

"How's that?"

"I really don't know too much about her, except that Molly found her beaten up outside of Albuquerque a few months back."

Logan was pensive for a moment, his demeanor changing in a heartbeat.

"Have the bastards been caught?" Logan asked coldly.

"I don't know."

Matt watched his younger brother and knew that beneath his easy-going personality was a determined man. He had never met anyone who possessed Logan's innate sense of justice; it was no wonder he became a lawman. Logan's reputation was well known—he was a man who got the job done no matter what the odds. And Matt trusted Logan's tracking skills as much as Nathan's or his own.

Both he and Logan had learned survival and hunting skills from Joseph Running Bear, an old crotchety Kiowa who had worked at the Ryan's ranch when they'd first settled in Texas. Uncle Joe had taught them more about the land and the creatures on it, man included, than Matt had learned in the last ten years on his own.

Losing the old Indian a few years ago had felt almost like losing a father. Men like him didn't come along every day. Matt still wondered why Joe had left the Kiowa, but the old man had refused to speak of it. He suspected it was tragic in nature. Misfortune seemed to touch almost everyone at some point in these parts.

Matt glanced at his brother again. Logan had abruptly returned from Virginia City a year ago, announcing he planned to stay on at the ranch and help out. Matt had never asked, but he suspected something had happened to cause Logan to walk away from his deputy position so easily.

The last few months were the first time Matt had spent any time with Logan in several years. His brother could be deceptively charming, but underneath the charm was a steely resolve to work hard and not let anyone get too close to him. Matt knew he was much the same way.

He couldn't recall ever meeting a woman Logan was interested in. But then, he'd never brought one home either, never staying in one place long enough to form any serious attachments.

But today he'd brought a woman home, two in fact, and one of them was definitely getting under his skin like no female had in some time. He really needed to get his head on straight because it was his job to protect Molly from men like him, not pursue her himself.

"Who's Molly?" Logan asked. "How did she and Claire end up here?"

"You're not going to believe this," Matt said quietly, "but Molly is Molly Hart."

"Molly Hart?" Logan questioned, bewilderment clear on his face. "The same Molly Hart who was killed years ago?"

Matt nodded slowly.

"How the hell can that be?" Logan asked in disbelief.

"I'll tell you what I know, but keep it to yourself. I doubt Molly wants the past floating around."

Matt had told his pa everything earlier in the evening because he felt his father needed to know, and now he'd tell Logan because he knew he could trust him to keep his mouth shut. Hatred toward the Indians still ran deep in this area of Texas despite the fact the Comanche and Kiowa were no longer a threat. Sometimes such disgust rubbed off onto captives trying to live once again amongst their own people.

Matt never quite understood it. Captives were often in bad shape, physically as well as mentally, and it didn't help when the family and friends that desperately sought their return couldn't handle what had happened to them. Especially when the captives were women.

When Matt finished the story of Molly's return to the living, Logan shook his head in amazement.

"An empty saddle is better than a mean rider," Logan said.

Matt looked at him, confused.

"That's what I always thought about Davis Walker," he elaborated. "He was always too stinkin' mean to his horses. Someone should've told him so years ago. But Cale, Joey and T.J. had other things to worry about, I suppose, than puttin' their daddy in his place."

"I'll agree Walker isn't the most upstanding citizen, but then none of us is a saint in these parts."

"Speak for yourself." Logan grinned.

"When I think of a saint, you're definitely at the top of the list," Matt said. Then, more seriously, "The big question is why? Why would Davis Walker hire a posse to attack the Harts, kill them and take Molly? The only motive we have is that he was supposedly sweet on Molly's mother."

"Sounds like enough to me. I've seen worse crimes prompted by a lot less."

"Yeah," Matt said tiredly, "so have I." He just hated to think Walker could have done it. He knew the possibility weighed heavy on his pa as well.

"Have you talked to Pa yet?" Logan asked.

"Earlier. He didn't have any ready explanations. He wanted to talk to Ma because he thought she might remember something. He did say Davis was never really himself after his wife died in childbirth."

"T.J.?" Logan asked, arching an eyebrow.

Matt nodded.

"Guess that would explain T.J.'s self-indulgent bent. His mama wasn't around to set him straight."

"Self-indulgence is probably one of T.J.'s better qualities," Matt said grimly.

"Well, you've managed to surprise the hell out of me, and that doesn't happen too often these days."

"Let's get some sleep." Matt stretched out on the couch. "We can figure out how to handle this tomorrow."

Logan sighed. "Something tells me I'm gonna be on this floor for a while. We should move to the bunkhouse until Ma finishes redecorating those rooms upstairs."

"Getting soft in your old age?"

"No, just realistic. Don't tell me you haven't noticed there are two young and pretty women sleeping in our beds right now?"

"Stay away from Molly." Matt's voice was quiet, but laced with an unspoken threat. Until the words were out, he hadn't realized how possessive he felt towards her. Taking a calming breath, he added, "Sorry, that didn't come out right. I'm just thinking we need to look out for her until she gets settled somewhere. There must be a few young ranch hands around these parts that might make a suitable husband for her."

Logan raised an eyebrow. "You're lookin' to find her a husband?" He laughed. "When did you become her guardian angel? Because I gotta tell ya, Matt, you weren't lookin' at her like an angel a few minutes ago." Logan's drawl always increased when he talked nice but was leveling a punch where you least expected it.

"What's that supposed to mean?"

"Nothin'," Logan shrugged. "But I'm not blind, and I know you sure as hell aren't. I saw her standing there only wearing one of your shirts. You want to find her a husband? I don't think that'll be a problem.

But you'd better make damn sure what *you* want before you start tryin' to take control of her life."

"What I want isn't at issue here. She's been through hell. I intend to make sure her life is nothing but better from this point on."

"I think I'm gonna enjoy this," Logan said, lying down on the floor.

"Enjoy what?"

Logan laughed again. "Watching you play matchmaker."

"Go to sleep."

His brother chuckled one last time before falling silent.

Chapter Eight

Molly awoke, sunlight shining through the windows. She was restless after her late-night run-in with Matt, not just because of her new awareness of him but also the fact that she hadn't slept in a bed in ten years. It was entirely too soft. Throwing a blanket on the floor, she'd finally found sleep in the early-morning hours on the firm wooden planks.

The images that had filled her dreams came back to her. She was at her folks' ranch, before the night when everything had changed in a heartbeat. In the afternoon sun, she was hanging on the side of the corral, Emma beside her. Emma's dark curls were so beautiful in the sunlight, and Molly couldn't resist twisting them around her finger in the dream.

It's so good to be with you again, Emma.

Her sister had smiled up at her, one of her cheeks dimpling. Emma's dimple always appeared when she was very happy. The smile warmed Molly's heart. Then a rider appeared in the corral. It was Matt, and he was trying to break a horse. Only Matt wasn't young as he had been that summer ten years ago. This time he was older, like he was now.

Remembering the dream made her heart ache for Emma. So much time lost. Hopefully, it wouldn't be long before she was able to see her again. Molly rubbed her eyes, trying to clear the last fog of slumber from her mind.

Susanna had left a simple dark brown dress at the foot of the bed, along with several white undergarments. Molly pulled on stockings, bloomers, and a light petticoat, then shrugged into a shift, buttoning here and there, slightly confused by it all. Not since she was a young girl had she dressed in this manner. Soon, the garment was in place.

Amused to look like a female again, she twisted her hips, causing the skirt to twirl back and forth around her ankles. It had been ten years since she'd worn anything like this. The thought brought a lump to her throat and her eyes burned.

Molly took a deep breath, suppressing the urge to cry. Reaching for her boots, she noticed how faded and dirty they were. But it was all she owned. She pulled them on, knowing they appeared mismatched with the dress, and wondered why she cared. *Matt.* She cared how she looked to Matt.

Before she could dwell on that thought further, she shifted attention to her hair. It was hanging in disarray around her face. It still wasn't as long as she would have liked, since Elijah had always insisted she keep it short during the time she'd been with him. She started to pull the curly mass behind her head then let it back down in frustration. Her experience in doing her hair in a way that might appeal to others amounted to nothing.

In a way that might appeal to men.

In a way that might appeal to Matt.

Molly let out a breath of frustration. She was acting foolish. It was likely Matt would hardly notice her at all.

Opening the bedroom door, she walked toward the front of the house. Hearing voices in the large parlor room, she paused at the threshold before entering. The conversation abruptly ended and everyone turned to stare at her. Heat crept up her neck, and her face felt flush.

Susanna and Claire stood off to her right, Logan and Matt to her left. Matt was visible from the corner of her eye but she couldn't bring herself to meet his gaze, so instead she focused on the older man standing directly across the room from her. Molly knew it was Matt's father, although she remembered seeing him only once or twice as a child.

An imposing figure, Jonathan Ryan's height equaled his sons, his shoulders just as broad, but his wrinkled face and gray hair showed the years he'd spent battling the land. His blue-green eyes—so much like Matt's—settled on her, and his expression softened. Molly's throat tightened as her emotions began to fall apart.

"Molly," Jonathan said quietly. "God Almighty. I've never seen someone rise from the dead, but your pa always said you had as much grit as the boys. I guess I'm not surprised you survived. Welcome home, child."

Molly hands shook so she hid them in the folds of her dress, twisting her fingers around the soft material.

Jonathan walked over to her and placed his hands on her shoulders. "You're welcome here as long as you like," he said gruffly.

With a pounding heart, Molly nodded. Clearing her throat, she finally found her voice. "It's good to see you again, sir." It sounded as if she were a frog attempting to talk.

Jonathan released his hold on her. "You must be hungry. Let's get everyone some breakfast, then we can talk more."

Molly glanced at Claire, observing she too wore a dress, cream-colored, with her blonde hair tied with a ribbon. Claire was quite lovely but Molly felt like an unkempt rag doll.

As everyone walked toward the dining room, Logan approached. He quickly gave her a hug, her stiff body swept awkwardly into the embrace.

"I didn't know who you were last night," he said, his voice and eyes full of warmth. "I guess saying 'It's good to see you' is a bit of an understatement."

She pulled back, beginning to relax.

"I knew it was you last night," she said. "You and Matt look too much alike." Logan released her and stepped aside because Matt suddenly filled the space between them.

Molly chanced a glance at him finally — her breath catching at the forcefulness of his gaze on her — and was surprised to see he was annoyed. She guessed it was from her appearance.

"Yeah, but I'm the good-lookin' one," Logan drawled.

Molly grinned, unable to stop the spontaneous gesture. Logan had always been easy enough to get along with, and that obviously hadn't changed. In the next moment, however, Matt ushered him away, putting his hand on the small of her back and guiding her across the hallway to the dining room. The touch made her smile vanish.

Matt's presence was something she'd never considered during the days and nights — the endless weeks — that she'd contemplated returning home.

She had certainly hoped to see him, but in all honesty, she'd imagined him how he was. The man who touched her now was an altogether different story, as was her reaction to him.

Part of her wanted to turn toward him, lean close, close enough to be surrounded by his scent — soap and sun and a more subtle masculine smell — and blanket his strength around her. The other part of her wanted to run and never look back. These yearnings she was beginning to develop for him would only get her heart into trouble. Despite her inexperience with men, she knew that much for certain.

Protecting herself from attachments had made surviving the last ten years bearable — almost. Nothing, and no one, had ever remained constant in her life.

So much had changed, and it was clear that in no time, she'd be on her way again. She had thought Texas was her destination, but her home was no longer here. Her folks were dead, their ranch abandoned, and her sisters gone. Nothing remained except to deal with Davis Walker.

"The only thing you're better looking than is an armadillo," Matt said as they entered the dining room.

Pulling out a chair for Molly, he directed Claire into the one beside her, then he and Logan sat across from them. Jonathan settled before a large window — bright sunlight filled the room with the promise of a new day — and Susanna was opposite him at the other end. The large table, made of a dark wood with intricate carvings around the edge, was filled with shiny white plates and silverware that was clean and straight. The matching chairs were broad and heavy.

A long table sat against one wall and a tall china cabinet guarded the other, filled with glasses and tableware that made Molly feel apprehensive. Eating had never been such a complicated affair for her. The previous night she and Claire had eaten in the kitchen with Susanna, suiting Molly perfectly well.

"I've always thought armadillos were handsome little fellas," Logan replied blandly.

A sudden thought occurred to Molly. "Claire, have you been introduced to Logan?"

"Yes," Claire answered, leveling a cool gaze at Matt's brother. "Just before you came in."

Logan grinned, then winked.

Molly was surprised to see Claire's cheeks become pink. Rarely did Claire react to anything.

"Did you sleep well?" she asked quietly, leaning close to the young woman who had become her travelling companion. But Molly suspected Claire's presence was temporary, as were all relationships in her life.

"Yes. I was fine."

Molly's discomfort was probably not half as much as what Claire was experiencing, being in a strange place with people she didn't know.

Matt and Logan bumped elbows as they started to eat, with Logan getting in an extra jab just for good measure.

"I keep forgetting you're a lefty." Exasperated, Matt dodged another elbow. "But you don't seem to have a problem forgetting I'm older than you."

"I can take you," Logan boasted over a mouthful of scrambled eggs. "Anytime, anyplace. You name the day."

Susanna leaned toward Molly and Claire. "Just when I think they're grown adult men they remind me I haven't lost my boys yet." Then, in a louder voice, "Will the two of you switch seats?"

Matt moved and sat directly across from Molly. She glanced up and caught him watching her. She almost dropped her fork.

"There's something I've wanted to know all these years," said Logan, "and now that you're here, Molly, maybe you can answer it for me. During the summer when we were all at your pa's ranch, who exactly stole all my clothes one afternoon after we'd broken a bunch of horses and gone swimming in the holding pond?"

Molly coughed, swallowing her eggs with effort. "Well," she hesitated, "that would have been Emma."

"Emma?" Logan asked, astonished. "Little seven- or eight-year-old Emma?"

"My little sister," Molly said in an aside to Claire.

"And the sweetest little girl you could ever meet," Matt added. "I wonder who gave her the idea to steal Logan's clothing." He looked directly at Molly.

"You can't blame me for that one," she said defensively. "It was all her idea. Although, she might've had some help from Joey or Cale."

Susanna laughed. "What happened?"

"Mrs. Hart eventually took pity on me and threw me a bed linen," Logan said.

Molly cleared her throat. "There might have been another reason Emma did it, now that I think about it. Both of us heard talk of your...well, that you have a mark, on a certain place on your body. A birthmark? I think Emma might've been overly curious."

Susanna smiled. "Yes, he was born with it. Matthew has one too," she added conversationally.

Matt and Logan both turned a dark shade of red. Although Logan's birthmark didn't interest her, she couldn't help but wonder what Matt's looked like, and where exactly it was located. She supposed she now had a blush to match everyone else's.

Molly remembered she wanted to ask Jonathan and Susanna about the death of her folks. Matt must have sensed her thoughts.

"Have you and ma talked about the night the Harts died?" he asked.

"Yes." Jonathan set his coffee cup down, his expression becoming grim, and looked at Molly. "I wish I could tell you something more specific, but the truth is, we were all devastated by what happened. There was no reason to suspect anyone your folks knew." Pausing, he sighed. "Least of all Davis Walker. Although it did seem odd to me at the time that he didn't help us investigate what happened, and he didn't offer to help search for you. But then again, Matthew was out searching day and night."

"You were?" Molly's attention shifted to Matt. "I thought you said Cale found the girl who was killed."

"That's true," Jonathan said. "Matthew got himself so worn out I nearly had to tie him down to get him to rest. That was when Cale found the body we thought was yours."

She supposed Matt's perseverance shouldn't have surprised her, but it did. His eyes, ever shifting from light blue to a gray-green, met hers. For a moment, she sensed how hard it had been on him all those years ago, trying to find her and failing. She wanted to say something to him but couldn't find the words.

Instead, she turned to Susanna, sitting beside her. "Did my mama ever confide in you?"

The older woman hesitated. "Well, no, not really. Matthew told us about the letter you have from Davis, written to her. I'm not sure if you ever knew this, but your mother was engaged to Davis before she married your father."

Stunned, Molly murmured, "I had no idea."

"Why didn't anyone ever say anything?" Matt asked.

"Well," Susanna responded, "it just never seemed appropriate to talk about. It was in the past, after all. When we all lived in Virginia, Davis and Robert were good friends. When Rosemary became involved with Robert, an obvious strain was put on that friendship. But things seemed to sort themselves when Davis married Loretta. Of course, now that I think about it, it was strange that Davis settled so near to the Harts when we came out here to Texas."

Molly thought of the letter she'd retrieved from her survival kit. Had her mother been involved with Davis again while in Texas? Had she still felt something for him? But she was gone now, along with the truth about what happened all those years ago.

But Davis Walker still lived. What would he say if she were to ask him about it? Molly decided if it came to that, she would.

"But what about here in Texas?" she asked Susanna. "Was Davis involved with my mama here?"

Susanna shook her head slowly. "I don't know. I truly hope she wasn't."

"I'll do some checking around," Matt said. "See what I can find out."

"So will I," Jonathan added. "In the meantime, you young ladies are welcome to stay as long as you like. Where are you from, Claire?"

"The New Mexico Territory, sir."

"You girls sure traveled quite a ways alone. Do you have family waitin' on you?"

Claire paused. "Of a sort."

Jonathan nodded. "Well, when you're wantin' to get home, we'll get you there, one way or another."

"Thank you," Claire said. "But I wouldn't want to trouble anyone."

"Nonsense. The spring roundup'll be startin' here in a few days, but we'll work somethin' out." Jonathan stood, throwing his napkin on his now-empty plate. "C'mon, boys. This ranch doesn't run itself."

"Don't I know it," muttered Logan, standing also. "Ladies." He grinned in Claire's direction as he left the room.

Matt hesitated.

"Don't worry," Susanna said to him. "I'll keep an eye on them. I thought we could write to Molly's sisters this morning."

Molly smiled in gratitude. "Thank you, Mrs. Ryan."

"I'll check back later," Matt said. With one last glance, he turned and departed also, his right leg stiff and the limp she noticed the day before more pronounced.

Molly thought to ask Susanna about it, but decided she would rather ask Matt directly. It would give her an excuse to talk to him later. They had ten years of catching up to do.

And she was becoming more and more curious about what had happened to him during that time.

Curiosity. Yes, that was it.

Or so she told herself.

Chapter Nine

It was mid-afternoon when Matt found Molly in the barn. At first he didn't think she was there — he only came looking for her in this particular place because his ma said Molly had wanted to check on her horse. Then he saw her, inside the stall that held her animal. Sitting near the gate, she leaned against one of the walls, dozing. He stopped and watched her.

She wore the same dress as she had at breakfast, the dark color hugging curves — despite the ill-fitting garment — that he was trying hard to ignore. *Try harder.* Her brown hair curled softly around her face; her long lashes drew his gaze to the handful of light freckles sprinkling her small, straight nose. His gaze dropped to her mouth. Her soft, rosy lips were entirely too appealing. What the hell had happened to the little girl?

Guilt washed over him unannounced. She must have been nothing less than terrified, ripped from her family and her home, forced to live within a culture so different from her own, only to find the promise of freedom violently taken from her at the hands of a filthy comancheros trader. Then, finally, to be saved by an absent-minded miner who had dragged her south into the middle of nowhere.

It was a miracle she had survived at all.

It was a miracle she still retained any trace of sweetness to her, but he remembered her fortitude and enthusiasm for life when she was a child. She hadn't been one to dwell on problems. And he didn't doubt such an attitude had kept her strong in the face of such devastating challenges.

But as she sat before him, quietly slumbering, her innocence and vulnerability cut him to the bone. If only he'd stayed with her that night, so long ago, he might have spared her the hardships of the last ten years.

A gunshot cracked through the air. Matt jumped to his feet, looking toward the ranch house. A full moon illuminated the hill where he'd found Molly digging in the dirt to bury her survival kit. The distant sounds of social chattering and laughter gave way to screams and more gunfire.

"What's going on, Matt?" Molly's voice, laced with fear, barely penetrated his thoughts.

"I don't know." Her pale dress caught the corner of his eye as she moved to stand beside him.

It was essential he get down there and do something. His mind raced to where his gun was located, in the bunkhouse near his saddlebags. He needed to get it as quickly as possible. He faced Molly and grasped her shoulders.

"Don't go near the house, do you hear me? Stay here and stay undercover. I'll come back for you when it's safe."

Molly nodded, but her eyes were fixed on the confusion a quarter-mile away.

Matt moved away from her.

That was the last time he saw her alive.

Until yesterday.

Molly stirred, then opened her eyes. When she noticed him she quickly stood, pushing her hair back and adjusting her dress. "How long was I asleep?" she asked hastily.

"I don't know. You probably shouldn't take naps in the stalls with the horses, though. You could get hurt."

She patted her horse's neck. "Pecos wouldn't harm me." But she opened the gate and stepped out of the berth anyway. "She was a gift from Elijah, from one of the rare times when he actually struck gold. He bought her from a trader who said he'd gotten her from one of the finest horse breeders in Mexico."

Pecos nuzzled Molly's neck, making her laugh. "I'd say she's the best friend I've had for the past year or so."

Matt crossed his arms and leaned a shoulder against a thick wooden post. "Mind me asking why you didn't stay put that night?"

She rubbed her palm along Pecos' nose, clearly enjoying the horse's closeness. "You just left me standing there. I know I should've stayed put, but I became worried about Emma."

"So you came down to the house?"

"Not right in the open, since there were men everywhere. But one grabbed me...after that I don't remember what happened. Can I ask you something?"

Matt nodded.

She took a steadying breath. "How did my folks die?"

Matt ran a hand through his hair, then repositioned his hat. He'd never been one to sugarcoat things, so he wouldn't start now. Especially not with Molly. She deserved the truth.

"Your father was shot in the head. Your mother in the chest." The stillness in the barn was only interrupted by Pecos' occasional snickering. "By all accounts, it appeared your ma threw herself in front of your pa."

Molly became quiet as she considered what he told her. "So she tried to save him?"

"That's what everyone concluded."

"Everyone?"

"Ranchers, neighbors, cowhands. They came from miles around to search for the men who did this. And they came to search for you."

Her blue eyes shone, her expression watchful and serious. And sad. Gone was the girl who ran and hid in the hills and gullies surrounding the Hart ranch, the girl who caught snakes better than any ranch hand, the girl who dreamed of living on her own one day in the wild, open prairies of Texas.

"Tell me about your time with the Comanche," he said.

A ghostly smile formed on her lips. "Do you remember the stories Cale would tell me about the abduction of Cynthia Ann Parker?"

"Yeah, I remember." He also recalled telling Cale to stop filling her head with tales certain to scare a young girl, but by then Molly had already been quite taken with them.

"She was abducted from her home as a child and grew up within a Comanche tribe. She became the wife of Peta Nocona and bore him three children. Have you heard of her son, Quanah Parker?"

Matt nodded. Quanah Parker had led his tribe, the Kwahadi, to the reservation in a surprising act of surrender two years prior. The man understood more than most that the Comanche couldn't fight the tide of change overtaking the land, and he'd wanted his people to live. Matt couldn't help but respect the courage it must've taken for him to reach such a decision. The Comanche were wanderers. Life on the reservation often took its toll, for the very spirit of the Indians was frequently crushed from being forced to stay in only one place.

"I was with Kwaina," Molly continued. "I often wondered at the irony of that."

"You knew him?"

She shook her head. "No, not really. I saw him a handful of times. He was in the party that originally took me, but he wasn't really a man of violence, and disagreed with the torturing of captives."

"Were you tortured?" he asked quickly, his world shifting uncomfortably once again. The thought sickened him.

"No, I was fortunate. I was adopted into Bull Runner's lodge and lived with his two wives, Coyote Woman and Rain Cloud, and his two daughters, Sits On Ground and Running Water. There was also a grandfather, Bird Fly High, who lived with us. He gave me my Comanche name, *Canauocué Juhtzú*."

"Bird?"

"Yes," Molly replied, her surprise apparent. "Cactus bird, actually. You speak Comanche?"

"Not really. But you pick things up here and there."

"It got to the point where I could only speak Comanche."

"You forgot English?"

"I guess you could say that. I just stopped using it, and soon it was lost to me." She shrugged. "But Elijah helped me relearn it." Smiling sheepishly, she added, "He refreshed my memory of cuss words before tackling anything else."

Matt grinned. "I suppose you blame me for teaching them to you in the first place."

"Not just you," she said. "Cale, Logan, Joey — they had colorful vocabularies as well."

"Colorful vocabularies? That's a mouthful for someone who recently forgot English."

"Elijah took book learning seriously."

"He taught you to read?" Matt asked.

"No." She laughed. "I had to teach him to read."

"Sounds like a lot of work."

"It was," she agreed. "But I had a lot of spare time on my hands."

"Explain to me again why Bull Runner wanted to give you back."

Molly continued to stroke Pecos while she spoke. "After I'd been with the Kwahadi for several winters, Rain Cloud suggested I participate in a ceremony known as girls-becoming-women, in which the girls hold onto the tail of a horse and attempt to run with the animal. But I didn't want to do it. I still considered myself a captive and always hoped I'd be rescued or somehow escape."

Matt flinched inwardly at her words. There was never any hope of a rescue because no one had known she'd lived and needed saving.

"To run the race would make me a Comanche woman," Molly continued. "I refused to accept them that much. But in the end, Bull Runner insisted, thinking it was a good idea. Sits On Ground, his oldest daughter, also was running in the race. She and I were about the same age. So, I ran."

Matt swore under his breath. "You could have been trampled to death."

"It was a little scary, but I did well. A little too well, I guess. I began to receive a great deal of unwanted attention from many of the warriors in camp."

"Why?"

"I was now considered available, and the fact I was a white captive didn't seem to make any difference."

That bit of news didn't surprise Matt. Molly was a striking woman. Any man, red or white, would have noticed her.

"Eventually, an offer of twenty horses was left in front of Bull Runner's lodge by a warrior named Snake Eater. It was a huge overture, and Bull Runner was very happy about it. But, he was confused as to which daughter Snake Eater wanted for his wife. For that many horses, Bull Runner was prepared to give all of us to him, myself as well as Sits On Ground and Running Water."

"How old was Running Water?"

"A few years younger than me."

Matt shook his head. Forcing girls to marry at such a young age was barbaric in his mind. That Molly was one of those girls only increased his disgust.

"But it turned out Snake Eater only wanted me," she continued. "It really made no sense, since having many wives was of great importance to most Comanche men."

Matt saw what Molly obviously couldn't. Snake Eater wanted her, and only her, and he made sure Bull Runner wouldn't refuse him. A swift and possessive jealousy gripped him, a feeling so unfamiliar that all he could do was stare at Molly, stunned by the rawness of it.

"Sits on Ground wasn't happy about the turn of events," she said, oblivious to his reaction. "She felt snubbed and rightly so. Offers were rarely made for captives—usually the father had to make his own proposal to a warrior to get him to take the woman or girl off his hands. Sits On Ground began being very difficult."

"Did you want Snake Eater?" The question was out before Matt thought better of it.

"No." Molly stroked her horse again. "I told Sits On Ground she could be his wife, if she wanted him, but Snake Eater insisted he would only accept *me*. That's when Bull Runner offered to return me to my people. He said he was fond of me and he really didn't want to let me go, but my presence was causing him embarrassment with his domestic matters. He could've just traded me to another lodge within the tribe, but for some reason he was willing to do more than that."

Matt was grateful Bull Runner had treated Molly so well. If only he hadn't left her with Jose Torres.

"How did Snake Eater react to this?"

"He wasn't too happy. I was taken with a raiding party into the New Mexico Territory. Snake Eater was among the warriors riding. For a moment, I thought he might steal me, but Bull Runner was there, and he made sure there wasn't any trouble."

"He obviously didn't stick around to make sure Torres would take care of you." Thinking of it darkened Matt's mood.

"No. Why do you limp?"

The change of subject threw him. He never spoke of it, had told his ma very little, his pa even less. But Molly had just shared her difficult past with him. He knew it wouldn't be right for him to put her off.

"I've been with the Rangers the past few years. About six months ago, I was captured trying to bring in a Mexican named Cerillo who was murdering and looting his way throughout much of the Texas-Mexican border. My leg was injured. It's only just healed."

"He tortured you?" Concern clouded Molly's blue eyes. "For six months?"

"No, it was about four months, actually." Matt tried to smile, but memories of that time still afflicted him, still left him shaking and covered in sweat after awaking from all-too-real dreams in the middle of the night.

"Did you escape?"

"No, a friend of mine got me out." Matt knew he owed his life to Nathan Blackmore.

"You managed to survive. Sometimes that's all there is in a situation in which nothing else bears remembering."

He sensed she spoke of herself as well as him.

Survival. When life was reduced to that, not much else mattered.

"Let's get some supper," he said. "I'm sure everyone is wondering where we are."

After a final goodbye to Pecos, Molly left the barn with Matt behind her. The wind whipped around them as darkness began to blanket the land. Abruptly, she turned back. He bumped into her before he could stop.

Smiling up at him, she tucked her unruly hair behind one ear. "I'm glad you're all right, Matt. I'm sure your folks and Logan are grateful to have you back. And I'm grateful I was able to see you again."

Her admission put him at a loss for words. It was all so damn unfair. The ten years Molly lost were gone forever. He still couldn't reconcile that she lived—a vibrant, breathing woman, standing just inches from him.

"Is there someone...?" her voice trailed off.

"Someone?"

"Someone special to you." Her earnest expression held him spellbound.

"You mean a woman?" He shook his head. "No."

"Never?"

He considered her question, the weight of the past pushing against the barriers of the present. He shook his head again.

She acknowledged him with a slight nod. Her gaze settled beyond his shoulder as a gust of wind pushed against them. "Do you believe in the greater good?"

"I'm not sure what you mean."

"That there's a purpose to the workings of this life."

"Believe me, I can see no good reason for what happened to you, Molly. And if I could go back, I'd make damn sure I took you away that night, and tied you up to keep you safe."

She laughed, but the sound was somewhat disheartening. "You knew me well back then, but in the end, I don't think you could've stopped what happened. The Comanche believe the dead still walk the earth. Maybe my folks had other business to tend to. Maybe I'll meet up with them again someday."

"For ten years I thought you were dead," he said thickly, his eyes locking with hers. "There were many times I dreamt of you." The unexpected constriction in his throat made him falter. "I wanted more than anything to bring you back."

She grabbed his hand, the touch jolting him. Without warning, she leaned forward and kissed him on the cheek. The warmth of her lips ran straight through his body. The shock of her soft curves pressing into him overwhelmed his male senses.

"Thank you for remembering me," she whispered.

As she moved away, another gust of wind slammed into him. His body felt raw and exposed. He wanted her heat and tenderness to touch him once again.

Matt couldn't move.

There had been women in his life. Fine women, fast women, some beautiful, some simply interested in the fury created between the sheets. Matt hadn't been a man to deny himself, not if his partner was experienced and willing.

But he *would* deny himself with Molly, even if it killed him. She wasn't experienced. She deserved better. She deserved a chance to explore what she wanted on her own.

Matt cared for her—he always had—but he wouldn't take advantage of any affection she might possibly still have for him. She had kissed him in sisterly gratitude, he would do well to remember that. She needed more than a dried-up Ranger plagued by nightmares, a Ranger withered and worn before his time.

Chapter Ten

Matt reined in his horse near the main house, then dismounted. He'd spent all morning repairing a collapsed roof on one of the line shacks. With his stomach growling for food, he was about to enter the house when he noticed Molly on horseback in the larger of the two corrals. He didn't recognize the man with her. Tying off his horse, he walked toward them, but Logan came out of the barn and cut him off.

"Who's that with Molly?" he asked.

Logan squinted. "Well, let's see. His name is Howie, I think. Howie Martin. Yep, that's it."

"*Who* is Howie Martin?" Matt asked ominously. He didn't like the gleam in his brother's eyes.

"He's workin' the Callahan ranch. Came by to return some of our beeves that wandered onto their land, so I didn't want to pass on a great opportunity."

"And what would that be?" Matt knew Logan was deliberately trying to provoke him.

"A potential suitor for Molly."

Matt stopped short, and Logan just laughed. "You said we ought to marry her off." His brother slapped him on the back and they continued to approach the corral.

Molly sat on Pecos, bareback, talking to Howie while he tried to mount his horse, also without a saddle. But the youth, blond-haired and wide-eyed, couldn't seem to get the animal to settle down.

"Molly's quite a good rider," Logan said just for Matt's ears. "I suggested she teach Howie how to ride bareback. I think he's fairly taken with her, don't you? Although I wouldn't mention matrimony just yet. Wouldn't want to scare him off."

"Howie doesn't look old enough to shave yet." Logan's meddling irritated him. What he'd said about doing right by Molly was one thing; seeing the reality of it was something else entirely.

"Yeah, I know," Logan conceded. "That's why I asked him how old he was. He claims he's nineteen. God's truth," he added, straight-faced. "He also pointed out, in front of Molly I might add, he's making forty-five dollars a month from the Callahans. The lad seems solid."

Matt swore under his breath as Logan walked off, grinning from ear to ear.

"Howie, you've really got to calm down," Molly was saying. "If the horse won't stop moving, you won't be able to get on."

"But you jumped on yer horse while she was movin'," Howie said in exasperation.

"I don't think you're quite ready for that."

Molly's hair was gathered at the base of her neck and hidden by her hat. Although the graceful lines of her posture caught Matt's eye, it was the glimpse of bare leg peeking from beneath a light blue skirt that drew his gaze, annoying him. It bunched up far too much. Why wasn't she wearing stockings?

And why was she riding bareback in a dress anyhow?

"Molly," he said loudly.

Startled, she looked over her shoulder at him, then smiled and waved. At that moment Howie managed to hoist himself onto his horse but in mere seconds was thrown to the ground. He groaned.

"Howie?" Molly turned her attention back to the youth. "Are you all right? It's all about balance. I thought you'd ridden since you were six."

He dusted off his backside and stood. "Yeah, but it's a lot easier with a saddle to hang onto."

"Howie," Matt said, "I'm sure the Callahans are wondering what happened to you. You better get on back."

"Who're you?" he asked.

"Matthew Ryan."

At that the boy's eyes widened even more. "Really? It's a great pleasure to meet you, Mister Ryan." Howie immediately moved to the edge of the corral where Matt stood casually resting arms on the wooden fence. Howie shook Matt's hand enthusiastically. "I've heard a lot about you, sir. You're a legend in these parts, ridin' with the Rangers. Was it really true you killed a bear while fightin' off hundreds of Kiowas? And did you kill a two-timin' trader from five hundred yards with only one shot right between his eyes?"

Molly moved her horse closer. When Matt chanced a glance at her, he caught her smiling.

"Tall tales, Howie," he said. "Don't believe everything you hear."

"Gosh, I sure would love to hear about some of your adventures," the boy gushed.

"Maybe some other time." Matt felt uncomfortable with such adoration. There was nothing in his life he would label an adventure. Too much death and violence had been attached to it.

"Could I bring some buddies?" Howie asked, latching onto the prospect.

Matt thought Logan would love that—more potential husbands for Molly. But Howie seemed more interested in him at the moment, not a pretty young woman. The boy needed to get his priorities straight, having all but forgotten Molly. Logan would probably howl at that too, but Matt felt oddly reassured by it.

"I'll think about it," Matt said. "Now get going."

"Gotcha." He excitedly shook Matt's hand again. "I'll see ya, Mister Ryan." He walked his horse out of the corral to where he'd left his saddle. Belatedly, he remembered Molly. "Oh yeah, bye Miss Molly. Thanks for the ridin' lesson." He waved a few times before cinching his saddle atop his horse, hoisting himself up then heading south.

"Logan asked me to teach him," Molly said, frowning. "Do most ranches normally have such poor riders?"

Matt grimaced. "No, not usually." He walked along the fence to the gate, watching as Molly gracefully slid from Pecos' back. Finally the skirt was where it ought to be. He held the gate while Molly walked through.

"Do you always ride bareback in dresses?" he asked.

"No, of course not. It was more awkward than I thought it would be."

"I was in search of lunch before I was sidetracked. Wanna join me?"

"Sidetracked by what?" She fell in step beside him.

"You." He looked directly at her.

A lovely blush brightened her face, which pleased him inordinately. He grinned as he glanced around the ranch his father had built from nothing over the years.

Matt was fifteen when his folks had left Virginia and come to Texas, looking for a fresh start after the Civil War. He still remembered living out of a little shack, he and Logan helping their pa chase down and rope the wild longhorns roaming everywhere in abundance. For the first time, it dawned on Matt what an incredible gamble the old man had taken.

All for the love of a woman. His father's devotion to Susanna Ryan was unsurpassed in these parts. He was a tough son-of-a-bitch when he wanted to be, but he made no bones about why he worked as hard as he did. "It's all for you, darlin'," Matt had heard his pa say on more than one occasion. His ma's response was always a bashful smile, a reaction only his old man could ever elicit.

"There's an old shack on the property not far from here," Matt said as he guided Molly around to the back of the house. "It's where we lived when we first came here from Virginia. Maybe we could ride out some afternoon and have a look."

"I remember living out of our wagon for a time. Our families had so little when we came out here."

"I often wished Robert Hart had never brought any of you at all."

A wistful expression crossed Molly's face. "I knew this was home the moment my feet hit the dirt."

Matt stared into her blue eyes.

Home.

"Do you still feel that way?" he asked, intensely curious. After all she had been through, it was a wonder she didn't hate everyone and everything associated with her ordeal for the last ten years.

She hesitated. "I'm not sure. Home isn't a concept I'm familiar with anymore."

Turning, she climbed the few steps to the back porch. Matt followed her through the door that led to the kitchen. They both simultaneously removed their hats. The elderly Mexican cook glanced over her shoulder when she heard the door open.

"Rosita," Matt said. "Sorry to bother you, but I'm looking for somethin' to eat."

Pursing her lips, Rosita wiped her flour-dusted hands on her apron and walked toward them. "*Señor* Matt, I just cleaned up lunch."

Matt looked down at her. Rosita was very short, but far from meek or helpless. She and her husband had been at the SR for years. Juan was one of the best horse wranglers they employed. Their children had since scattered to the wind, much the way Matt and Logan had; his ma had pointed that out one day not long ago. He knew his mother would like nothing better than to see him settled somewhere, preferably close. "To see my grandchildren," she had said.

But Matt just didn't see himself with offspring. What he'd seen of youngsters caught in the crossfire of Indian wars, and the brutality in general of this land, had convinced him that children were better left to the worries of others.

"And is this the *señorita* Juan was speaking of?" Rosita shifted her attention to Molly. "He say you are *muy bien* with the horses. You ride like an Indian, he say. My Juan, he not impressed by many people, but you…all through lunch he talk about you."

"Thank you," Molly answered.

"So, you both sit down." Rosita ushered them to a long table flanked on each side by a wooden bench. "I make you something to eat." She walked back to the stove and began spooning something into bowls. "What is your name?"

Matt sat next to Molly on one side of the table. They would both be able to speak to Rosita this way, he told himself. He ignored the fact that being near Molly was just plain nice.

"Well, it's Matt," he answered innocently. "I thought you knew that."

Rosita fixed him with a glare. "Oh, you Ryan boys. You never get a wife with such a smart mouth. I tell my Juan he must teach you boys some charm. *Sí, sí*," she said loudly, raising her arms for emphasis, "charm. Not a *señorita* who could resist you then, since the good Lord already blessed you with a handsome face. It is almost wicked, I say." She set the steaming, aromatic bowls before them.

"Thank you, and my name is Molly."

"Where you come from?" Rosita asked earnestly.

Molly cleared her throat, glancing at Matt. "Mexico?"

"Molly is an old friend," Matt intervened. "She's been away for many years."

Rosita ignored him. "Where in *Méjico*?"

"Well, I lived mostly in the mountains," Molly replied.

Rosita planted a fist on each hip. A spoon extended from one hand and dripped sauce onto the floor. Molly let out a sigh. "Before that," she added, "I lived for many years with the Comanche."

The Mexican cook's eyes widened.

Matt started to eat the bean, corn, and tomato stew flavored with chili peppers. He was too hungry to wait while the women spoke.

Rosita put a plate of flour tortillas before him and a pitcher of water. He poured a glass for Molly then for himself.

"Well, that explains how you came to ride so well," Rosita finally said. "The Comanche, they are expert horseman. They teach their women to ride?"

Molly nodded while spooning the stew into her mouth. She suddenly coughed.

"Spicy, *sí*," Rosita said. "You drink water."

Molly took a big gulp, then reached for a tortilla.

"You'll get used to Rosita's cooking," Matt said to Molly, smiling at her watery eyes. "You won't get sick eating this stuff."

"I think I'm sick now," Molly wheezed.

Matt laughed. "What do the Comanche eat?"

"Buffalo, berries, nuts, more buffalo." Molly gulped more water. "It's really very good, Rosita. Thank you." But her voice was still strained.

The petite woman waved her off with a smile. "You eat it all. You look too thin. Those Indians starve you?"

"Not on purpose," Molly replied. "But some winters were long."

Matt finished his portion, then started to stand so he could get a second helping when Molly's hand on his arm stopped him. She slid her bowl before him and beckoned him back into his seat.

"You should eat more. Rosita's right—you're too thin."

"Isn't that better than too fat?" she asked with an amused glint in her eyes.

When he continued to glare at her, she reached for another tortilla and began eating it. He ate her stew while Rosita busied herself around the large kitchen.

"You have no marks from the Comanche," Rosita said. "They no mark you up?"

Molly shook her head. "No. I was treated well, for the most part."

"How old when they take you?"

"I was nine."

"You lucky to come back."

"Yes, I know."

"I know men attacked. The Indians, they scalp them. Some don't die." Rosita shook her head. "They wear a hat to hide it."

"Anyone in particular you know?" Matt asked curiously.

"Juan meet a man at the Bautista ranch a few months back. He was ugly as a mangy dog. Juan, he certain the man was scalped many years ago."

"Do you remember his name?" Matt questioned.

Rosita paused, thinking. "Whitaker he say. *Sí*, that was his name."

Matt turned the information over in his head. A connection to Walker seemed unlikely, but it was a place to start. He'd talk to Dawson first. The foreman knew most of the ranches in the area and would probably know who this Whitaker was, whom he might have worked for in the past.

"What are you thinking?" Molly interrupted his thoughts.

"Nothing you need to worry over." He wanted to involve Molly as little as possible in the search for the man or men who killed her folks.

Standing, he grabbed his hat and made to leave. "*Muchas gracias*, Rosita."

Molly came up quickly behind him, following him outside and down the steps. "Wait," she said. "Do you think this man Whitaker could have been involved in the attack ten years ago?"

Matt placed his hat on his head, then stopped to look at the young woman running after him. "Molly, do me a favor."

"What?"

"Trust me. I'll take care of this. I don't want you involved."

"Why not?" she asked, her irritation evident.

"Because you should be looking to the future, not looking for the kind of vermin that would commit such cold-blooded crimes. You should think about finding a husband and making a house full of babies instead."

"Is that why you think I came back? To find a husband and live happily ever after?" Pushing her hat onto her head, she rested her hands on slender hips hugged by a dress the same color as the sky, a dress his mother had undoubtedly given her. This one fit annoyingly better than the brown one.

With curves like hers, Molly would have no trouble having a whole bushel of babes. The thought irritated him, imagining some other man enjoying those curves.

"If you decide to go see this Whitaker man, will you promise to take me with you?" Her voice was firm.

"I'm not going to make a promise like that."

"You need me," she argued. "I was the only witness to all of this. I might remember something that could be useful. I came back hoping to see my family again, and all I got were grave markers. I have nothing, Matt. Nothing save my horse, a few meager supplies, and what little gold I have left from Elijah. Maybe that makes you think I'd be looking for a man to take care of me, but that couldn't be further from my mind. What I want right now is simply the truth. And then, maybe, I can begin to consider the future."

Matt saw the determination in her eyes, but he also caught a clear glimpse of the shadows. The scars of the past ten years flashed to the surface; they had lain hidden deeper than even he had suspected.

He wanted to wipe the fear from her haunted eyes. He wanted her safe. He wanted...things he shouldn't.

"I'll think about it." He could give her that much, at least.

"Hey, Matt." The yell came from near the corral. Matt looked over his shoulder at Dawson. "Blackmore's ridin' in."

"Thanks." His gaze came back to Molly.

Her face, shaded by her hat, was still etched with concern.

Such a little sprite she'd once been, stirring up emotions within him he'd never expected — affection, fondness, protectiveness. Such a resolute woman she'd become, stirring...damn, he really didn't want to dwell on that. Nothing good would come of it.

"Why don't you come and meet Nathan?" he said, walking toward the man approaching on a dark horse. Perhaps his friend would be interested in Molly. On the heels of that thought came an irrational impulse to usher her back into the house to keep her from the eyes of any of the men on the ranch, including Nathan, but he forced himself to resist it.

He couldn't have it both ways. His mind, however, was beginning to lean to the possibility that he knew wasn't a possibility at all, a circumstance he wasn't sure he could live with if he ever let it occur.

As he stood beside her and waited for the man who had saved his life, the hard reality of his own truth slapped him in the face.

He wanted Molly for himself.

Chapter Eleven

By mid-afternoon Molly trailed behind Matt and Nathan as their horses picked a path along a streambed, its course surrounded by scrub cottonwoods. The warm day under the cloudless sky heralded the hot summer soon to arrive.

Molly pushed her hat back slightly and turned her face to soak up the heat of the sun. Having lived intimately with the land for so long, even one night spent at the Ryan ranch, as nice as it was, had her feeling out of rhythm. Now that she was outside in the open spaces, she felt more herself.

Since Matt and Nathan discussed something she couldn't hear, she focused her attention instead on the various birds darting to and from the many trees surrounding the stream.

While with the Comanche, she had often watched the many birds abounding out in the wild. Their freedom made her envious. Sometimes at night, when the loneliness and fears were the most prevalent, she would imagine she was a wren flying high, fast and free. Her soul would lift to the wind, soaring above the land. Or, so she imagined. Perhaps they were foolish daydreams, but they kept her sane when the grief of being torn from her family threatened to overwhelm her.

Her Comanche grandfather, Bird Fly High, had noticed her interest in birds from the beginning and often talked to her of them. A quiet, soft-spoken man, a bit stooped but still strong, he always helped whenever they moved camp, aiding her and the other women and girls in dismantling the teepees and strapping the heavy cedar lodge poles to the horses and donkeys. Then, he would usually walk rather than ride atop a horse, always saying he liked the exercise for his old bones.

"You watch the *tiriejuhtzú* with a keen eye," Bird Fly High had said to her one day.

Molly had simply nodded in reply.

"To understand the *juhtzú,* one must have a sharp mind, able to discern the smallest of details from a larger landscape. It can be a difficult medicine because you must be careful not to keep your head in the clouds too much. Are you a dreamer, *tiriejuhtzú?*"

Molly had grasped most of what he'd said. Everyday her comprehension of the Comanche language had expanded as she'd paid attention to the women and children speaking around her. But she'd always hesitated to voice the language herself, fearing a loss of connection to her own people.

So she'd answered, "*Jaa,*" and left it at that. Bird Fly High had nodded in approval and clasped her shoulder, telling her with his touch that he understood her.

A part of her missed the old man, and she wondered if he still lived. The thought of not ever knowing saddened her. He had taught her many things—about Comanche lore, about the land, and especially about birds. For the first time, a sense of gratitude filled her for knowing him.

Matt and Nathan splashed their horses across the stream then took to a well-worn trail, the route winding its way through several low-lying hills covered with juniper and cottonwood trees. Spring was in bloom and green engulfed the land.

She was glad Matt hadn't excluded her from this excursion. While his desire to protect her from the ugliness of what had happened to her folks warmed her, it was already too late for that. She needed to be here. In the end, he must've realized that.

When this was all over, she would need to think of her future. The thought left her feeling adrift. Where would she go? Claire had decided to stay at the SR instead of accompanying the three of them to the Bautista ranch, but Molly knew at some point her friend would need to return to the New Mexico Territory. Perhaps she should go with her, and then continue on to California to see Emma and her aunt. She had no reason to stay in Texas anymore, but the thought constricted her chest.

She was back in trousers again because it was far more comfortable, but she found she missed the dresses. Not that looking like a woman had anything to do with it. But, if she had to be honest, it rankled her a bit that Matt still treated her as if she were nine years old. Maybe he was right. Maybe she really was searching for a husband and just didn't realize it.

If that were true, then why did she care less what Nathan thought of her clothing, but Matt's opinion nagged at her?

Molly glanced at Nathan. He'd been cordial enough when Matt introduced them earlier, but it was quickly apparent, even with Molly's limited experience with men, he wasn't a man of ease and openness. A black hat covered dark hair, and a scar on his left cheek made him appear menacing. She could only imagine how he'd acquired it.

He was as tall and lean as Matt, but his eyes carried shadows from which his soul seemed unable to escape. Engaging in small talk with the man gave every indication of being a futile task since there appeared to be nothing lighthearted in either his demeanor or his personality.

Matt and Nathan slowed their mounts so she could ride abreast of them on the far right.

"You and Nathan have something in common," Matt said to her, his horse drawing close. Their legs touched, and Molly savored the brief contact.

"What would that be?" she questioned hesitantly.

"Nathan was held captive by a band of Comanche also."

"You were?" Surprised, she leaned forward to look at the man on the opposite side of Matt. "How old were you?"

"Older than you, from what Matt tells me," Nathan answered. "You're fortunate to have survived. And even more blessed to have found your way home."

"I suppose that's true." Molly knew fate had been against her through the years, but somehow she'd never lost faith in eventually finding her way home. "Which tribe were you with?"

"The Kotsotekas. I was held for about eighteen months before I was able to escape."

"How did you manage that?" How had he done what she'd only dreamed of doing night after night?

"One of the women helped me."

90

"How could one of the women have helped you? They weren't allowed at any of the councils. They weren't even allowed to have medicine."

"I wasn't a boy when I was captured. One of the Indian women took a liking to me and convinced me to start acting daft. After a while, the warriors began letting me accompany them on hunting parties, so I started deliberately getting lost trying to return to camp. Each time I delayed my return a little longer, until one day I just never returned. They naturally assumed I was lost, and therefore didn't come after me, at least not until it was too late."

"How did you know where to go once you were free?" Molly's biggest fear if she ran off—and after a while there had been plenty of opportunities—had been that she would become hopelessly lost.

"I knew where I was, and I'd been making mental notes of landmarks as the tribe moved from place to place, so it only took me four days on foot to reach a white settlement."

"Is that how you got the scar?" An hour ago she never would have guessed how much she and Nathan had in common. She knew male captives, especially older ones, were often not treated well. Some were beaten, overworked, even maimed.

"This one was the least of what they did to me." A muscle in Nathan's jaw flexed, and his expression became shuttered again.

"You always could get out of any scrape," Matt said.

"I got lucky. The woman saved my life. I guess it just disproves most Texan theories that the Comanche are all barbarians."

"But they are barbarians, aren't they?" Molly remarked. "Maybe not as bad as the Tonks. The

Comanche children would whisper stories about how the Tonkawas would boil the arms and legs of any Comanche they captured, eating them. As far as I know, the Kwahadi didn't eat their enemies, but I do recall one time when some of the men returned from a war party with a Ute prisoner. The way they tortured the poor man...it turned my stomach. I couldn't watch." She still had visions of the moment when some of the older women cut off his eyelids, blood pouring down his obscene-looking, wide-eyed face. Afterwards, she'd run back to Bull Runner's teepee and had tried to keep herself from heaving.

"I wouldn't feel sorry for that Ute, Molly." A trace of anger filled Matt's voice. "I've no doubt he did his fair share of butchering."

"You're probably right." She glanced at him, wondering why of late he seemed edgier than usual. But then again, how would she know what was normal for him?

Nathan regarded her. "How did you get back to Texas? Matt said a miner took you into Mexico."

"Elijah Hardin saved my life, and for that I owed him. I tried to tell him about my family, but I couldn't speak much English at first."

Thinking she heard Matt swear she looked at him, but his face was turned away from her. She caught a fleeting smile on Nathan's lips. Both men's behavior was odd. Matt's good spirits appeared to be fading with each passing moment, while Nathan showed himself to be slightly more human than had at first been evident.

"It's tough speaking English when no one will speak it back to you," Nathan remarked.

Molly nodded. "For a while I tried not to speak Comanche. I guess it was my way of rebelling against them, but the English eventually went away. Elijah helped me relearn it while I was with him."

"What happened to him?" Nathan asked.

"He spent a great deal of time searching for gold in his mines." She remembered her solitary existence with the reclusive old man. "It was a strange twist of fate that he died one night in his sleep, considering how many risks he took in abandoned mine shafts and caves. I woke up one morning to find him cold and stiff."

She took a steadying breath, and continued, "So, I buried him, gathered up our belongings, and made my way out of Mexico. One of the reasons I never left Elijah, or the Comanche, was because I didn't think I could find my way out of the wilderness. But, surprisingly, I knew more than I realized. Like you, I'd noticed landmarks and had watched the stars for many years." Then, almost as an afterthought, she added, "Hunting rattlesnakes was frequently uneventful."

"What was that?" Matt asked, his tone almost accusing.

"Can you fathom how boring it was to live with an old man in the mountains, with no one else to talk to," Molly replied defensively. "The nights were the worst. It was too easy to let the loneliness overwhelm me, and I refused to be afraid of the creatures of the night. So, instead of waiting for them to pounce on me, I would hunt them down after sunset. Not to kill them, of course. Well, I did have to kill a few snakes, but that couldn't be helped."

"Why the hell didn't the old man look out for you?"

Molly winced at the outrage in Matt's voice. "I wanted to live, and Elijah couldn't protect a dog if he wanted to. Don't you remember how good I was with my slingshot? I made myself another one."

"Yeah, I remember that thing, and I also remember the rattlesnake you tried to kill with it when you were nine years old. If I hadn't snatched you when I did, it would have grabbed hold and never let go."

"Maybe." She probably shouldn't tell him about her other rattlesnake incident while with the Kwahadi. Smoke might come out of his ears. The image made her smile.

"Just promise me one thing," Matt said firmly. "No more going near snakes."

"Even if I'm hungry?" She couldn't resist teasing him, reminding her of their relationship years ago. He'd been amazingly tolerant with her, considering how much she badgered him with questions, trailing after him to learn all he knew. She wasn't sure what she felt now, but the air fairly crackled between them, making her feel uncertain but also more alive than she could remember in a long while.

Nathan laughed. Molly grinned at him, thinking he wasn't so bad after all.

"Do you really think I'd let you eat a snake?" Matt asked. "I can look after you better than that."

"I never asked you to look after me. No one has looked after me for ten years, and I managed to survive just fine."

"You may as well give it up, Matt," Nathan said. "She can probably cook up a better meal than you anyway."

Matt's only response was silence. Despite his dark mood he rode with ease, his gloved hands casually holding his horse's reins.

"What did you eat when Cerillo had you?" she asked.

Nathan gave his attention to Matt, apparently curious as well.

"Not much." Matt kept his gaze on the terrain ahead. "A snake would have been a feast."

"Now you understand," Molly said quietly.

Matt's blue-green eyes fixated on her. "How did you manage it? How did you keep from going crazy?"

She wrinkled her brows in concentration. "I saw the suffering of other captives, so I learned to keep my mouth shut and do what I was told. They worked me hard, but all of the Comanche women worked hard. They lived a difficult life. My Comanche mothers did show me some kindness, which helped. Every night I would look to the stars though and imagine that somewhere my family watched the very same sky, that you watched the same sky." She smiled at him. "It made me feel connected somehow."

"You survived what many young girls and women couldn't," Nathan said.

"So did you," Molly said to him. "And so did Matt," she added, noting Matt's gaze had softened. An immense gratitude overcame her. She was glad to have found him again.

"Did you hear that, Ryan?" Nathan joked. "She's comparing us to young girls and women."

"Works for you," Matt drawled.

"Next time I'll just leave you in that hell-hole Cerillo built especially for you." But there was no heat in Nathan's words, just a tinge of consideration.

"I'll always be grateful you didn't," Matt murmured.

Molly wished she could say something to ease the memories in Matt's mind, but experience had taught her that time was sometimes the only remedy to soften the edges of a painful past.

* * *

By late afternoon they came to the Bautista ranch, nestled in a valley surrounded by flat-topped buttes. Men on horseback moved back and forth, attending to a group of longhorn cattle imprisoned within a corral. Matt knew the men were readying the animals for branding, reminding him that soon the SR would need to begin their spring round-up as well.

After a few inquiries, they learned Whitaker was in the bunkhouse. As they approached the one-story wooden structure, Matt told Molly to wait outside while he and Nathan questioned the man, thinking to spare her from what could become an unpleasant encounter. In Matt's experience, whenever a man was cornered, he came back fighting. And usually lying, to boot.

But at the last minute, he almost brought her inside with them. Despite the fact she was back to wearing the trousers and baggy shirt he had first discovered her in a few days ago, she was still far too feminine-looking for his peace of mind. He didn't want the other ranch hands hassling her. With nagging doubts, however, he told her to stay put.

Molly wasn't happy about it, if the mutinous expression on her face was any indication, but she remained astride Pecos. Grateful she held her tongue, Matt didn't miss the flash of anger in her eyes. A fire brimming. He decided it was better to deal with her anger than her sweetness. He could handle her wrath more easily than innocent gestures of friendship and gratitude. The kiss on the cheek still had his head spinning, tough and unfeeling Texas Ranger that he was.

He entered the bunkhouse with Nathan behind him. Several men milled about inside, the air thick with smoke, sweat, and the stench of unbathed bodies.

"We're looking for a man named Whitaker," Matt said to the men staring back at them.

"Why's that?" one of the younger ranch hands asked.

"We just want to ask him a few questions." Matt took in the group of men, trying to decide if they would give him and Nathan any trouble.

The young ranch hand jerked his head toward an older, thickset man standing behind the long table at the center of the room. The man scowled. "Thanks a lot, Jenkins, you piece of chickenshit."

Jenkins and the other men left, clearly not fond of Whitaker, and Matt waited until they were alone. Peripherally he was aware of a few whistles outside. The young cowpunchers obviously spotted Molly. A sense of urgency pressed on him to end this encounter as quickly as possible.

"I understand ten years ago you worked for Davis Walker, at his ranch up near the Red River," Matt said.

Unshaven and with skin darkened from the sun, shadows cloaked Whitaker's face from the grimy hat he wore. When he spoke, Matt noticed a few front teeth missing.

"Who're you?" the man demanded.

"The name's Matt Ryan. Ten years ago there was an attack on the Hart Ranch, west of here. Two people were killed, and a little girl abducted. Would you happen to know anything about that?"

"For Christ's sake, I can't remember what I did yesterday, let alone ten years ago." Whitaker laughed in disgust.

"Did you attack the Hart ranch for Davis Walker?"

"You're barking up the wrong tree, son. I ain't got nothin' to tell you. Why the hell would you want to stick your nose in something that happened so long ago? It'll only bring you trouble."

Matt stared at Whitaker, every instinct telling him the man was involved, somehow. Perhaps a shot in the leg would help him talk faster, but that would be messy.

Closing the distance between them, he yanked off the man's hat in one fluid motion, confirming Rosita's account that the man had been scalped. The top of Whitaker's head was scarred and mottled, gray hair growing haphazardly from the sides only.

"You sonofabitch!" Whitaker roared. "You stay the hell away from me or I'll kill you."

"Is that a promise?" Matt asked dispassionately. "What happened to your head?"

"Looks like an Indian haircut to me," Nathan drawled. "And none too recent."

"It's no crime to survive a scalpin'." Whitaker grabbed his hat back from Matt and put it on his head.

In a heartbeat Matt drew his six-shooter and pinned Whitaker to the back wall, his left arm choking the life out of the man while he pointed the gun right between Whitaker's eyes.

"I'm not a patient man. I wanna know why Davis Walker told you to attack the Harts, and why you took one of their daughters."

"All right," Whitaker rasped. "I'll tell you what I remember. Just get your goddamned hands off me."

Matt stepped back and the older man stumbled, rubbing his neck and coughing. Matt kept his gun drawn and heard Nathan ready his rifle.

"We was only told Walker wanted us to attack the Harts. He never spoke to us hisself. We was s'pposed to be paid a hefty sum, but we was all cheated in the end."

"I heard most of the other men were killed," Matt said. "You're damn lucky to be alive in the first place."

The man was silent.

"Who told you to attack the Harts?" Matt asked.

"I dunno. I never actually talked to him. Word was just passed around among the men. We all needed the money, and Hart was stealing Walker's beeves anyway. He needed to be taught a lesson."

"By killing him?" Matt asked. "How do you know he was stealing cattle?"

"It was common knowledge."

Matt would have to ask his pa about that, but he found it unlikely Robert Hart was rustling cattle. What could possibly have been the reason? Had he been in need of money that badly?

"Why did you take the little girl?" Matt demanded.

"We was told there was something extra in it if we snatched the middle girl and dropped her near the Brazos River."

"Who told you?" Matt's restraint was wearing thin.

Whitaker shrugged. "I don't remember. It was a long time ago. It was just somethin' one man passed on to another."

"Were you the one who shot Robert Hart?" Nathan questioned from behind Matt.

"Shit, I don't remember. Everyone was all in a frenzy. And his damn wife was screamin' and going on."

"Is that why you killed her, too?" Matt was on the verge of smashing Whitaker's face with one of his fists.

"She threw herself in front of him, the dumb woman," Whitaker cried. "There wasn't any way we could've saved her. Jesus H. Christ! You can't hold me responsible for any of this. It's not like there's anyone left who gives a shit anyway."

Matt hid his disgust at the callousness of the man's attitude.

"But I wasn't the one who shot 'em," Whitaker continued hastily. "One of the other men did it. But you won't be able to nail him since the Comanche killed him shortly after that anyways."

"What did Walker say when he found out what happened?"

"D'ya think I hung around to find out?" he yelped. "I'm not a stupid man."

"That remains to be seen." Matt wondered if he should believe Whitaker's story or not. His gut told him he wouldn't likely get anything more of value out of the man, who had probably told all he could remember.

"Who's that girl?" Whitaker asked, a note of worry creeping back into his voice.

Matt didn't need to turn around to know it was Molly. He wondered how much she'd heard. A quick glance at her pale face and stunned expression told him she'd witnessed enough.

"He's the one," Molly whispered. "The one who grabbed me."

"What's she talkin' about?"

"I'm the middle girl," she said angrily.

Whitaker swore loudly.

Chapter Twelve

Matt and Nathan rode south about a half-mile, with Molly trailing behind them. The orange tint of the sky signaled the impending sunset while the air began to buzz with the sounds of the night. Matt thought Molly had become too quiet since leaving Whitaker. As they pulled a few horse-lengths ahead of her, Nathan finally spoke.

"What do you plan to do about Davis Walker?"

"Damned if I know," Matt replied.

They rode in silence while the final sliver of sun disappeared below the horizon. In the muted haze of twilight, Matt contemplated the woman riding behind him, the woman who had changed his life in the span of only a few days.

"What do you plan to do about Molly?" Nathan asked, as if reading Matt's mind.

"Tie her to a bedpost," he muttered.

"Would that be any bedpost in general, or just yours?"

Matt glanced at Nathan. There was a mischievous gleam in his friend's eye.

"It's not like that," he replied. "I intend to do right by her."

"You're gonna marry her?" Nathan raised an eyebrow.

A slight shake of his head was all Matt could manage. "Can't."

"Why? Is she already married?" Nathan clearly wasn't ready to let the subject drop.

"No." It was like instructing a child. Matt reminded himself it wasn't Nathan's fault he felt so conflicted when it came to Molly's future. "She's been through a lot. She needs a man she can trust, not one who just wants to get between the sheets with her."

Nathan laughed, looking relieved. "All right. Now we're getting somewhere."

"What's that supposed to mean?"

"I just wanted to understand how you feel about her."

"I don't feel anything for her," Matt shot back. "At least nothin' that merits any attention. She's vulnerable. I won't take advantage of it."

"I suppose you feel guilty about what happened to her ten years ago."

"Why shouldn't I? I left her alone when Whitaker and those men attacked her home. I never helped her during the years she was with the Comanche."

"Your problem, Matt, is you always take on too much responsibility for what goes on in this life. You did it countless times when we were in the army. And, although you never told me, I'm sure it was one of the reasons Cerillo was able to nab you as well. Let it go. You've got a woman in front of you that doesn't come along every day. Are you going to piss it all away because of a sense of guilt, or because you feel too honorable to touch her?"

It wasn't that he felt too honorable to touch her. It was quite the opposite. He feared it would be the most dishonorable thing he could do.

His friendship with Molly had been real years ago. He didn't doubt she had cared for him, might still care for him now. Wouldn't it confuse her to use that affection for his own ends? Would she respond to him simply because he desired it? The idea of coercing her didn't sit well with him. Not after what the last ten years had wrought.

Eventually, Molly would come to terms with all that had happened, and then it was very likely she'd walk away from him. He supposed he really couldn't blame her. But if he had to be honest—something he seemed determined to avoid when it came to his growing feelings for her—then he had to admit that maybe he wasn't protecting Molly at all. He was shielding his own sorry hide in the event she left him, again. Only this time, it would be of her own free will. So much for honorable intentions.

"I think we part ways here." Nathan reined his horse toward the east. "When I'm finished in Fort Worth I was planning to go to California to visit my sister, so I'll stop in on my way back. Molly, it's been a pleasure." Nathan tipped his hat to her as she caught up to them.

"Thank you, Nathan," she said, her mellow voice drawing a response from deep within Matt. "Especially for your help back there with Whitaker."

"You take care of yourself," Nathan said. "Take some advice—let go of the past and try to settle down. In the end, I doubt Davis Walker is worth the trouble of putting your life on the line tracking down scum like Whitaker. In my experience, Walker's past will kick him in the ass one day anyway."

Molly smiled, but her demeanor was somber. "I'll keep that in mind." Clearing her throat, she continued, "I have to be honest, you've completely surprised me. When we first met, I thought you a hard and unfeeling man, but you've managed to prove me wrong on each account. And I genuinely didn't think you liked me at first."

"Nothing could be more wrong. In fact, if Matt doesn't do right by you, then you might see me again."

A confused expression crossed Molly's face.

"Get the hell out of here, Blackmore," Matt warned.

Nathan laughed. Guiding his jet-black horse closer, he said in a low voice, "Take a chance, Matt. You deserve some happiness after Cerillo."

Nathan clasped Matt's shoulder briefly, then disappeared into the quickly encroaching darkness, his midnight black horse blending seamlessly into the night. His words hung in the air.

Take a chance.

Matt stared at Molly as she watched Nathan's departure, the certainty of wanting her so very clear to him now. But she was young, and alone. He knew that unless she came to him of her own free will, he could never live with himself if he touched her.

Hardening his resolve, Matt rode beside her as they headed west.

* * *

Matt guided his horse through the darkness with Molly behind him. Pushing forward, he wanted to get them to a small creek before stopping for the night, but upon reaching the flowing water they encountered another camp.

105

At first, Matt tried to simply skirt around the three or four men surrounding a blazing fire, their horses grazing in the dim flicker of the orange light, but then he caught sight of one of the men and couldn't believe his eyes.

"What's wrong?" Molly guided Pecos closer to his gray-flecked gelding.

"The spirits must be out to haunt us tonight, because one of those men is Davis Walker."

She snapped her head around. "Are you sure?"

"Yeah," Matt replied wearily. He took a deep breath. "Molly, let's just keep on goin'. There's nothing to be said tonight that will help anybody. In the end, Whitaker didn't tell us much more than we already knew, so we really don't have any more proof of Walker's guilt than we did yesterday."

"It's just not right." Her voice shook with anger. "He's had the last ten years of his life. He took all of that away from my family."

"Hey! Can we help you fellas?" one of the men around the campfire yelled to them, having finally noticed their presence.

"Davis, it's Matt Ryan," he said, trying to keep his voice neutral. He hoped the exchange would be brief, and that Molly wouldn't do or say anything rash. As an aside, he said to her, "Maybe you better let me do the talking."

Glancing at her face, visible from the firelight, he saw the flash of displeasure reflected in her eyes, but he also saw something else. She was afraid.

"You don't have to worry," he said. "I'll protect you."

"I'm not concerned about myself. I'm worried for you. Please be careful."

Stunned by her words and the panic in her voice, further discussion ended as Walker approached their horses. Reluctantly, Matt dismounted.

"Matthew Ryan? Well, I'll be damned. How are you?" Davis reached out and Matt couldn't see any way of avoiding the handshake.

Matt hadn't seen Walker in several years, but he hadn't changed much. He was still tall, with a paunch now hanging over his belt buckle. His hair was thin and graying, but his eyes were still shrewd. Davis Walker wasn't a man to be underestimated. Something in Matt's gut clenched. He didn't want Molly around him.

"I'm fine," Matt answered noncommittally.

The other men stayed near the fire, but Davis gestured to them. "That's Hal Lewis, Charlie Brewster, and George Sawyer. Maybe you remember Georgie? He used to work at the Hart ranch years ago, when all you boys were there."

Matt didn't have to turn around and look at Molly to know she had tensed at the mention of her folks' ranch. He glanced at Sawyer, nodding slightly.

Matt did remember him, although Sawyer had been just a lad ten years ago, not much older than Matt and Cale. From the looks of things, though, he hadn't changed much. There was something a little wild in the man's eyes and his lanky body appeared poised for violence. Matt remembered he was a little crazed back then, and he found his opinion to be much the same now. Why was Sawyer hanging around with Walker these days? Something about it nagged at the back of his mind, but he'd have to think on it later.

"I didn't realize you have a little lady with you, Matt," Davis remarked when he noticed Molly's presence. "Did you finally settle down?"

"No." He would have lied, but he didn't think Molly would understand. She was safer if the other men thought she belonged to him, but getting her riled up wouldn't get them out of here any quicker.

"You both want to join us?" Davis asked. "We're headin' back to my ranch in the mornin' — we could ride together."

"No thanks," Matt replied. "We're planning to keep going for a while yet."

Davis winked, laughing. "Sure thing. Can't blame you for wantin' a little privacy."

"Miss, you're welcome to stay here," George Sawyer said, a gleam of defiance in his eye.

Matt's dislike for the man grew. "We really should be on our way."

"What's your name, miss?"

"Now, Georgie, keep your britches on." Davis laughed again. "You'd think he never saw a woman before."

"Not one as pretty as you, miss," George said.

"She's with me," Matt said, his voice flat and definite. He couldn't fathom why Sawyer challenged him, and it didn't sit well that he eyed Molly.

"Heard you were hurt recently down south, Matthew," Davis remarked, obviously trying to change the subject. "But you look well enough now. You plannin' on going back to the Rangers, or you gonna stay on to help your pa?"

"I haven't decided yet."

"Wish Cale would come home and help his old man out. Your pa is lucky to have you and Logan, even if it's just for a short while."

"Where is Cale these days?"

"How the hell should I know? Last I heard he was a goddamn bounty hunter in Colorado. I'm sure he must make good money, but I don't see a cent of it. That boy never showed me much respect. And he never could stay in one place long enough, except maybe to take a crap. Well, at least I still have T.J. and Joey."

Davis glanced at Molly, realizing his language. "Sorry, miss. Sometimes I forget myself. What's your name, honey?"

Matt thought quickly for a lie, but she answered before he could, her voice clearly defiant. "It's Molly."

Matt swore to himself.

"Molly. Well, that's a nice name. I knew a Molly once." Davis reflected on that for a moment, then he slapped Matt on the shoulder. "Guess some things are better left in the past, eh?"

The urge to punch Davis came swiftly, an unnatural reaction since Matt had never been one to respond impulsively in the heat of battle. Standing very still, he steadied his breathing and reminded himself the other men might overpower him, leaving Molly on her own. He needed to think of her first.

"Well, Miss Molly," George said, his voice sickeningly sweet, "if you ever get tired of being Mr. Matt's woman, you're welcome to warm my blankets. I'd take real good care of you."

"Don't mind Sawyer," Davis said in disgust, "he's a lot of bluster."

Movement in the dry foliage behind the group of men abruptly caught Matt's eye, bringing his senses to full alert. Before he could determine the culprit, something flew past his head and into one of the bushes. Molly slid off her horse, running toward the shrub. Matt saw the slingshot in her hand. He pulled his gun.

"No, Molly!"

But it was too late. The other men heard the rattle at the same time Matt did.

As Molly neared the darkened perimeter of the encampment, Matt watched her do a strange sleight of hand as she grabbed the snake quickly. One hand gripped the creature's heart-shaped head from behind, the other held the long, thick body as it writhed in agitation.

"Jesus," Matt said in a panic as he rushed after her, "put it down."

She turned to face the stunned expressions of the men.

"Mr. Sawyer," she said, contempt evident in her voice, "I can take care of myself." She was stronger than Matt realized, given her control of the thick and twisting reptile. She held the snake out farther, which caused the men to jump back. "I would've cut its head off, but it's bad luck to kill a snake within the boundaries of camp. An old Indian superstition. I certainly wouldn't want to give any of you bad luck."

As she carefully released the snake, all of the men stumbled backwards, hastily trying to get away from the very poisonous serpent as it slithered away into the dark night.

Matt held his ground.

The damn woman wanted to kill herself. Only the fact they had an audience kept him from shaking some sense into her.

Bending to retrieve her slingshot, she didn't even look at him as she moved past Davis and the other still-agitated men. "Let's go," she said.

Matt paused, trying to control his temper. "Gentlemen." He turned and followed her.

Chapter Thirteen

As Molly rode behind Matt in the shadowed night, she let Pecos find her own way. Weary and cold, she wanted to get as far away as possible from Davis Walker and the other men before stopping. She and Matt hadn't spoken, but they seemed to be of the same mind.

The rush of energy from grabbing the snake had worn off, leaving her limbs weak. The mental weight of facing the man possibly responsible for the murder of her folks also pressed on her. It was all too much to worry about at the moment, so she tried to quiet her thoughts. But for some reason, the night Bull Runner and the other Comanche warriors took her to Jose Torres' camp kept playing through her mind.

There had been an instant when she thought Snake Eater might kidnap her. There had also been a flash of clarity when she was certain he would kill her instead.

The transaction with Torres was completed. Bull Runner negotiated for blankets, guns, and ammunition in exchange for Molly. In the oppressive darkness, only torchlights illuminated the contorted, savage-looking faces of the Comanche men, painted as they were for a war party. Molly had never seen the Kwahadi men appear so much like wild animals. As she stood next to Torres, she felt sick to her stomach. Drunk, he kept leering at her.

Her eyes locked with Snake Eater. His angry gaze pierced hers as he whooped and hollered. All of the warriors began circling around her and Torres, the pounding of the horses' hooves shaking the ground beneath her. The display confused her, but one look at Torres' frightened expression confirmed her suspicion this was an act of aggression by the Kwahadi men.

Later, she would remember with grim satisfaction the fear in the trader's eyes, but at the moment she wondered in a panic if they were after her, or Torres. When she saw Snake Eater's calculating eyes focused upon her, she knew she was the target. She counted her life in heartbeats.

The warriors continued in their circular path, shrieking and yowling, the constant movement making her dizzy. Then Bull Runner intervened, riding into the center of the frenzy. Giving her one last look, an expression almost of regret on his face, he forced the other warriors into the foreboding night before riding off himself. Her labored breathing echoed in the sudden, deafening silence.

That night she was favored, and not just with Snake Eater. Torres thankfully passed out not long after the noisy display.

Molly listened to the sounds of the night – the chirping crickets, a hooting owl, the distant cry of a coyote. The creatures of the night didn't scare her. They were predictable in their own way, once their patterns were understood. But men weren't predictable, and some men had altered the course of her life so drastically she wondered now how she had ever survived it.

When an old bedraggled man dropped a large bag of gold on the ground for Torres, Molly hardly believed he meant to buy her. Who would think she was worth so much? Especially as she sat there in the dirt, her face swollen from the beating Torres had given her.

But the trader grabbed the gold, then kicked her between the shoulder blades to get rid of her. Stumbling over to the old man, she didn't dare hope he wouldn't hurt her. A wild display of gray hair covered his head, and his eyes flashed with kindness when he inspected her.

"You gotta name, miss?" he asked.

The familiar language hung just beyond her reach, her mind struggling to unlock it.

The old man pointed to himself. "Elijah Hardin."

Molly nodded, then pointed to herself. "Canauocué Juhtzú."

Elijah's expression became disgruntled. "I can see you're white, in spite of those Indi'n clothes and that thick coat of grime all over you. You gotta white name?"

The meaning of the words teased her, leaving her with memories of a time when she spoke in that tongue. Tears sprang to her eyes as she grappled with the name that existed only in her dreams, a haunting recollection of a time so very long ago. "Molleeharrt."

"That's better." Elijah nodded. "You can't talk Indi'n. You hear me? It just ain't right."

Molly frantically searched her mind, but she couldn't remember any more of the English words she'd spoken as a child. She attempted to ask Elijah to take her home using Comanche phrases, but that only seemed to aggravate him more.

"Ne tzaréja Komantcia. Ne tza que Komantcia." She tried telling him she had been with the Comanche, but wasn't really a Comanche. He misunderstood her.

"You can't go back," he said as he started to walk away, leading his two mules behind him. "You're white, it ain't right. So come on. You'll just have to come with me. I paid a fair amount for your freedom, so you can stay with *me a while, cook and clean up, to pay me back. Then, I'll figure out what to do with you."*

"Ne miar equihtzí neririeté...muyienaet. Taabetzaróehquit!" She pointed east to make him understand. Her home was to the east. "Taabetzaróehquit!" She needed to go toward the sunrise.

"We'll do fine if you just stop talkin' Indi'n," Elijah muttered, heading south.

Molly stood, unmoving, as frustration threatened to overwhelm her. What should she do? As tears streamed down her face, she glanced back and saw Torres counting his gold pieces. There really was no choice. She knew she'd never survive on her own and certainly never find her way home. All she could remember about home was that it was to the east!

Helpless once again to change the path of her life, and too weak to overcome yet another obstacle, she followed behind Elijah as quickly as her battered body would take her.

Elijah was a bit peculiar, and while he literally abandoned her for days while mining, the remainder of the time he entertained her with his suspicious views about people and places. It soon became clear to Molly why he lived the life of a hermit. But he did teach her English, night after night, by the light of the fire until the language she'd always known flooded back into her awareness. Elijah's sudden death came as a shock.

Molly awoke that bright summer morning to find the elder man still asleep on his blankets. Although they had a small shelter, they frequently slept outside when the weather was clear.

They'd been fortunate these past few weeks. Crisscrossing paths with a trader recently, Elijah had bought a chicken, enabling them to enjoy an occasional fresh egg.

"Wake up, Elijah," Molly said, trying to locate the cast iron pan. She walked over to nudge him.

His stillness caused her to pause and look at him again. He wasn't breathing.

"Oh, no." Molly fell to her knees beside him and tried to shake him. "Elijah, wake up." What should she do? How could she help him?

"Please, Elijah." Tears blurred her vision. "Please don't leave me."

A sob escaped her. She tried to stay in control, but it was clear the old man was very much dead. Leaning her head on his stiff shoulder, she let the grief pour out of her unchecked. She despaired that he'd died, and the pain of the last ten years overpowered her.

Much later, numbed by her anguish, she sat next to his remains and absorbed her state of complete isolation. It was a frightening moment. A conversation she and Elijah had recently had came back to her.

He had told her it was time he took her back to her family, realizing now it wasn't right he had kept her with him for so long. He promised soon they would set out, heading back to Texas.

Tears escaped puffy eyes and rolled down her cheeks.

A flock of wrens swooped from above and landed on a thorny shrub. Each chubby bird sat perched with its short tail held straight up to the sky. They sang a rhythmic series of musical notes.

Chewee-chewee-chewee-chewee.

She watched the brown-headed birds with their long, slightly curved beaks and a white stripe faintly visible above each eye. The remainder of their bodies was spotted, a mixture of brown, white, and black, and they possessed finely-streaked whitish underbellies. Molly wondered what it would be like to be a part of such a flock, to not be alone.

The wrens abruptly took to the sky, fluttering their wings to the north. Molly took it as a sign.

It was time to go home.

But first, she needed to bury Elijah. Her only knowledge of such things came from the Kwahadi, so she laid Elijah to rest as befitted a Comanche warrior.

Dressing him in his best clothes – a faded pale shirt and dirt streaked trousers – she brought his knees to his chest and wrapped a thick blanket around him, securing it with a rope. Dragging his body to the nearest rocky outcrop took the better part of the afternoon, and Molly heaved and sweated during the effort.

Facing his body to the east, she filled the space around him with large rocks and dried brush. She placed his most prized possessions near him – his mining pick, his tobacco, and a small sack of gold. The remainder of the gold and silver she kept for herself. Maybe it was selfish, but she knew she'd need it to return to Texas.

She also couldn't bring herself to kill the mules – she'd need them as well. Elijah would just have to walk in the afterlife. She hoped he wouldn't be too cross with her.

Molly still hoped Elijah wasn't angry with her. She had sold the mules in Albuquerque for a good price.

* * *

Matt stopped and dismounted from his horse.

As Molly watched him, a sense of security overcame her, a sense of protection. It was an odd feeling, long absent from her life.

Matt didn't have to help her, and yet he had. And, she suspected, would continue to do so. He didn't have to defend her, and yet she hadn't missed the slight movement of his hand poised near his gun holster when George Sawyer had started haggling her. She was certain Matt would have fought all of those men, including Davis Walker, on her behalf if it had come to that.

To have such an ally on her side was a new experience for her. And so was the fear something might happen to him.

While Matt removed the saddles from the horses and led them to a nearby stream, Molly gathered wood and pondered over her jumbled feelings for him. He then fed and brushed the animals, so she worked on the fire. Once she had a good blaze going, she took a small copper pot to the stream and filled it, then set the water to boil. Pulling several bags from her belongings, she began preparing a meal.

Matt hobbled the horses nearby on a grassy clearing. Approaching the fire, he dropped his saddlebag nearby.

"I have food," he began, his voice hard and clipped.

"No, that's all right." She wondered at his curt behavior. "I'd like to make you something to eat."

"Boiled snake?" His tone was downright snide.

"I beg your pardon?"

"You haven't changed, have you, Molly. You're still chasing snakes and stupid ideas. You're gonna get yourself killed." The proclamation was loud and clear, hanging in the air between them.

Shocked by his outburst, it was as if he'd thrown a cold bucket of water on her. "You think chasing Davis Walker is stupid?"

He threw his hat to the ground, then ran a hand through his dark hair. "I don't know what to think about Walker. Believe me, I'd love to bring whoever did this to justice, but at what price? You're alive,

Molly, beyond all odds. Maybe you should just walk away, and not look back. Start over somewhere, get married, have children, be happy. Stay alive."

"You just want me to walk away." She stared woodenly into the fire. "Leave Texas." Then, before she could stop herself, "Leave you?"

Their eyes met, and the longing in Matt's sent a jolt of awareness clear to her toes. He wanted her. There was no mistaking it. She felt frightened and victorious at the same time. He saw her as a woman and the thought left a nervous warmth in her belly, but fast on its heels was an overwhelming apprehension about what this meant between them.

He shook his head. "Don't look at me like that."

"Like what?"

"I won't let anything happen between us."

"What are you saying?"

"Nothing good can come of this."

Molly stood, her face burning from humiliation. "What makes you think *I* wanted something to happen?"

Matt stared at her from across the fire, his eyes flashing with fear. Yes, the man looked afraid. Molly couldn't imagine why.

"You've been a good friend to me," she said quietly. "And I've appreciated everything you've done since I returned to Texas. I don't expect...anything more." But as soon as she said it, she knew it wasn't true. "I'm sorry you misunderstood," she lied. But he hadn't. God help her, somewhere in the last few days she'd fallen hard for him.

His shrouded gaze darted from her to the fire then back to her. His jaw flexed, as if he were going to say something, but he didn't.

She walked back to the stream, needing to get away, needing to hide while she cleared her head. She told herself she would retrieve more water, but it wasn't until she leaned her hand into the stream that she realized she'd brought nothing in which to carry it.

She attempted to compose herself as embarrassment washed over her. Had she been so transparent that Matt could guess her thoughts so easily? She would simply have to bury her feelings, something she had learned all too well during the past ten years. Bracing herself, she returned to their small camp.

Matt sat by the fire, watching her. "Molly." His voice broke the crackling silence of the flames separating them.

"I'm not really very hungry after all," she interrupted. "I think I'll just get some sleep." With hardly a glance toward him, she lay down on her bedroll, pulled a blanket tight around her shoulders, and willed herself to the oblivion of her dreams.

* * *

Matt watched Molly's backside as she completely shut him out. It was for the best, he knew. She was so young, so innocent. For a moment, a mere brief moment, he had thought she was offering him…what? His deepest desires? What a load of hogwash that was. Molly and his deepest desires had no business even being in the same thought together. He swore at himself for even connecting the two.

Molly had become attached to him, and who could blame her? She needed his friendship, not his lust. He was angry at her for endangering her life with that damn rattlesnake earlier, but he was also angry at himself for even acknowledging the possibility of what lay between them. He'd actually said the words to her, and she left no doubt how uncomfortable such a prospect made her feel.

Nathan had told him to take a chance, but Matt could not, and would not, take advantage of her heart or her trust. Hadn't her very faith in life been shaken? He'd be damned if he'd shake it further.

* * *

After a restless night, Molly awoke at dawn. A mist shrouded the area, reminding her of the endless days she'd spent with the Comanche. Donning a long coat to ward off the morning chill, she set off in search of more firewood, hardly glancing at Matt's sleeping form nearby.

In no time she started a fire, heated more water and added ingredients from her saddlebags — mesquite-bean meal, sunflower seeds, and several prickly pear apples.

Matt roused. "Mornin'." He sat up and rubbed his face.

"Good morning." She concentrated on stirring the food. "You're welcome to some of this." She nodded toward the copper pot. "But it's Indian food."

Matt sat forward on his haunches, extending his hands to the fire to warm them. He'd slept in his clothes, his indigo shirt rumpled and untucked. "I don't have anything against Indian food. I appreciate you makin' it."

She let out a breath. He was her friend; she didn't want to be at odds with him. Perhaps she would just have to learn to live with wanting something more between them. "I've been thinking."

Matt's gaze settled on her.

Maybe there'd be nothing more than brotherly love between them, but that didn't stop her heart from beating faster when she had his complete attention. Everything about him called to a level far more basic and primitive than was proper within the boundaries of mere friendship.

"I'd like to return to the spot where the Comanche attacked the men who took me," she said.

Matt sat back on the ground and reached for his boots, shaking them for critters. "Do you think you could find it?"

"I'm not sure. Would you remember the general location?"

"Maybe." He shoved first one foot then the other into the soft leather footwear. "What do you think we'd find there?"

She shrugged. "I don't know, but it seems like a place to start."

"All right," he agreed. "We should stop at the SR first."

She nodded. "I'll see if Claire would like to come."

It wasn't a good idea for them to be alone together anymore. That she would make a fool of herself again, she had no doubt.

Chapter Fourteen

Just after midday, Matt's horse followed Molly's toward the main house of the SR. They had hardly spoken during their return ride.

Immediately, he noticed the strange brown horse tied at the front of the house. His first thought was Logan had found another potential husband for Molly, putting him in a foul mood. Not that he wasn't already in a grumpy disposition.

He and Molly dismounted, then he handed both horses off to a boy named Lionel, recently hired. Molly preceded Matt into the house before he could catch up to her. Once inside, he saw the visitor shaking Molly's hand, a man with short wheat-colored hair and features very like Davis Walker. It was Cale.

Cale's attention shifted to him. "Matt, good to see you."

Matt smiled, shaking his hand. "It's been a while. How you doin'?"

"As decent as can be expected."

Matt noticed Logan and Claire were present, as well as his folks. "I saw your old man last night."

"I'm on my way to see him now," Cale said. "I was ridin' by, so thought I'd stop in and say hello."

"Matthew," his mother said, "how did things go at the Bautista Ranch? Did you find the man you were looking for?"

Matt nodded. Molly began removing her coat, so he stepped forward to help her. The look on her face made him feel he'd invaded her privacy. He took her coat anyway.

"Whitaker was the one who grabbed her," he said, hanging the long duster in the hallway then returning to the parlor. "But beyond that, he didn't offer any conclusive evidence." He wasn't sure how much to say in front of Cale.

"Anything I can help with?" Cale asked.

"We haven't told him yet," Susanna said.

Cale narrowed his gaze. "I'm getting the feeling I've walked in on something."

"You've always had a knack for timing." Logan settled on the couch beside Claire.

"Cale," Jonathan cut in, "you've met Molly, but I don't think we made it clear who she is."

Molly removed her hat, but remained near the entrance to the room. Matt watched as she pushed self-consciously at her hair. He had a sudden desire to pull her close.

Cale looked once more at her. "Have we met?"

"Yes." She hesitated. "I'm Molly Hart."

Cale's expression hardened and his eyes shifted to Matt. "I'm not appreciating the humor."

"It's not a jest, son," Jonathan said. "It seems all these years, what we believed happened to Molly was wrong. The body you found wasn't hers."

Cale flicked his gaze to Molly. "How the hell did that happen?"

"Another girl was killed," Molly replied. "It was her body you found."

"Where've you been?" he asked.

"I lived with the Comanche for eight years."

Cale stared at her, clearly stunned.

"She's only just returned to us," Susanna said. "It was a shock to everyone."

"It's a mighty big one to me," Cale said. "I was certain that body I found was hers. Whose was it?"

"Her name was Adelaide," Molly replied. "She was frantic that night and wouldn't stop screaming. The Indians were very brutal when they killed her."

"I found the cross," he responded, an urgency to his voice.

"I left it with her, to ease her journey."

Cale went silent, his eyes flashing like a wild animal backed into a corner. His angular features hardened into an unflinching line as he attempted to process Molly's return from the dead. Matt understood. He'd felt the same utter disbelief just a few days earlier.

"C'mon," Matt said to him. "Give me a hand outside, would you?" He'd tell Cale about the suspicions involving his father without everyone listening.

As Matt left the room, he lingered on Molly's lovely face. A slight sunburn reddened the freckles scattered across her petite nose. Her blue eyes watched him with apprehension and concern, undoubtedly cloaked with thoughts of the past.

A past unresolved, full of pain and loss and heartbreak.

Molly's heartbreak, he told himself. What he had felt then—what he felt now—was secondary to the welfare of the woman before him.

The woman.

No longer the little girl who had lived for years in his memories, she was a real flesh-and-blood woman who tugged at him in ways others never had. He didn't understand it, but angry common sense refused to let him dwell on the remarkable significance of her return into his life.

* * *

The men decided it would be better to ride out to the location of Molly's abduction in the morning. Cale left for the Walker ranch, but agreed to return at dawn to help them pinpoint the exact locale, since it was he who'd found little Adelaide's body in the first place.

Matt avoided dinner. In fact, Molly noticed Matt had managed to evade her completely since they'd returned that afternoon. She supposed he had things to attend to around the ranch. She really shouldn't be so sensitive.

Leaving her bedroom—she and Claire were now on the second floor in the spare rooms Susanna had recently redecorated—she tiptoed next door in her ivory nightgown and robe to Claire's room and knocked.

The door opened.

"I could use some company," Molly said. "You weren't sleeping, were you?"

Claire shook her head. She wore a similar gown, her blonde hair braided and hanging over one shoulder. "Come in." She stood back from the doorway. "I was just reading a bit. Susanna has been so nice to let me borrow from the collection in Mr. Ryan's office."

Molly sat down on the edge of the bed, covered by a lacy coverlet. Claire's room was as lovely as her own, the décor very soft and inviting. A large poster bed consumed half of the floor space, opposite a stone fireplace. A dresser, two nightstands, and a narrow desk completed the furnishings. Light green cotton curtains hung across the window on the far side.

Molly liked her room, as well as Claire's, but felt a wistful longing for Matt's quarters. She supposed he was back sleeping in his own bed. Best not to think about that right now.

"How are you?" Molly asked. They hadn't had much of a chance to talk lately.

"Fine."

"Have you given any thought to returning home?"

Sitting in a chair across from her, Claire nodded. "Yes. I'm thinking of leaving very soon."

"I thought as much." Molly was surprised Claire had stayed with her as long as she had. "Do you want to talk about what happened before I found you?"

Claire hesitated. "You have more important things to think about. Do you think Davis Walker was really responsible for the attack?"

Molly hooked her bare heels on the frame of the bed, and rested elbows on knees, her chin in one palm. "I don't know. That man, Whitaker, he definitely was the one who grabbed me that night. His voice was very distinct. And then Matt and I saw Davis as we were riding back last night."

"What happened?"

"It was quite by accident. Matt wanted to avoid him altogether, but he saw us."

"Did he know who you were?"

"No. I don't think so."

"What do you plan to do?"

She bit her lip. "Stay here for now. I have nowhere else to go, at least not until I hear from Mary or Emma. Then, I suppose I'll visit one of them." Looking at Claire, she said, "If you want, I'll return to Santa Fe with you. I owe you that, for coming here with me."

"Actually, I'm from a town east of Santa Fe called Las Vegas. It sits right on the Santa Fe Trail."

"Well, then I'll go *there* with you."

"That's not necessary. Mr. Ryan has arranged for one of his ranch hands to escort me. Besides, it's very comfortable here with the Ryans. You should stay put."

"Yeah, comfortable," Molly mumbled.

"Is something wrong? Has something happened?"

Pausing, Molly tucked her hair behind an ear. "A misunderstanding."

"About what?" Claire moved to sit beside her on the bed.

"Matt and I, well, we were alone together last night, and…"

The look of shock on her friend's face stopped Molly short. "Oh no," she continued, "it wasn't like that. I mean, I think Matt thought *I thought* it should be like that, but it wasn't."

"I'm not sure I'm following."

"Me neither. Do you think Matt is handsome?"

"I suppose. Do you?"

"I…think so."

"I understand."

"You do?" Molly wasn't accustomed to girl-talk.

"Have you ever been with a man before?"

Molly shook her head. "Have you?"

"No, but let's just say I probably have more knowledge on this subject than you."

"How could that be?"

Claire hitched her feet on the bedrails as well. "I have this dream. It's farfetched, really."

"What is?"

"I want to be a doctor."

"That's not farfetched," Molly said.

Claire grinned sheepishly, then shook her head. "I have no money, and I'm a woman. I can't enter medical school with either of those strikes against me. And there's something else—I was raised in a brothel."

"You were?" Molly didn't know what women in brothels acted like, but she was fairly certain quiet and soft-spoken Claire wasn't one of them.

"Please don't say anything to the Ryans," Claire said quickly.

"Is that why you were beaten?"

"It's a long story. My mama runs a saloon, and...there are always men in and out. Some are the good sort. Some aren't. Promise me you won't tell the Ryans. They've been good to me, and I would hate for them to think the worst."

Molly squeezed her friend's hand. "I promise."

Relief played across Claire's features. "Now, back to your dilemma. From what I've observed, most men—men like Matt and Logan—prefer women who aren't too fake."

"Too fake?" Molly frowned.

"Well, they haven't stuffed their gown to make their bosom appear bigger than it really is, or put so much rouge on their cheeks that they look like a candied cherry."

"How is this supposed to help me?"

Blowing out a breath and leaning her chin into a palm, Claire sighed, "I have no idea. Men come to the saloon and pay for sex. It's a pretty simple transaction. Did anything like that occur with the Comanche?"

"Not that I know of, but then, most men claimed several wives. I suppose if a wife displeased a warrior, he would simply move on to another one."

"That's convenient, for the men at least. What about the women?"

"It wasn't for a woman to decide," Molly said.

"It never is, is it?" Claire pulled her braid over her shoulder and began to fiddle with the ends. "Do you want Matt to notice you?"

"I'm not sure."

"Well, there is the issue of pregnancy to consider."

"Pardon?" Molly asked weakly.

"You do understand what happens between a man and a woman, don't you?"

Molly thought of the dogs mating in the Kwahadi camp. Of course, during harsh winters, most of those dogs were eaten. "I have some idea."

"If you have sex with Matt, you could become pregnant. Do you think he would marry you?"

Molly shrugged. The thought had never occurred to her.

"There are ways to avoid pregnancy," Claire continued, "but men are particular about women they intend to marry. If you make love with Matt, then leave him, another man might not be so willing to wed you. Even worse, you could end up with a child outside of matrimony."

So many complications, Molly realized, and none she'd considered. But perhaps Matt had. He undoubtedly had more experience in these matters.

"But if you decide it's still worth it, then it might not hurt to drop some bait."

"What do you mean?" Molly asked, intensely curious.

"Make him want you, more than reason will allow."

"How?"

Claire sighed. "Well, sex is probably at the top of most men's desires, but you should safeguard that. To be certain, he can get that anywhere."

That was a disconcerting thought. A stab of jealousy of every nameless, faceless woman Matt had ever encountered, or would encounter, filled Molly.

"What about making him jealous?" Claire asked, as if reading her thoughts.

Molly shook her head. "I know little about attracting men, let alone making them jealous. And honestly, does that work?"

Claire shook her head, thinking again. "Probably not. What if you play hard to get?"

"He's happy to avoid me of late. If I play hard to get, I may never see him again."

Claire laughed.

Molly smiled, too. Nothing had changed about her situation, but she definitely felt better having talked about it with someone.

"Maybe you should take him away, get lost in the wilderness, just the two of you," Claire suggested. "If he can't find his way back, he'll be forced to rely on you. Maybe if you don't feed him, in his weakened state he'll realize he can't live without you." Claire clearly warmed to the idea.

Molly giggled, something she hadn't done in such a long time, not since the days with her sisters. "He's a Ranger, Claire. How lost do you think I could make him?"

"Maybe if he hit his head on a rock."

More laughter ensued.

"Will you promise me something?" Claire asked.

Wiping her eyes, Molly nodded.

"Will you tell me if you find something that works?" Her friend's expression was almost wistful. "I'd love to hear a happy ending."

Molly sobered. "Yeah, so would I."

A happy ending. Such things didn't exist in either of their worlds.

Chapter Fifteen

The next morning, following breakfast, they set out. Jonathan and Susanna, Logan and Claire, Cale, and Matt. Molly took the lead, but Cale helped when her memory faltered. Matt stayed close. Molly tried to ignore his presence, but he was always at her heels.

Maybe he really did have feelings for her, Molly considered, warmed by the thought. Maybe Claire's suggestions weren't as ridiculous as they had sounded the previous night. Perhaps Matt simply needed nudging in the right direction. Molly dwelt on that during the long morning ride west into land that had long been the stronghold of the Comanche.

She recognized the scenery and memories tugged at her. She wore a dark blue cotton dress with a full skirt, at Susanna's insistence, though she found the clothing tight and somewhat constricting. Molly had the sudden urge to strip down to her chemise and ride bareback. She had done as much while with the Kwahadi. How startling it was to wish, even for a moment, that she was back with them. But the yearning was there, pulling her into a past she had thought long dismissed in her own mind.

As Pecos climbed a low hill, Molly scanned the horizon from beneath the brim of her hat. "I think this was where the Comanche attacked."

"I found the girl's body about five miles from here, to the north," Cale said.

Molly glanced at Cale Walker. He was tall, broad-shouldered, and as solid as Matt. His facial features were fairer, but she saw the same unyielding look in his light blue eyes. She knew he was close in age to Matt—twenty-seven, twenty-eight?—but, like Matt, he seemed much older, hardened by life and heartache. She wondered what sadness Cale carried within him.

"Let's spread out and have a look," Matt suggested.

"I think I'll ride to where I found the body," Cale said. "I'll meet y'all back here."

"Agreed," Matt replied. "Logan, why don't you and Claire scout the southern part of the valley. Pa, you and Ma take the east. I'll follow you, Molly."

Everyone nodded, then set off in their respective directions.

After she and Matt had ridden for a time, they entered a thicket of juniper and mesquite trees on the valley floor. Matt moved his horse beside hers. She couldn't help remarking, "If you're trying to avoid me, you're not doing a very good job of it."

Matt glanced at her, his gaze sharp. "I'm not trying to avoid you."

"You don't have to worry. When this is all over, I'll probably go to my Aunt Catherine's in San Francisco. I suppose I can find myself a good husband there and have a bunch of babies. Does that reassure you?"

She couldn't be certain, but she thought she heard him swear under his breath. "That *is* what you want for me, right?" she pressed.

"I just want you to be happy."

"I'm not sure happiness is a possibility anymore. Is it possible for you to be happy? What are your hopes for the future?"

They rode in silence while he reflected on her question. At length, he finally answered, sounding somewhat bewildered. "I guess I've never had any long-term goals, now that I think about it."

"You joined the army, that was a goal," she prompted.

"In a way."

"What about the Rangers?"

"It served a purpose."

"Which was?"

"To help the helpless."

"That's an admirable dream," she said.

He shook his head. She took the chance to steal a good look at him. Steadfast and powerful, he was a force to be reckoned with, and he was so easy on the eyes that it made her heart ache. The strong lines of his profile, the lanky ease of his body as he rode — the visions burned themselves into her head and her heart. He was but a dream to her, a dream of masculine strength and beauty, a man and a vision of a man. So close, yet completely out of her reach.

"For the last ten years, Molly," his eyes met hers, "I think I've been running from you."

His admission confused her. "I don't understand."

"When I thought you died," he said slowly, precisely, "something inside of *me* died. We were friends back then, I think you know I cared a great deal about you. You can't imagine how devastated I was when Cale brought that body back, when everyone thought you'd died in such an inhumane and agonizing way. It killed something inside of me. And for ten years, I've run from it, trying to hold it at bay, trying to keep it from tormenting me." In a ragged breath, he uttered, "The guilt tore me apart."

Molly listened and began to understand. It filled her heart, knowing how much he'd cared, but emptiness followed close behind, because it was clear now why he would never touch her.

"I won't use you to heal my wounds. You've suffered enough, but I'll do everything in my power to help you find your own happiness." His words and his gaze pierced her.

What had happened to him? It was as if he believed in nothing anymore.

"You're wrong," she said angrily, refusing to let the damn man off so easily. "I suppose it's true I've suffered, but not as much as you. Despite everything, I still believe in the power of the human spirit. You obviously don't anymore. And if that's true, then you're not the Matt I remember, because the Matt I knew would never give up. He would've lived life, embraced it. There *is* cruelty in the world—I suspect you've seen far more of it than I have—but what's the point in living if we let it beat us? You asked me how I survived all these years. It really boils down to one word—hope. Without that, I would have lain down and died during those early days with the Comanche. But I refused to accept that. And I came back."

"But to something much different than you thought," Matt said, his tone frustrated.

"Yes," she agreed. "That's true. But the Kwahadi did teach me something. The world is ever-changing. The land, the seasons, they always brought something new. If you couldn't adapt, you died. It was as simple as that. You can't fear change."

But what she saw in his eyes *was* fear. "What happened to you?" she demanded, startled by her own level of resentment with him. "Why are you so afraid?"

"If you must know, it's not fear, it's regret. You come back and throw my entire life upside down. You look at me with the innocent longing of a child."

"I'm not a child," she replied abruptly.

"That's the problem. I'm doing my damnedest to do right by you, but you're determined to needle me about it."

"So, I'm nothing more than a pest to you?"

"That's not what I meant."

It *was* childish, but Molly kicked Pecos into a gallop and left Matt behind. It would seem they couldn't even have a conversation anymore without arguing.

As Pecos broke through the surrounding brush, she abruptly reared, nearly throwing Molly to the ground. Holding tight, Molly glimpsed a flurry of movement, animals everywhere. Pecos took off at a dead run.

Molly thought it was a bear she saw. Yipping and barking filled the air. Chancing a look over her shoulder she saw not a bear but a stampede of cattle behind her, behind them a pack of coyote or wolves at their heels. Pecos darted back and forth, avoiding cactus and brush. Molly's hat went flying from her head. The frightened animals continued running hard.

Gunshots rang out but Molly couldn't be certain from which direction. Pecos ran at breakneck speed to the south. On a slight rise before her, Molly saw Logan and Claire still atop their horses, watching her. Claire, her brown riding dress blurring with that of her chestnut-colored mount, was trying to contain her agitated horse while Logan aimed a rifle in Molly's direction.

"Get down!" he was yelling. "Get out of the way!"

Molly would have tried, but she had little control over the path her horse chose. The animal ran on pure instinct. Without warning, Pecos cut to the left, throwing Molly to the ground. The impact knocked the breath out of her, but she struggled to stand, aware she was in danger afoot.

The cattle, ten or fifteen at least, barreled toward her. From nowhere, Matt broke ahead of them. Leaning his arm down, Molly knew he meant to haul her onto his horse. She prepared to grab him, but as she did her foot slipped and she fell back hard, losing her grip on his arm. Matt reared his horse, and his feet hit the dirt as he roared something at her, but she couldn't make it out. Her eyes focused on the animals that were almost upon her.

In a panic she tried scrambling up the hillside, but the dirt was too loose. All at once the snorting longhorns and Matt were on her. In a split second it was over, and she realized Matt had covered her with his body, her face smashed into the dirt.

The heavy animals had trampled him, not her.

Twisting underneath him, she rolled onto her back, his body still covering hers. "Matt? Matt?" His face rested near her breasts. With a hand on each side, she tried to raise his head. "Are you all right?"

He raised his eyes to her, clearly dazed, and tried to catch his breath. "Never better," he choked out, but she didn't miss the wince when he moved slightly.

Logan and Claire appeared, having run down the hill. "Don't move, Matt," his brother said.

"Wasn't planning to," he replied, his voice strained.

His hat was gone, so Molly touched his face, burying her fingers into his hair. Placing a palm on his forehead, she tried to comfort him since he was clearly in pain.

"I think your foot might be broken," Logan said.

"No shit," Matt muttered.

"How're your ribs?" Logan asked.

"My legs took the beating."

"Claire, give me a hand," Logan said, trying to straighten Matt's leg.

Molly watched as sweat broke out on Matt's forehead and the veins on his neck bulged as he struggled to contain the anguish the movement caused. Instinctively, she wound her arms around his shoulders, trying to take some of his suffering into herself. Without thinking she placed her face into his hair, kissing him, murmuring to him. His arms tightened around her. Tears burned her eyes.

"I'm going to roll you over," Logan said.

Reluctantly, Molly released Matt as he moved away from her. Claire came to her side. "Are you hurt?"

Molly sat up, feeling only a little bruised. "No, I'm fine."

Jonathan and Susanna approached, both dismounting quickly. "What on earth happened?"

Susanna asked, bending down beside the two of them.

"Those damn coyotes spooked a herd of beeves." Logan scanned the surroundings once more. Dark clouds had formed in the sky and the wind was starting to pick up.

"I think we need to get Matt back to the ranch," Molly said.

"I can ride," Matt said. "Just get me to my horse."

Jonathan handed his gun to Susanna, then moved to help Logan get Matt into the saddle. Claire guided Molly to her feet.

Cale rejoined them. "What happened?"

"Stampede," Logan said. "Matt's foot might be broken."

"Want me to have a look at it?" Cale asked.

"Didn't know you were a damn doctor," Matt said, grimacing as he settled into his saddle.

"I spent some time with an Apache medicine man. But maybe I'll just let you suffer."

Matt swore under his breath.

"Claire might be able to help," Molly offered, looking earnestly at her friend.

Claire hesitated before saying, "I do have some experience with setting broken bones."

Cale nodded. "Two hands are always better than one. We'd best get back to the SR though, since it'll probably need to be wrapped. Storm's blowin' in and I don't think we should linger. But I did find somethin' useful."

"What's that?" Jonathan asked, securing his hat against a gust of wind.

"A pile of bones, buried under a ridge. Looks like several men. No way to tell for certain, but it could've been the ones the Comanche killed—the ones who took Molly. Someone went to a lot of effort to hide the bodies." Cale glanced at the coming storm, his own expression troubled. "That's why we never found 'em."

"Let me talk to him, son," Jonathan said to Cale. "We can't be certain your pa had anything to do with this." His gaze settled on Molly. "I'm not discounting what you think might've happened, Molly, but this is serious business. No sense flinging accusations until we're certain."

She nodded, knowing he was right. The wind blew hard now.

"Let's get going," Susanna said loudly. "Matthew's foot needs attention."

Logan retrieved Pecos, as well as Matt's hat and Molly's, and they all began a slow journey back to the SR. Molly rode close to Matt, not caring if anyone said anything about it. Not caring if he said anything about it.

Rain began falling in sheets. Luckily everyone had thought to bring a long coat since the weather often changed without warning. Drenched, with water streaming from their hats, they rode slowly across the flat open plains. Molly worried about Matt. Susanna frequently checked back on him, but he always assured his ma he was fine.

Jonathan and Susanna took the lead, followed by Matt and Molly riding side by side, then Claire, Logan, and Cale. Molly had to admire Matt's strength because it was obvious he was in pain. His foot dangled from the side of his horse.

"Why don't you let me guide your horse in, Matt?" Molly yelled, trying to be heard over the torrential storm. "It might give you a rest."

He looked at her. "I'll be fine," he said resolutely.

"It's not a crime to let someone help you."

"You're one to talk."

"What's that supposed to mean?"

"All I've ever wanted to do was help you," he said. "You don't like it any more than I do."

All of sudden she laughed. What else could she do? She was cold, wet, and tired. Her folks were dead, she was homeless, and Matthew Ryan was just plain irritated with her. He did have an injured foot, she reminded herself, so she supposed the man could be justified his bad temper. If she could just forget how nice it had felt when he held her, when she had indulged herself in touching him. She wanted to again. She wanted the warmth, the connection. She wanted him, and no one else.

"What's so funny?" He glared at her.

"When did you become such an ornery cuss?"

He scowled. "Don't talk like that. You're a lady now, not a child."

"Well, thank God you finally noticed," she declared, smiling into his face.

"I've noticed. All I've done is notice," he muttered, turning away from her, but she heard it.

And it gave her hope.

Chapter Sixteen

It was late in the day when they arrived at the SR. Dark clouds still hung oppressively in the sky, but the rain had finally stopped. Molly went upstairs to change out of her wet clothes while Susanna, Claire, and Cale tended to Matt, who had been moved to his bed by Logan and his father.

Susanna had been gracious enough to supply Molly with several dresses and undergarments, a nightgown and two pairs of new shoes. She laid her drenched garments on a chair and quickly donned a pale yellow dress that buttoned down the front. As she hurried back downstairs, she knew the reason for her haste. She wanted to make sure Matt's foot would be all right.

Hearing Jonathan and Claire in the parlor, Molly peeked into the room. An elderly woman was seated comfortably in one of the overstuffed chairs, a blanket over her lap.

"Molly." Jonathan gestured to her. "Please come and meet Mrs. McAllister."

Molly moved forward and the woman grasped her hand with bent fingers and large knuckles; Molly wondered if it was painful, and lessened the pressure in her hold. Mrs. McAllister's face bore heavy wrinkles and her thin lips spread into a painted-on smile. A heavy mass of gray hair was pinned atop her head, and although she appeared frail and petite, the scrutiny in her eyes as she scanned Molly from top to bottom left Molly thinking the woman was not what her appearance would seem to convey.

"You can call me Elizabeth," she said, a southern twang in her voice.

"It's a pleasure to meet you." Molly stood back when the woman released her hand at last.

"Mrs. McAllister was caught in the storm," Jonathan said. "She'll be stayin' the night with us."

"Thank you so much, Jonathan," Elizabeth said sweetly. "I always appreciate your hospitality, and it will be nice to have a visit with Susanna. It's been lonely in my big old house since Charles passed on. I didn't expect this storm, however. Came quite out of nowhere."

"I best check on Matthew," Jonathan said. "Molly, would you and Claire mind keeping Mrs. McAllister company?"

"No, not at all," Molly replied.

"Claire, we'll have you set to go in the mornin'," Jonathan added before he left. Then he was gone down the hallway.

"You're leaving tomorrow?" Molly asked in surprise.

"I think it's time. Mr. Ryan has made arrangements for Lester Williams to take me."

Molly nodded, glad that Claire would be returning home, but also saddened at the thought of her departure. Claire's still-wet hair had been braided again, and she'd changed into a blue and white striped dress.

Feeling chilled, Molly moved closer to the blaze burning brightly in the stone fireplace.

"A young woman shouldn't be out and about alone, in the wilderness," Elizabeth said. "Too many Indians."

"But I thought most of the Indians in this area had been moved to reservations?" Molly asked.

"That's what they say, but don't you believe it. I'd bet my mama's fine china there are still some of them out there."

Molly wasn't sure what to say, but something in Elizabeth's tone told her it was a subject best not pursued.

"So, are either of you young ladies betrothed to the Ryan boys?" Elizabeth asked.

Molly frowned. "No, ma'am. The Ryans have just been kind enough to let us stay on a bit."

Elizabeth nodded. "Ryan hospitality is well known in these parts. They're good people. Where are you girls from?"

Molly wasn't sure what to say, but suddenly felt a need to safeguard her past. Claire saved her the trouble of lying.

"New Mexico."

"Oh, that's still a territory, isn't it? I hear it's a lawless land, full of bandits and outlaws, and more of those blasted red men. They're like vermin, crawling all over this land. I just can't abide their presence." She waved a gnarled hand in disgust.

Claire raised an eyebrow in Molly's direction.

Molly remained silent.

"It's a shame about Matthew's injury," Elizabeth continued. "Did he fall from his horse?"

"No, ma'am." Molly cleared her throat. "It was a cattle stampede." Then she asked Claire, "How is his foot?"

"It's not broken, just badly bruised and swollen. Cale is wrapping it now. He's going to be fine."

Elizabeth nodded knowingly. "No one believes me, but cattle are dangerous animals, there's no doubt about that. But Matthew is young and strong. I'm sure he'll be up and around in no time. I'd always hoped my Lizzie would marry one of those boys."

"Lizzie?" Molly asked. A quick stab of jealousy sent a jolt through her stomach. Or maybe all she needed was some food.

"My dear sweet daughter." Elizabeth smiled. "She's away at boarding school in Richmond. She's my only child, and I've missed her so. But she's to return soon, and I have no doubt she'll have plenty of men interested in courting her. She's quite lovely. It's a shame Matthew had to leave the Rangers, but perhaps it's God's plan." Whispering, as if they shared a beloved secret, she went on, "I'm sure Lizzie will catch his eye, and I wouldn't be at all bothered if she were to become a Ryan."

Molly thought she'd had quite enough. Forcing a smile on her face, she said, "I'd best check if Susanna might need help. You must be hungry, Mrs. McAllister." Molly didn't think she could stand there another minute and listen to her go on about her daughter and Matt. "I'll see if Rosita has started supper." Turning quickly, she left the room.

She made a silent apology to Claire as she escaped to the kitchen.

* * *

Matt lay back, his head propped up with pillows. Cale had wrapped his foot, but the swollen injury throbbed and he took another steadying breath. At least it wasn't the same leg Cerillo had mutilated. Now, both his legs were shot, but he

146

didn't regret it. He couldn't think of what would've happened to Molly if he hadn't managed to shield her from the crazed animals.

Logan entered the room, carrying firewood, then proceeded to stoke the fireplace on the far side of the room. Soon, flames grew in strength.

"Ma doesn't want you to catch a chill," his brother said, standing.

Matt noticed Logan still hadn't changed out of his wet clothes since they returned. "You're the one who's gonna catch a chill. Go clean yourself up."

"You never did get it, did you?" Logan grinned. "You're ma's favorite. I could be passed out in the pantry with pneumonia, but ma would still insist I fetch some peaches for you."

Matt suppressed a groan as he tried to shift his position. "Then where the hell are my peaches?"

Logan laughed. "Get your own damn food. Pa has Dawson making a crutch for you. Should be ready tomorrow." Then, out of the blue, he said, "Claire's leavin' in the mornin'."

Alarm shot through Matt. "Is Molly going with her?"

Logan shook his head slowly. "Pa's gonna send Lester with her." He went silent.

As the panic over Molly leaving gradually faded, relief flooded Matt. He could hardly chase after her in the condition he was now in. Damn. What was he going to do about her?

"I'd take her myself," Logan said reflectively, "but Pa's countin' on me for the roundup, especially now that you're useless."

"Lester's a good man. I'm sure Claire will be fine." Selfishly, he was just happy that Molly was staying.

"Yeah." Logan turned back to the fire, poking it with an iron rod. "Mrs. McAllister's here."

"I guess somethin' good came of getting laid up after all." Matt shifted his position again. His injured limb was propped up on a pillow, but pain still spread in all directions any time he tried to move his backside.

Standing, Logan rested his hands on his hips. "Yeah. You're lucky all the way around. You hungry?"

"I don't know." He leaned his head back and closed his eyes. He didn't like being stuck in bed. He'd just recovered from an extended bed rest from his *other* leg injury. He didn't particularly look forward to it again.

"I'll send Molly to keep you company."

Matt opened his eyes a slit, wondering what his brother was up to. Still, he wouldn't mind seeing her. But he really should mind. Hell, he was too tired and in too much pain to care. Seeing her would be damn nice.

"She's been asking about you every five minutes for the last two hours," Logan added, walking to the doorway. "I think Ma would be glad to lock the two of you away, but I wouldn't mention it to Mrs. McAllister. She's got her sights on you for Lizzie."

Matt did groan aloud now, rubbing his face. "I'm not good husband material."

"Don't I know it. You're too much a mama's boy."

Matt threw a pillow at his brother, but it hit the door as it closed.

* * *

Molly knocked before entering Matt's room, balancing the tray of food with her free hand. She took the muffled response—or was it a dog barking?—as a signal to enter. Kicking the door closed behind her, she noticed a pillow on the floor. When she finally looked up, she almost dropped the tray.

Sitting upright on the bed, his injured foot resting on a pillow, Matt was shirtless and quite obviously pantless, with a pile of bedcovers bunched at his waist. His appearance reminded Molly of every creature's will to survive—barely leashed power with a watchful wariness as potential prey entered its vicinity. His exposed chest was broad, muscled, and dark hair curled downward. With gleaming eyes he watched her, the scrutiny intense and distinctly primal.

"Are you always in a bad mood?" she asked in defense, then realized her poor manners. "I apologize, I'm sure your foot pains you." Walking around the bed, she handed him the tray. "I've brought you some food."

Despite his position, he easily lifted the tray from her, his stomach muscles clenching, drawing her eye to the strength and grace of his body. With effort, she attempted to quiet her wayward thoughts.

"Thank you." He set the food on the center of the bed.

"Logan mentioned you could use some company, but if you want me to go...," She sensed that being alone with him might not be such a good idea. If Mrs. McAllister knew of his state of nakedness, she'd probably faint on the spot. The image brought a smile to her lips.

"What's so amusing?" he asked.

"I probably shouldn't say." She glanced back at the closed door. "But Mrs. McAllister would probably comment on how improper it is my being here with you. Seeing as how you have no clothes on and all," she added, in case her meaning wasn't clear.

Matt laughed.

Molly liked it, having heard so little of it since they'd been reunited.

"Then you definitely better stay," Matt said. "That woman sticks her nose into too many people's business."

"I got that impression." She turned and dragged a heavy wooden chair closer to the bed and sat. "What did Cale say about your foot?"

"He didn't think it was bad." Matt swallowed a piece of bread and drank half a glass of milk. "But it might take a week before the swelling goes down."

"I should thank you for trying to protect me. Those cattle came out of nowhere."

"Yeah. It doesn't take much to spook 'em. The storm and the coyotes were a bad combination."

"Do you think the bones Cale found are the men who attacked?"

"I don't know." Matt picked up the potatoes and carrots with his fingers instead of using a fork, quickly consuming them. "He didn't find anything more that would've been useful in identifying who they might've been. But if they're the same men, then someone went to an extra effort to conceal the bodies. That means someone early on in the search got out there and disposed of them before the rest of us came along."

"Do you remember who that might've been?"

Matt shook his head. "No. Honestly, it could've been anyone."

She fell silent.

"Logan said Claire is leaving in the morning," Matt said, popping pieces of torn chicken meat into his mouth.

"It would seem so."

"You thinkin' of goin' with her?"

"No, I thought I should stay a bit longer yet. I'd still like to know what happened to my folks."

"We may never know that." Matt wiped his greasy fingers with a cloth napkin, then pushed the tray aside. He'd managed to eat the large meal so swiftly.

"I realize that." Frowning at the empty plate, she asked, "Do you want more food?"

"No." His unrelenting gaze focused on her, making her uncomfortable.

"Then maybe I should leave." She stood.

"You don't have to," he said quietly, "unless you want to."

Hesitating, she replied honestly. "I'm not sure what I want."

She stepped toward the bed, then shook her head and turned to flee but Matt reached for her. His large, callused fingers burned the skin around her wrist where he held her. Her heart pounded and she swayed, light-headed.

"Molly." His deep voice caressed her. The sound of her name on his lips was enough to ignite a desire in her body so sharp she almost gasped aloud. "I don't have any answers for this."

"I don't recall asking a question." Her voice, husky and full of wanting, didn't seem to be her own.

"You're young, and I have far too much experience to understand what this is."

151

She still couldn't look at him. "So, you prefer women with experience?" Claire had said men came to the brothel to pay for sex, preferably with women who knew how to give pleasure. Did Matt frequent such establishments? And if he did, how could she ever hope to live up to such expectations?

"Molly," he said more urgently, pulling her around to face him. "What I prefer has nothing to do with this. You're a beautiful young woman who's been through hell and back the last ten years. It's my job to look out for you."

"Since when?" Good Lord, she sounded almost petulant.

"Since ten years ago," he responded impatiently. He took a deep breath before continuing.

His large, tanned hand still held her. She thought to pull away, but his thumb grazed her knuckles, moving back and forth in a way that felt far more than friendly. It dawned on her then that maybe Matt wasn't sure of what should or shouldn't be between them; maybe he was as confused, as attracted, as she. It was that very thought that made her feel bold, almost reckless, and she seized the feeling and the moment before common sense stopped her. Leaning forward, she kissed him.

One kiss, lips to lips, then she stopped, her mouth inches from his. Matt didn't move. Disappointment struck hard. It had been too forward, and now she'd humiliated herself. Indecision kept her frozen in place.

"I'm sorry —"

Matt's mouth covered hers, hard and unyielding. His hands dug into her hair, holding her in place while he kissed her. She fell against him and gripped his shoulders as his lips devoured hers. She couldn't breathe, couldn't think, she could only hold on while the storm between them exploded.

Molly started to tremble, overcome by the strength of Matt's desire. Her heart raced, her skin felt flushed, and her breasts reacted to the slightest movement of his body. Deep within her abdomen awakened a longing, a need that overcame reasonable thought...

Without warning, Matt stopped.

Molly opened her eyes, completely bewildered.

"This is dangerous," he said, his rapid breathing mingling with her own. "I'm not a saint, Molly. You make me forget right and wrong."

Reluctantly, Molly withdrew from him. She felt exhilarated, but also apprehensive at what had just occurred. Her innocence was distressingly apparent to her. Matt's lust was that of a man, and she kissed him in the artless way of a naïve young girl, but that was exactly what she was. Maybe Matt was right in denying what was between them. His kiss demanded a completion that left her filled with longing, but also uncertainty.

It would seem she wasn't ready to meet the demands of the flesh between a man and woman.

She stood, amazed her legs even held her upright. She walked around the bed and took the tray holding his dinner dishes, then hastily left the room.

Chapter Seventeen

Matt had only himself to blame for his restless, miserable night of sleep. He didn't know what hurt more, his foot or his own persistent arousal. He never should have kissed Molly, but once he had, he could think of nothing else.

She had lured him with one chaste kiss, obliterating his self-control and making him forget why he shouldn't touch her. With frustration, he knew touching her wasn't the end. It was only the beginning of a longer struggle to keep her at arm's length.

If there was any consolation in the situation, it was his certain knowledge that keeping his distance wouldn't be difficult. It was painfully obvious he'd overwhelmed Molly last night, and she'd likely want nothing to do with him while she remained at the SR.

Damn, that was why he'd struggled to stay away from her in the first place. His hunger had gone beyond proper and delicate in a flash. He would have gladly undressed her and learned every innocent inch of her. *Innocent.* That was why he couldn't touch her. She deserved better than a lustful encounter that Matt wasn't even sure he could control anymore.

He could marry her.

The thought stopped him cold.

He'd never wanted to settle down. Did he really want to now? Or were the recent longings for an anchored home life just fleeting desires? He had roots. The SR provided that.

Matt hesitated to act on impulse, for it went against his nature. Wait, watch, listen. That was what he'd always taught his men, in or out of battle. And patience. It could save a man's life.

Molly had left his room last night stunned to her very toes. It was clear she felt the pull between them, but it was also obvious she was nowhere near ready to face it. He really couldn't blame her.

Perhaps he needed to practice what he had so often preached—patience. Molly needed time to become accustomed to him. He needed time to decide if he could truly make a commitment to her, because anything less would be unacceptable for her situation. They needed a chance to get to know each other again.

Awaking at dawn, he decided keeping her at arm's length wasn't such a good idea after all.

* * *

Molly hugged Claire as she prepared to leave. They stood outside, in the early-morning light, while Jonathan and Lester Williams, an older man with a purposeful face, prepared the horses. Logan and Susanna also waited nearby.

"Send word that you're all right," Molly said, "and how I might reach you."

Claire nodded.

"We'll see each other again," Molly predicted.

"I hope so," Claire replied sincerely. Smiling past the awkwardness of the goodbye, she said quietly, "Matt didn't get hit in the head with a rock, but his injured foot puts him at a disadvantage. I hope it works out the way you want it to."

Molly shook her head. "I'm not sure that's such a good thing anymore." Thoughts of where their kiss might have led had haunted her sleep all night long.

Claire looked at her in surprise. "Then you can avoid him, and he can't chase you down?" she asked uncertainly.

"I suppose there's that, too." Molly laughed as tears unexpectedly filled her eyes. "I'm going to miss you."

Claire squeezed her hand, pausing for a moment before she mounted her horse. Logan moved to help her. Susanna stood next to Molly. "Have a safe journey, Claire," she said.

"Thank you, Mrs. Ryan. You've been very kind to me. Mr. Ryan, I appreciate everything, truly I do."

"Well, you come back and visit, you hear?" Jonathan said.

Logan stood back to let her and Lester leave.

He slapped the rump of her horse, then walked several yards away from the main house to watch them as they rode toward the west.

Soon, Molly would be riding away in the same fashion. The knowledge only left her feeling confused. She and Matt were obviously mismatched. Why would leaving upset her?

It was the uncertain future, she told herself. That's what it had to be. Because the other option filled her with trepidation...and excitement. It meant giving her body to Matt, sharing with him something she had only imagined. If that happened, then what?

Leaving would break her heart.

So, was her only choice to avoid Matt until she moved on?

Standing near Susanna, Molly almost turned to the older woman for advice. She certainly needed some, but the words caught in her throat.

"Molly, dear," Susanna said, "Claire will be fine. Lester has been with us for years. He's honest and trustworthy, a fine man. He'll see her safely home."

"I'm sure you're right."

Matt's mother gazed at her intently. "Is something else bothering you?"

Molly forced the words out in a rush. "Mrs. Ryan, what does a woman do when a man is interested in her?"

Susanna looked surprised. "Is one of the ranch hands bothering you?"

Molly shook her head. "No. Not exactly."

"Well, if the man is worth his salt, he would court you, then propose marriage." Susanna paused. "In these parts, however, there are exceptions to that, but a woman should be certain of her situation before letting...certain liberties be taken."

"Liberties?"

"Hmm." Susanna frowned. "Who is it, Molly? That boy, Howie, from the Callahan Ranch? I could have Jonathan have a talk with him."

"Oh, no. That's all right."

The older woman grasped Molly's hand. "You've been away from this way of life for some time. It'll take a while to readjust, but you're also a very lovely young woman. I don't doubt you'll receive a lot of attention. From men, that is."

Molly nodded.

"Just remember," Susanna continued, "you can take the time to choose. Men are not all created equal."

Logan joined them. "What makes you say that, Ma?"

"A woman's choices can haunt her all her life."

Logan grinned. "Right. Isn't the same true of a man's choices?"

"Yes, of course," Susanna said. "Just take your time, Molly. There's no rush. You're welcome to stay here as long as you like. And if you'd like me to invite Howie for dinner, I'd be happy to."

Logan raised an eyebrow.

"No," Molly said, "that's not necessary."

"If you change your mind, let me know." Susanna released her hand, then returned to the house.

"Would you like some advice from an unequal man?" Logan asked.

Molly laughed. "I don't know."

"Whatever you do, don't let Matt think it was his idea."

"Why?"

"I probably shouldn't say this." Logan's face was so much like Matt's—hard planes and dark hair and the same blue-green eyes—but his personality was far more relaxed and open. "He seems to think he should be plannin' your life for you, to make up for the last ten years of missin' out."

"I suppose he's just trying to help."

Logan put an arm around her shoulders and walked back toward the house with her. "Matt would never admit it, but he's happier than a possum eatin' a yellow jacket to see you."

"Matt? Happy? That's not what I'm getting from him."

"Yeah, that's my point."

"I appreciate the advice, but I'm not sure I understand your point."

"Give 'im a run for his money. Make him earn it."

She shook her head in confusion.

Logan turned to face her. "He's determined to see you married and settled to ease his guilty conscience, to make sure there's a good man lookin' out for you, that you're happy and safe. But I don't think that's what you want, and I don't think that's what he wants, either." He knocked her shoulder with a friendly thump of his fist.

She went slightly off balance.

"I could always do that to you as a kid, too." Logan walked back toward the corral, leaving her on the front porch.

Still not completely clear about what Logan was trying to tell her, she did know she couldn't avoid Matt. The truth was, she really didn't want to. She marched into the house and went straight to his bedroom.

* * *

Matt was finishing the large breakfast of eggs, bacon, potatoes, and biscuits Rosita had brought him when a knock came on his door. Thinking it was the elderly Mexican woman returning for the tray, he was surprised when Molly entered after he yelled, "Come in."

He didn't know what to say. Surely she would want to avoid him after last night. And evading him wouldn't have been hard, considering his injured foot.

She appeared...well, pretty. He couldn't stop staring at her. The calico dress hugged her curves in all the right places. Dark, chestnut hair framed her face and her blue eyes sparkled with determination.

"Claire and Mr. Williams just left," she said in a rush. "I told Rosita I'd fetch your tray." She came around to his side of the bed and stood next to him. As she leaned over he caught her scent, a hint of roses and fresh air. In a fog, he handed her his breakfast dishes.

"I'll be back once I deliver these to the kitchen." In a flurry, she left the room.

Matt didn't have a chance to collect his thoughts before she returned. She carried a wooden crutch. "Dawson just finished this. Get up and get dressed," she commanded. "You should go outside for a while."

She moved to his bureau and pulled out a dark blue shirt and a pair of brown trousers.

"I can dress myself," he said hoarsely, still surprised she was giving him the time of day.

Walking toward him, all flushed and full of feminine energy, she frowned. "I don't think so. Would it be all right if I cut a slit up the right side of these pants so we can get them over your foot?"

"I suppose." He was trying to keep up with her rapid train of thought.

She left again in search of scissors. When she returned, she put her hands on his thighs to help him swing his legs over the side of the bed.

"Molly." He flinched in surprise. Trying to remove her fingers, he did his best to ignore the heat of her palms.

"You need help." She pushed his hands away.

Involuntarily, he groaned as his injured leg left the comfort of its pillow.

Once he was upright, Molly moved quickly to put the shirt on him, feeding his arms through the sleeves, then rolling the cloth to his elbows. As she shifted to the front buttons, he stopped her.

"I can do this myself." If he didn't, he was afraid he might grab her and do more than kiss her this time. Diverting his attention to the pain throbbing in his foot helped to cool the urge.

Holding the pants up, she leaned down to fit his legs into the holes.

"Molly." He pulled the trousers from her hands. "Give a man some privacy."

"I don't want you to hurt yourself," she calmly replied.

"I think I can manage."

"I can assure you, I won't see anything I already haven't. Comanche men wore very little, especially on the war path."

Matt stared down at her; she gazed right back. What was she up to? She wasn't giving him an ounce of space. And the thought of her surrounded by scantily clad men needled him.

"I wonder how they put up with you," he muttered, leaning over to put his good leg into the trousers.

She laughed. "Sometimes I think the Kwahadi wondered that too. They didn't like snakes in camp, but I did have a knack for catching them."

He struggled with his injured foot. She crouched down to help, and he reluctantly let her. Their hands touched.

"You're going to get killed one day if you keep messin' with snakes."

"It's mostly the harmless ones. Believe it or not, I do know the difference." She stood. "Can you pull them up now?"

He glared at her. She threw her hands up. "I won't look." She turned around and rested her hands on her hips.

He glanced again at her backside, noting the nice flare of her waist. Balancing on his good foot, he yanked the trousers up.

"I was actually bitten by a rattlesnake when I was twelve or thirteen," she said casually.

Matt sat down on his bed again, having accomplished his goal of getting dressed. "What?"

"There was this cave. Running Water and I were playing, and she ran inside. When I came up behind her there was the biggest rattler I'd ever seen in my life, coiled and ready to strike. He was the meanest-looking thing I'd ever seen."

Matt felt cold. "You can turn around."

"Oh." She faced him again and smiled. "Everything buttoned and tucked?"

"Yeah." Morosely he asked, "What happened with the snake?"

"I tried to save Running Water. When I turned to push her out of the cave, the snake bit me in the heel of my foot. I still have a scar. Would you like to see it?" She lifted her right foot.

"That's all right. Obviously you didn't die."

"Obviously." She grinned, and the room seemed brighter. "But I was quite ill. The shaman, Esa-tai, prepared great medicine to save me. But honestly, I think I must have received very little poison. The snake had struck me through thick moccasins. There was much talk when I recovered to change my name to Snake Charmer instead of Cactus Bird."

"I think I'm going to be sick." Matt didn't like hearing about her near-death stories.

"Really?" she asked with concern. She quickly handed him the crutch. "C'mon, let's get you outside so you don't make a mess in the house. Your mother is busy enough as it is." Then, with a twinkle in her eye, she added, "When you feel better, maybe I can scare up a few snakes to entertain you."

* * *

Molly spent all morning with Matt, walking with him as he hobbled around the ranch, checking the horses, monitoring the progress of chores to be done, conferring with Dawson about the upcoming spring roundup. Molly learned this would be a joint effort with several surrounding ranches. Men from each outfit would be present to herd the longhorns to a common holding area, and then they would cut out their own animals for branding and potential movement to markets in Kansas.

"You sound disappointed about missing the roundup," Molly remarked as they headed back to the house for lunch.

"I never really thought about it, but yeah, I guess I am a bit."

"Why does that surprise you?" She deftly sidestepped a pile of horse droppings as her calico dress swirled around her legs.

"I've never pictured myself as a rancher." He moved easily on the crutch, but his pale face belied his apparent strength and Molly knew he was exhausted. After lunch, she would insist he rest.

"Why? Your pa runs quite a spread here."

"He does," Matt agreed. "But I haven't stayed put in one place for the last ten years. I'm not sure I would know how."

"It's been much the same for me." The sudden longing for a home hit her hard, constricting her throat. She scanned the plains beyond the house; the long yellow grass and colorful wildflowers swayed in the wind. Taking a deep breath, she knew she could always count on the land to calm her.

In silence, they ascended the steps to the porch—Matt taking them a hop at a time—and entered the house.

Lunch was cold roast beef, fresh bread, and potato salad. There was also a selection of pickled hot peppers which Matt ate in great quantity. Molly watched him with alarm.

"Are you sure you should eat so many of those?" she asked, sitting beside him. Susanna sat at one end and Mrs. McAllister was across from her. Jonathan and Logan were out and about, and wouldn't return until dusk.

"It's not as if I'll be doin' any kissin' later," he said casually, grinning at her and winking.

Embarrassed, her face warmed and she suspected she was as red as some of those peppers.

"He's always liked spicy food," Susanna remarked. "I pity the woman who marries you, Matthew. You won't get many goodnight kisses."

"A man isn't lookin' for kisses at night," he said.

Molly's eyes widened before she could stop the response. Why was he talking like this, in front of his own mother and Mrs. McAllister, no less? Her cheeks burned hotter.

"Matthew Ryan, I would like you to behave yourself for our guests," Susanna admonished.

He just grinned, spearing a piece of roast beef and putting it in his mouth.

"Oh, Susanna," Mrs. McAllister said, "he's fine. Men are just more direct in these parts. More simple. I fear Lizzie will have to readjust to that notion, but I have no doubt she will. She'll make a fine rancher's wife."

When Molly looked at the woman, she was annoyed to find Mrs. McAllister directing her words at Matt.

"Do you think you'll be settling in these parts, Matthew?" the woman asked.

While Matt attempted to swallow the mouthful of food he chewed, Molly answered for him before thinking better of it. "Matt isn't the settling-down kind of man, are you?" She glanced at him.

He just raised an eyebrow in response.

"Most Texas Rangers find freedom in not being tied down to one place," she continued. "Makes sense, really. Criminals don't stay put, so neither can the men who chase them."

"Oh, I don't know," Matt replied. "I suppose I could settle down if the right woman came along." He looked straight at her.

"Just as I suspected," Mrs. McAllister said smoothly. "Lizzie is returning home in three days. I know she would love to see you, Matthew. Perhaps you could come for dinner one night? When your foot is all healed, of course."

Matt downed a large gulp of lemonade. "Do you think Lizzie even remembers who I am?"

Mrs. McAllister laughed in a dainty, feminine way.

Molly thought it sounded like a songbird bent on deceit.

"Of course. You have quite a reputation in these parts. In all of Texas, I would daresay. A fine officer in the United States Army, an honorable Texas Ranger. Susanna, you should be terribly proud of him."

"I am," Matt's mother replied warmly. "But I do wish you would consider doing something a bit less dangerous," she said to her son.

"Of course," Mrs. McAllister agreed. "And when you've married, you'll want to present your bride with a fine house and enough land to do right by her."

"I suppose every woman in north Texas is highly interested in how much land her husband can acquire," Matt said dryly.

"Well, Elizabeth is right, Matthew," Susanna said. "It's important to build a legacy on which future generations can profit. Your father has worked hard to make the SR into what it is today. I know he'd like to see you and Logan take it over one day."

Matt became contemplative.

"Every father wants his sons to follow in his footsteps," Mrs. McAllister added. "It was my Charles' greatest disappointment that we should only have one child, and a girl at that. But we have wealth in our land—Lizzie will bring much to a future husband."

"If she has so much," Molly interrupted, annoyed at how threatened she felt watching Mrs. McAllister's blatant attempts at matchmaking, "why does she need a husband? She could just run the ranch herself."

"Run it herself?" Mrs. McAllister asked weakly. "That's simply not acceptable. It's a man's job to take care of such things. A woman only has the position her husband affords her."

Molly was about to ask how important position could possibly be out here in the near desolation of this part of Texas, but common sense buzzed in her ear and she held her tongue.

"I'm sure Lizzie will find herself surrounded by many interested men, Elizabeth. Probably so many you'll not know what to do." Susanna smiled, clearly trying to calm the atmosphere.

Mrs. McAllister nodded serenely. "Molly, dear, where is it that you're from? I'm still not sure I caught that."

"Molly is an old family friend," Susanna replied. "We haven't seen her in some time, but we're so glad to be getting reacquainted with her now."

"So, you're from Texas?" Mrs. McAllister asked.

"No," Molly replied, "I was born in Virginia. My family traveled here when I was seven."

"So many of us came out here after the war," the woman said with authority. "It was a place of new beginnings, although not as grand as it is now, before the Indians were removed from the land. You and the army did a fine job, Matthew."

Molly stilled. The U.S. Army, and Matt, had been responsible for uprooting the existence of the Comanche, indirectly forcing their path toward the reservation. She could no longer deny the trace of affection she held for the Kwahadi. It had been a hard life, and some members of the tribe had not been kind, but Bull Runner had shown fairness and concern when dealing with her. While Sits On Ground had struggled with normal sisterly competition, Running Water had become quite attached to her. She wondered if the young girl still remembered her, possibly even missed her.

"It was a reluctant job." Matt glanced in Molly's direction. "Both sides had valid reasons behind what they did. Nothing was ever clear cut."

"On the contrary," Mrs. McAllister argued. "They were barbarians, living like animals, breeding among whites to contaminate us from within."

"Elizabeth, I think that's enough," Susanna said sharply.

Molly wasn't hungry anymore. "If you'll excuse me, I think I'll take a few apples to Pecos." Rising, she left swiftly, making haste through the kitchen but once she got to the stables, she realized she'd forgotten Pecos' treat.

Chapter Eighteen

Matt found Molly in Pecos' stall again, although thankfully she was awake this time. Standing near the animal's neck, she rested her head against the friendly mare, crooning softly to her. Matt stopped before them.

Spying him, Molly said, "You look exhausted. You really ought to get some rest this afternoon."

"I hate to admit it, but I think you're right. Look, Molly, about Mrs. McAllister…"

"I'm fine. Really."

"That woman has always been bigger than her britches and prejudiced beyond belief. Don't ever get her started on the issue of slavery." He held his hand out to Pecos, and the horse's wet snout coated his palm. "Don't let her get to you."

"But there's some truth in what she said. I've never really thought about it until now, but I think a part of me will always be Comanche. A part of me will never forget."

"No one's asking you to."

"But people like Mrs. McAllister will never accept me, will they? Is the sentiment the same with everyone in these parts?"

Matt paused. "I can't say for certain, but memories are long and the Comanche terrorized this area for some time. People aren't likely to forget that." He pushed his hat back. "Molly, I didn't say this before, but maybe now's the time. It's probably best if you don't talk much about where you've been the past ten years. Some folks just won't understand."

Molly's stricken expression made him feel lower than dirt.

She recovered quickly, however, and nodded. "You can get on back to the house now," she said thickly, "I'll be all right. I think I might ride Pecos a bit. She needs to stretch her legs."

"One of the ranch hands can ride her." He didn't want to leave just yet.

Molly shook her head. "I think I need to stretch my legs, too."

"Will you play a game of chess with me tonight?" he asked in a vain hope to engage her company later.

Molly opened the stall door, forcing Matt to move aside as she led Pecos out of the stables. "I've been living with barbarians. When would I have learned to play chess?" she asked bitterly.

"I'll teach you," he said behind her.

"I'll think about it." She efficiently saddled her horse and was gone before Matt could catch her.

Damn his injured foot.

* * *

Molly stayed away for several hours, the freedom and solitude a balm to her spirit. The whisper of the wind, the all-encompassing blue sky, and the endless plains brought her back to her life with the Kwahadi, a life that had taken her from childhood to the beginnings of womanhood.

It had been a life of hardship—bitterly cold winters, hungry nights when food was scarce, the constant togetherness of living in a crowded teepee with Bull Runner's family. But there had also been sweet summer days, buffalo hunts in which the women often accompanied the warriors, games and mayhem, funny stories and gossip from the older women while they ground, cut and dried the food they gathered and hunted nearly every day of their life. There had been joyous births and sad deaths. It had been a life, and the Kwahadi had been no better or worse than any other people. They loved, they laughed, they feared as much as any other. They were human, and Molly could never think of them otherwise.

The sun beat down as she rode, and after a time she couldn't resist the urge she'd been trying to ignore since she and Pecos had set out. Stripping out of the calico gown, she tied the blouse around her waist. The chemise undergarment still covered her upper body. Pulling the saddle from Pecos she dropped it to the ground, leaving only the blanket on the mare's back.

Casting off the remainder of her dress, she sprang onto Pecos. The action pleased her, and the memory of doing it countless times before reminded her the past belonged to her. It couldn't be erased. She was Molly, but she was also Cactus Bird. Two different lives, existing within the same person.

As one, girl and horse rode, streaking across the earth, flying as if they were a bird hovering above the ground. Together, they soared like a wren seeking its home.

* * *

Molly finally returned to the SR at dusk. Wearing her dress again, she approached the dining room, and supper, with a certain amount of dread.

She really didn't want to dine with Mrs. McAllister again, but to her great relief the woman had left that afternoon to return home.

"I think it was time for her to get back to her ranch," Susanna said. "You'll have to forgive her, Molly. Some people will never change, I'm afraid."

Molly sat next to Matt again; across the table were Logan and Dawson, and Jonathan sat across from his wife.

"How was your ride?" Matt asked, leaning close.

Molly smiled, noticing the silver flecks in his blue-green gaze. "Long overdue."

Once she spoke, it dawned on her the words might hold another meaning.

Clearly Matt thought so, too, if his intense gaze was any indication.

Rosita entered and began serving dinner—a mouth-watering beef stew filled with potatoes, carrots, onions and peppers, alongside blue corn muffins and apple pie for dessert. The upcoming roundup dominated the conversation. The men discussed how many beeves they would need for market, supplies coming and going, and the general state of the ranch.

Molly remained silent and simply listened, aware of Matt's easy presence beside her. His movements, his voice, every aspect of him resonated within her, calling to her. He was achingly familiar and yet completely unfamiliar. The man he had become was a new and dangerous creature, utterly compelling. And utterly terrifying? Not Matt himself. But she couldn't deny that what could be between them filled her with unease. It was such completely new territory for her.

When dinner ended, Matt silently guided her into the parlor and to the small table in the corner that held a chess game. A fire crackled in the hearth while a strong wind howled outside. Susanna went to the kitchen with Rosita while Jonathan, Logan and Dawson went into the study across the hall.

"You don't have to sit with me," Molly said. "If you'd like to join your pa and the others, it's fine with me."

Matt settled himself into the ornately carved wooden chair—there were actually longhorn cattle patterns along the side she noticed—and sighed. "They're just gonna smoke cigars and have a shot or two of whiskey. Then, there'll be more ranch talk. I'm not missing anything."

Molly stared at the chessboard and settled farther into the soft cushion of her chair. Her papa had played when she was a child, so she was acquainted with the game, but she had never really learned to play. "You really dislike ranch life?" she asked.

"No, that's not it. It's just always seemed so permanent. So many people rely on my pa."

"What's wrong with that? In the army and the Rangers, didn't your men rely on you?"

Matt agreed with a nod of his head. "Of course."

"But permanence scares you, is that it? Permanence would be a nice change of pace for me."

Matt's eyes held a gleam of amusement. "Are you ready for a basic lesson in chess?"

Molly assented, glad for the diversion. Except she wasn't sure what the distraction was—the chess game or Matt.

* * *

173

Matt played chess with Molly for over two hours. She was perceptive and quick—traits she'd possessed as a child—and he was hard pressed to beat her during their three games. In the soft glow of the firelight, he enjoyed watching her face as she focused on the game, her blue eyes shrewdly examining the board, her dark brows drawing together in concentration. Her hair was down and glistened in the muted light of the room, and while she calculated her next move, she'd bite her lower lip and rest her chin in a graceful hand.

Matt couldn't remember the last time he'd simply enjoyed sitting with a woman. Observing her, he appreciated the sparks of intelligence as she grew more and more accustomed to the game.

As the third round ended, she said, "I think you should get some rest."

He leaned back in his chair. He was weary—there was no doubt of that—but he was reluctant to leave.

"Do you need some help back to your room?" she asked.

"I think I can manage. Molly, what will you do eventually? Have you thought about where you'll go?"

"I imagine to Mary, or my Aunt Catherine and Emma, if they'll have me."

He expected such an answer. Still, it bothered him. Her leaving. His departure too, at some point. "What about your family's land?"

Male voices interrupted them as his pa and brother entered the room, followed by his ma.

"What'd you say, Matt?" his pa said. "Were you asking about the Harts' land?"

He nodded. The elderly man sat on the couch while Logan tended the fire. His ma snuggled next to her husband. Molly turned in her chair to listen.

"Well, by golly, I should've told you sooner, Molly. Upon your folks' death, the land was put into a trust for you and your sisters. When Mary married that fella Simms, I wrote to her and asked if she wanted it, but her husband was dead set on the territories—Arizona that is. So I was just waitin' on Emma. Now that you're here, though, I guess you should consider if you want it. I'd be happy to make a decent offer on it if you girls decide to move on."

"You mean I own the land now?" she asked.

"Well, not exactly," his pa answered. "It can only be owned by your husband. It's the same for Mary and Emma. As soon as you're married, the land can be deeded over straightaway."

"Oh."

"Is there any way around that?" Hope filled Matt that Molly might stay near.

"What on earth for?" his ma questioned. "Molly shouldn't live out there all by herself. If it comes down to that, you can just stay here with us, dear."

"Thank you, Mrs. Ryan. I appreciate that."

"Well, of course."

"How many acres do Molly and her sisters have?" Logan asked, still kneeling before the fireplace.

"Hmm, let me think," Jonathan said. "I'd have to rifle through the paperwork, but I'd say about twenty thousand acres."

Logan whistled. "You'll make some rowdy ranch hand happy one day, Molly."

"Is that all anyone thinks about around here?" Matt asked, irritated. "Just how much land they can get their hands on?"

"Times are changing, Matthew," his pa said. "There's talk amongst the ranchers about this new barbed wire fence. It could alter a lot of things, for the worse, some say, but I think mostly for the better. Land is important. Always has been, always will be. I'd be happy to have you stay close, Molly, but you don't have to decide right now."

"Matthew," his ma said, "you really ought to get some rest."

"I think I'll turn in as well." Molly stood. "Goodnight," she said to the others, then turned back to him. "Goodnight, Matt."

He tried to think of something to say to stop her, but she promptly left the room.

"Don't worry, I'll help you back to your room." Logan grinned. "I'll even help you put a nightshirt on."

"Like hell," Matt muttered.

Logan laughed and his ma reprimanded them with a single look before leaving the room with her husband. The image of his folks going off to bed struck him as odd. They were happy.

"Jesus, Logan," he said, "look at us."

"What's that supposed to mean?" His brother sat on the couch just vacated by their folks.

"We're grown men, still living with our ma and pa. Haven't you ever thought about getting married?"

"Yeah, sure. I almost did."

"What?" he asked in surprise. "Does Ma know?"

Logan shook his head. "Nah. It didn't work out. It's just as well."

"What happened?"

"She skipped town with some other guy."

"Then she obviously wasn't worth it."

Logan blew out a breath. "Yep. Barely escaped that one."

"Have you thought about settling down with another woman?"

"If you're talkin' about Lizzie McAllister, then you don't have to worry. She's all yours."

"I'm not interested in a fine society lady, all gussied-up and as smart as any man," he said, surprised by the echo of Molly's words from that first night when they were together.

"Then just do us all a favor." Logan stood to leave. "Start courting Molly and quick. I have it on good knowledge Ma's thinkin' of inviting Howie for dinner."

"Howie?" Matt asked, confused.

"That baby-faced cow wrangler Molly was teaching to ride bareback."

Now Matt remembered. He hardly considered Howie competition. Or was he? The truth was, Matt had never courted a woman in his life. The women he'd spent time with didn't particularly need courting, and he certainly wouldn't have stuck around long enough to endure it.

"Courting, huh?" he asked his brother. "Any suggestions?"

"Don't let Ma catch wind of it." Logan's ominous tone grabbed his attention.

"Why?"

"She was giving Molly her speech earlier, about waiting and taking her time in choosing a fella to shack up with."

"Ma told her to shack up with someone?" Matt asked, incredulous.

"Jesus H. Christ, Matt," Logan said in exasperation. "All the smarts must have been blessed to me. Of course, Ma didn't say it that way. But think about it. Molly lived with Indians for years. You know their marriages were loosely structured, and the men often took more than one woman. Molly's an easy target, and Ma knows this. She'll be all over the guy who's sweet on her. You'll be lucky to steal a kiss, let alone get up her skirt."

Matt shook his head at his brother's crude interpretation of what he wanted to do with Molly. While true, it also sounded crass and wrong. If that's all he desired, then he was the kind of man he was trying to protect Molly from. Hadn't he already stolen a kiss from her?

"You've really cast a new light on it," he said sarcastically. "Thanks."

"Anytime. Can I be the best man?"

Matt swore but Logan had already left the room.

Chapter Nineteen

The next morning, Susanna awoke Molly at dawn.

"What is it?" Immediately Molly worried that something was wrong with Matt.

"I'm sorry to disturb you, but I just remembered something and I simply had to tell you." Susanna sat beside her on the bed, still in her nightgown, her black and gray hair braided and resting over a shoulder. "Do you remember Sarah Pickett?"

"Yes."

"She lives within a day's ride from here. I can't believe I didn't think of it before. Perhaps she'll know something about your folks that might be useful, and I'm sure she'd be thrilled to know you're alive."

"Can we see her today?" Molly asked hopefully.

"I'll speak with Jonathan. I'm sure we can leave after breakfast. I'll meet you downstairs."

After Susanna left, Molly considered seeing Mrs. Pickett again. It would be nice to talk with someone from her past. The woman had been friends with her mama—was it possible she knew of a connection with Davis Walker? The thought motivated Molly out of bed.

* * *

By mid-afternoon Susanna stopped her horse in front of a modest, wooden house. Molly glanced at the surrounding cottonwoods swaying in the wind, noting how the slight breeze from earlier in the day was fast becoming blustery. She hoped they'd make it back before the storm overtook them.

A petite, older woman opened the front door and came onto the porch. Smiling, she wiped her hands on a white apron and waited with a questioning gaze.

Susanna dismounted, looped the reins of her horse around a wooden post and removed her hat.

"Mrs. Pickett? I don't know if you remember me. I'm Susanna Ryan. I was a friend of Rosemary Hart."

"Why yes, I remember you. I'm pleased to see you again." She reached out and clasped Susanna's hand with both of hers. "How nice of you to stop by. I don't get many visitors these days."

After securing her horse, Molly waited a few feet behind Matt's mother.

"Mrs. Pickett, I'd like you to meet Molly." Susanna turned around to include her.

"Please, call me Sarah. It's a pleasure to meet you."

Molly noticed the delicate wrinkles around the woman's eyes and mouth, as well as her soft, white hair pulled into a bun. Still, she appeared youthful and her skin glowed with warmth.

Memories filled Molly's head—fond recollections of a cheerful woman who helped Molly's mother adjust to a new life in Texas. Mrs. Pickett spent hours doing Mary's hair, teaching Emma how to write her letters, and attempted to teach Molly how to sew.

"May we speak with you for a bit?" Susanna asked.

"Well, that would be nice. Please, come inside."

They entered the simply furnished house. Molly noticed the cleanliness of the dwelling immediately. The living room consisted of two rocking chairs positioned before a stone fireplace. A wooden table with matching chairs sat near the cooking stove, and a bed covered with a colorful quilt was visible through another doorway.

Sarah turned the two rocking chairs around so they could all face one another, while Susanna brought a stool closer from the table.

"I wasn't expecting guests," Sarah said, "but let me at least set some water to boil for tea."

"That would be lovely," Susanna replied, "but not necessary."

"Nonsense. Please, sit down." Sarah moved to the kitchen area with a purposeful stride. She added wood to the stove, then used a pitcher of water to fill the kettle.

Returning to the empty rocker, she settled herself.

"I wondered if we could talk about Rosemary Hart," Susanna began.

Sadness played across Sarah's face. "I still think of her quite often. Did the young lady know her?"

"I did," Molly answered. "She was my mama."

Sarah froze. "You're *Molly Hart*?"

"Yes, ma'am."

Confusion played across Sarah's face. "But...Molly is dead."

"It was all a terrible mistake," Susanna interjected gently. "But she's returned to us now and that's all that matters."

"Oh, my word." Stricken, Sarah sat back and stared.

Molly reached out to touch the woman's hand. "It's good to see you again, Mrs. Pickett."

"You've been alive all this time? I can't believe this." The older woman grasped Molly's fingers. "Oh, child, what a miracle this is. Your mama would've died a thousand times over if she were alive and thought you lost all this time."

"That's why we've come," Molly said. "Can you tell me about her?"

Sarah release her hand and dabbed at the tears in her eyes. "Lord, it broke my heart when she and your papa were killed. They were such good people, and so kind to me. The work she gave me helped my Lou and me survive when he couldn't work. He was sick, you see."

"Is your husband…," Molly didn't know how to phrase it.

"He's gone, God rest his soul. He died of consumption several years back." Sarah took a steadying breath. "What would you like to know, my dear?"

"Everything, I suppose. But what I'm most curious about is if she ever told you anything about Davis Walker, especially during the summer before she was killed."

Sarah paused, tentative. "What do you know about Mr. Walker?"

"Only some…suspicions, mostly. Did Mama ever confide in you?"

The elderly woman hesitated for such a long while that Molly almost asked the question again.

"I suppose you've a right to know, and with Rosemary gone there's no one left to tell, but I must say, I don't feel right saying anything about it. It's not really my place, you see. Your mama carried a great burden, and I'm certain it affected her health. She could hardly stand to be outside in the sun after a while. You can't keep such guilt inside. It only festers."

Sarah glanced at Susanna. "Perhaps I should speak with Molly alone."

"No," Molly said. "I trust Mrs. Ryan."

Sarah nodded, a deep sigh releasing her earlier, cheerful self. "Very well. Your mama didn't confide in me right away, but, after a time, it became clear something distressed her greatly. I noticed it especially after Davis would visit her. One night, she broke down and told me everything.

"Your papa, well, he was away at the time. I never breathed a word of this to anyone, not even after your folks were killed. I was greatly conflicted about whether I should have spoken up then, but I finally realized it wouldn't help bring back all that was lost. And I wanted Mary and Emma to remember their mama as a good woman."

"What did she do?" Molly asked, a feeling of dread settling over her.

"Well, you see, she and Davis knew each other in Virginia. They were actually engaged to be married."

"Yes, I know. I recently learned of this."

"You did?" Sarah asked. "Well, then, maybe this won't be as much of a shock as I feared it would be." Taking a fortifying breath, she continued, "Molly, your mama was in the unfortunate position of loving two men. I hope you'll remember that and not judge her too harshly.

"When Rosemary met Robert, she told me she was immediately drawn to him. So, eventually she broke off her engagement to Davis and married

183

Robert. Within a short time, your older sister Mary was born. In the meantime, Davis married someone else and his wife bore him three sons. As I understand, she died in childbirth with the last."

"We all felt terrible when Loretta passed giving birth to T.J.," added Susanna.

"Rosemary as well," Sarah continued. "She tried to ease Davis' pain by caring for the babe, as well as for Davis and the other two boys."

"I remember," Susanna said. "She ran herself to exhaustion. I always thought it was because of Loretta, but I'm guessing there may have been other reasons."

"She told me all she'd wanted to do was help in any way she could. She felt badly for a long time about how things had ended between her and Davis. Her intentions were noble, but in the end being near him wasn't a good thing. There were still, well, feelings between them."

"Are you saying Mama carried on with Davis?" Molly asked in disbelief.

"I'm afraid so," Sarah said quietly.

Anger welled in Molly. "How long?"

"More than a year, it seemed."

Sitting back in her chair, Molly tried to fathom what her mama could have been thinking, carrying on with another man while she had a husband and child at home waiting for her.

"But that's not all of it, is it?" Molly asked, a sick feeling settling in the pit of her stomach.

"No, dear," Sarah said soothingly. "From the looks of it, I think you already know."

"What is it?" Susanna asked.

Molly's throat constricted around the truth, the final act in her mama's betrayal.

"Davis Walker is my father."

Chapter Twenty

Matt waited on the front porch, leaning on his crutch and eyeing the storm quickly building on the horizon. It was late in the day, and his ma and Molly still hadn't returned.

As Logan rounded the house, a gust of wind flattened his shirt against him. At the same time, Matt saw his pa approach on horseback.

His pa dismounted and Logan took the horse to the barn.

"Have you seen Ma and Molly?" Matt asked.

"No," his pa replied, immediately looking concerned. "They haven't returned yet?"

Matt shook his head.

"Damn." Jonathan glanced at the sky. "Your mother knows better. It's very likely she stayed put at the Pickett house. No reason to worry unless we have to."

His pa was right, but that didn't make Matt feel any better.

"How's the foot, son?"

"A nuisance."

His father laughed, then sobered. "I went to see Davis."

Matt looked at him in surprise.

"What happened?" Logan asked, rejoining them.

"I just wanted to ask him what he remembered of the situation surrounding Robert Hart's death ten years ago."

When his pa became quiet, Matt asked, "And?"

"He blathered on about that nonsense of Robert rustling cattle off Walker land, which I find hard to believe. Davis is a resentful man. I guess I never noticed just how much."

"Did he admit to wanting Hart killed?" Logan asked.

"No, and of course I didn't ask him. But a bottle of rot-gut later left him talking about Loretta in a way that turned my stomach."

"What did he say?" Matt asked neutrally.

"Loretta was a nice woman," his pa replied gruffly. "She sure as hell didn't deserve Davis. It doesn't seem he ever loved her. He described her as clingy and pathetic, blaming her for all his sons' bad habits." He shook his head in disgust.

"There were other things going on between Davis and Robert," he continued. "Some I knew about, but when I brought up what happened ten years ago, just casually mind you, he immediately went on a tirade about how I really never knew Robert. He brought up the cattle rustling, claiming Robert was changing the Walker brand to his own."

"But you don't think it was true?" Logan asked.

"No, I don't. Robert was as good and honest a man as you could find. Why would he steal from Davis? He didn't need the money. It's just too easy now for Davis to lay blame on a dead man to cover his sorry ass."

"So what now?" Matt asked.

"We keep Molly safe and away from Davis." Jonathan stood. "He's wallowing in his own bitterness — that may be all the justice we can ever hope for. I don't want him near any of the Hart girls again. I owe it to the memory of Robert and Rosemary to look out for their children. I know they would've done the same for me."

"This is ugly business, but I thank God every day for your mother," he continued, surprising Matt with an uncharacteristic display of emotional sentiment. "You boys really ought to settle down and start a family. Your ma wants to see some grandchildren and I have to admit, I wouldn't mind it either. Those things are important. A man shouldn't spend his life alone."

"Is this the short or the long lecture?" Logan asked dryly.

"Start bringing some women home, or I'll be forced to search them out myself," Jonathan remarked sternly. "You boys aren't getting any younger."

"God help us," Logan groaned, "they'll be plain, homely, and sturdy."

"Ah hell, you boys are too picky."

Matt spied two riders in the distance. "So much for Ma stayin' put." He nodded toward them, feeling relieved Molly was safe.

"The damn woman," Jonathan said under his breath. "What's she doin' out in this?" A jagged bolt of lightning shot from the dark mass of clouds.

Jonathan and Logan moved swiftly to meet the riders partway as Matt hobbled to catch up. Logan took the horses as soon as Molly and Susanna dismounted. The group proceeded quickly into the house.

As they entered the parlor, Molly shot upstairs and disappeared.

"What's wrong?" Matt asked.

His ma removed her coat. "Oh," she said, rubbing her forehead, "I don't even know where to begin. Molly needs some time, I think."

"Time for what?" his pa asked.

"Where's Rosita?" Susanna questioned. "Let me eat something first, then we'll talk."

As his folks left the room, Matt knew he didn't want to wait. Hopping upstairs, he paused at Molly's bedroom door then knocked. "Molly? It's Matt. Can I come in?"

The door opened and the bleak expression on her face immediately concerned him. "What's wrong?" he asked quickly. "What's happened?"

Standing back, she let him inside. Confused, he stared at the bedcovers thrown on the floor. Noticing his line of sight, Molly said, "Sometimes I can't sleep in the bed. It's too soft."

"So you sleep on the floor?"

"Not every night, just when I'm restless."

She turned toward the window to watch the storm dumping water and wind into the darkness outside.

"Did Sarah Pickett tell you something?" he asked.

She nodded, her body tense and rigid. With arms folded tightly before her, the dark dress she wore strained across her shoulders.

"On nights like these," she said, "Bull Runner would gather us inside the teepee. While he struggled to keep a fire going, each of the women would sit in a corner trying to keep the buffalo hides from flying up, but the wind made it in anyway. It was so damn miserable sometimes. There were times when I wondered if it wouldn't be better if I'd just died."

"I'm glad you didn't." He spoke resolutely, willing her to believe it was true.

She faced him. "Have you ever wondered about the reasons for your existence, Matt?"

"Molly—"

"Elijah often spoke to me of God. He even quoted the Bible, at least the verses he could remember from his own mama. There was always one that stuck in my head, something about do not place an obstacle in my path to Him. I'm beginning to think God Himself is placing as many obstacles as He can in my life."

"Tell me what Sarah Pickett said," Matt demanded.

"It seems Davis Walker is my father," she said in a rushed sob.

Matt crossed the room, discarded his crutch and took Molly into his arms. He held tight as she fell apart. "Are you certain?"

She nodded into his chest. "My mama told her," she cried.

He held her close, hardly imagining what any of this meant. The indecency of the revelation belied a grim logic. At the moment, however, all that concerned him was the woman in his arms. Murmuring her name, he offered protection with his embrace, trying to lend her the strength he regretted not giving her throughout the last ten years.

Releasing his own restraint, he touched her, running his hands down her back then into the soft mass of brown curls. He breathed in the scent of her hair—wildflowers and rain and sunshine. She fit him so easily. Not surprisingly, desire stirred but he took care that she wouldn't be able to tell. The last thing he wanted to do was send her running away from him.

Without words, he guided them to the bed, and folded her against him. He stroked her head while she fell into an exhausted sleep. As the rhythm of her deep breathing released a bone-deep tension within his own body, he leaned over and very carefully extinguished the oil lamp on the night table.

Then, he slept.

* * *

Molly awoke abruptly, alone on the rumpled sheets of her bed. Bright sunlight poured through the window. She still wore the same dress from the previous day.

Matt was with me.

He'd held her, and they'd slept, together, in each other's arms. Despite the painful revelations from Mrs. Pickett, Molly felt well rested. She might be able to tolerate the bed more frequently if Matt shared it with her. The thought quickened her pulse.

But the ever-present loneliness pressed on her.

Nothing in her life had been constant. Now, the man she'd always thought was her father—Robert Hart—wasn't. Davis Walker, a man she hardly knew, was. A man she suspected may have murdered her folks.

What should she do now? Susanna had told her the Ryans would shelter her for as long as she needed. Tears welled up in her eyes. She felt lost, cast adrift in the world. Emma, Mary, her Aunt Catherine—none of them would even recognize her now. They were but strangers to her. Elijah was dead, her mama and the man she thought was her papa were dead. And what of the Kwahadi? That makeshift family had slipped beyond her the moment Bull Runner had traded her.

God help her, a part of her hadn't wanted him to leave her. But she'd buried that yearning, along with a thousand others, over the years.

The tears flowed freely, clouding her vision, effectively shutting the world out.

* * *

"Matthew?"

Matt stopped at the threshold of the dining room and faced his mother. She sat alone, eating breakfast.

"Can I speak with you a minute?" she asked.

He nodded.

Appearing uncomfortable, she said, "Last night I brought food upstairs for Molly. And I...found you with her."

Matt shifted. It'd been a while since he'd been caught red-handed by his ma. Damn if he didn't feel like a boy caught with his hand in the cookie jar.

"I'm not going to pry," his mother continued, "but I will ask that you take care with her."

"You don't have to worry, Ma. Her well-being has always been important to me."

"Yes, I know. I remember how hard you took it when we all thought she was gone. But she's a woman now, and I know how scarce women can be in these parts."

Matt raised an eyebrow. "I think I can control myself."

"Well, I'm not questioning that. It's just that I can't help but think of Molly as a daughter, and I don't want to see her unnecessarily hurt."

"What about me?" Matt asked in a teasing tone. "What if I get hurt?"

"You're my son and I love you dearly, and of course I want you to be happy. If Molly can do that, then I'm behind this. However, you've been a closed book since you rode away from this ranch at the age of eighteen. You're a fine man, responsible and reliable, and your pa and I couldn't be more proud of your career in the army and the Rangers, but in the process you've buried your heart.

"Believe me, I hope you can find it again, but please be very careful with Molly's in the process. Please be very sure of your intentions before you become involved with her."

Matt stared at his ma. Leave it to her to cut to the chase and lay it all out before him. And, as usual, she was right.

"You're not using your crutch," she said. "How's your foot?"

"Getting better," he said, still humbled by her insight about him. "I can put a bit of pressure on it now."

Susanna rose and came to stand before him. She pulled him down toward her and kissed him on the cheek. "I love you."

He grinned at her. "Now you know why I've stayed away all these years. I was trying to escape my meddlin' Ma."

She laughed, pushing him away. "Get going. Or I might decide to meddle some more."

He kissed her cheek, then made his way to the kitchen.

Chapter Twenty-One

After a little cajoling, Matt talked Molly into a ride mid-morning. He knew exactly where he wanted to take her. As they approached the abandoned building sheltered by the shade of several cottonwood trees, he thought of the past but also the future. The woman riding ahead of him embodied both.

"Is this where you and your family lived before the ranch was built?" She glanced over her shoulder. A hat shaded her eyes, but Matt knew the deep blue depths waited to welcome him home.

He nodded, glad to see she was still herself despite the events of the previous day. She wore a dark blue dress, a simple petticoat bunched up around her knees as she rode, but the sight of bare leg didn't bother him today. With no one else around for miles, the inadvertent display was only for him. He vowed to behave like a gentleman, his ma's lecture notwithstanding, but that didn't mean he couldn't indulge himself the view. He suspected he could look at Molly for a long time to come.

She swung down from Pecos and tied the horse to a tree branch. "Do you need help?" She squinted up at him. The storm during the night had blown through, leaving sunshine in its wake.

"I can manage." He dismounted, landing on his good foot, which still sent a jolt of pain along his leg, always a reminder of his time with Cerillo. He pushed the shadows away. Today was about moving forward.

"Are you leaving on the roundup tomorrow?" She helped him with the bag of food he'd brought. Their arms brushed against each other and he enjoyed the contact.

"I was thinkin' about it," he replied, untying a blanket from his saddle. He could ride fairly well now, and he wanted to do his part with the ranch. He owed that much to his folks, but it would also mean time spent away from Molly.

"You'll be gone for a few weeks?" She took the blanket from him as well, then walked away before he could protest.

"Give or take a few days."

She spread the cloth on the ground underneath the shade of a tree, positioned the bag of food in the center, then sat on one side and removed her hat. He settled opposite her.

"You should be careful not to overdo it, but then I'm sure your ma has already told you that." Molly tucked her legs beneath her dress.

"Yeah," Matt said, smiling, "she's already lectured me on that and several other things." He'd decided not to tell his ma he planned to take Molly riding, alone. She probably would've wanted to chaperone them.

"You're lucky. Your folks are wonderful."

"Molly, you'll get through this." He reached out and tucked a strand of hair behind her ear. Her gaze softened.

Reluctantly, he let his hand drop away.

"Thanks for staying with me last night," she said.

"You're not alone anymore. I hope you know that."

She didn't respond, instead shifting her gaze to the flat horizon before them.

"I'm afraid we were found out," he added.

Molly looked at him expectantly.

"My ma discovered me in your room last night."

"She did?" Molly asked in alarm. "Well, you told her nothing happened, didn't you?"

Frowning, Matt realized he hadn't because if he had to be truthful, he'd *wanted* something to happen. And in the wanting he was as guilty as if he and Molly had actually made love.

"Don't worry. My ma has your best interests always in hand."

"Oh." A blush crept up Molly's cheeks.

Matt enjoyed her discomfort, savoring her reaction to being with him. He damn well liked everything about her.

To take his mind off more intimate pursuits, he reached for the bag and began removing fried chicken, bread, cheese, and two red apples. He also pulled out a dark bottle and two tin cups.

"What's that?" Molly asked.

"Wine. Even out here in the middle of nowhere, we're not so backward as everyone would have you think."

A smile tugged at Molly's mouth. "I wouldn't know. Of what's forward, backwards, or any which way, that is."

He popped the cork, poured the amber liquid into a cup and handed it to Molly. He filled the other cup, then clicked hers in a toast. "To only moving forward from now on."

Molly took a sip. "It's good." She licked her lips.

"Try and eat something." He didn't want his ma accusing him of getting Molly soused just so he could steal a kiss, although the idea did have merit.

In an easy silence they ate, drank more wine, and watched clouds move across the sky. After a time, Molly lay back onto the blanket.

"The wine's making me sleepy." She rubbed her forehead.

Matt cleaned up the remains of the food, set the bag aside, then reclined beside her. "A nap sounds like a good idea." He covered his face with his hat, then reached out and grasped Molly's hand. She interlaced her fingers with his and together they dozed, the calming silence of the wind lulling them to sleep.

* * *

Molly came awake with a start. Sitting up, she noticed it was late afternoon and that Matt still slept, if the low and constant snoring coming from him was any indication. Lifting his hat, she set it nearby and looked at the man who had stood by her in these strange and uncertain days since her return to Texas. If she wasn't careful, she'd come to rely on his presence too much.

But it was difficult to not want more from him, to not want it *all*. She watched his strong jawline and shadowed cheeks, mellowed in his relaxed state yet still exuding a masculinity that was a natural part of him. His broad chest rose and fell with each breath. A hand with long fingers rested on his stomach, the sun-darkened skin in stark contrast with the ivory shirt he wore. His long legs stretched out before him, his scuffed boots crossed at the ankles.

Molly could hardly resist. Leaning over him, she kissed him gently on the mouth. He tasted of chicken and wine, his lips warm, and the new growth of stubble pricked her chin. He stirred. A large hand reached up to grasp behind her head so she kissed him again.

He responded to her this time, both hands burrowing in her hair, drawing her down. Their lips fit together as if they'd always been made for the other, and Molly sank against him. His mouth moved over hers, drinking her in, and she followed his lead, meeting his overtures fully, determined not to waste this opportunity of getting him to respond to her. She shifted an arm and buried a hand into his hair, reveling in the feel of the thick tresses, wanting to touch him with intimate gestures she had only imagined. Lost in the sensation that being near him brought, she let her lips move to his cheeks, not caring as his whiskers poked, showing him with her response how much she desired him.

In one swift motion, he rolled her onto her back and covered her with his body. His tongue swept her mouth with a searing intensity, obliterating her ability to think. Grasping tightly to his shoulders, she clung to him and the lightning bolt of sensation released between them. She felt the hardness of him press against her and it didn't scare her. She simply wanted more…of this, of him, of Matt.

Abruptly he stopped and leaned into her shoulder, breathing heavily. "Molly," he whispered. "We can't."

"Why not?" She tried to bring his mouth back to hers.

"Not here. Not like this." He lifted his head to look at her. Then, he laughed. "If I thought all that wine would make you frisky, then I wouldn't have brought it. On the other hand, waking up to you draped all over me is the nicest dream I can imagine."

He kissed her again, sweetly, lingering over her.

"I don't understand," she said against his mouth, lifting her head toward his in an attempt for a deeper kiss. "Don't you want me?"

He pressed his forehead to hers, forcing her to stop her seeking. "Since the moment I laid eyes on you again." His breath mixed with hers.

He disengaged from her and stood, offering a hand. Disappointment and frustration welled up inside as he pulled her upright.

"This is best for you, Molly." He released her hand and she immediately missed his warmth and the fire only he could ignite within her.

"How do you know what's best for me?" She couldn't keep the irritation from her voice.

"A young woman has to consider her future. Rolling around in the dirt shouldn't really be a part of that future."

"You think this is amusing, don't you?" she accused, planting hands on hips and looking to the prairie beyond.

He grinned, then picked up a small rock and threw it into the distance. "I think it's sweet you haven't changed much, still rolling around in the dirt and all."

Was he serious? He says he wants her, but then likens her to the little girl she used to be. A little girl so long gone from her life, she could hardly remember what it felt like to be excited to greet each new day. Until now. *Until him.* He made her want so much more than she ever dreamed could be within her grasp.

Discouraged by the turn the day had taken, she walked over to the dwelling the Ryan family inhabited so many years ago. Stepping inside, she blinked a few times until her eyes adjusted to the dark corners. Four windows, with no glass or shutters, let light enter the one-room abode. A small cast-iron stove stood at one end, but other than that the room was empty save for dirt on the wooden floor and spider webs in abundance.

Molly slowly walked around the room. She ran fingers along the stove, the coolness surprising her. A shadow crossed the doorway and she saw Matt's large frame, his hat firmly in place, silhouetted as he leaned on the doorjamb.

"They took just about everything when they built the ranch house," he said. She couldn't see his face, could only hear his deep voice as he cornered her, much the way he'd cornered her heart, only to turn away from her in the end. "My pa always thought he'd clean the place up, make a little getaway for him and my ma."

"Why didn't he?" Her voice echoed off the walls.

Matt shrugged. "Never got around to it, I guess."

"Time is precious," she said quietly. "You shouldn't waste it." She knew that better than most.

Matt watched her, but whatever he thought he kept to himself. "Speaking of time," he finally said, "I'd better get you back to the ranch or else my ma is gonna think we were doing a lot more than kissing on that blanket."

Why is it when he spoke it was like a caress on her skin? Her heart raced and warmth spread throughout her body, most especially in her belly, making her ache for him.

A wistful longing filled her to be back on the ground, beside him, watching the clouds pass by and knowing that he was hers.

Chapter Twenty-Two

Matt and nearly all of the men who worked and lived at the SR departed the following morning. Susanna said they'd be gone at most ten days, working in tandem with several other ranches in the area to round-up the cattle grazing and surviving on thousands of acres of the surrounding countryside.

Unable to sleep, Molly stood on the porch to see them off in the pre-dawn haze. Matt's wink set her stomach to fluttering before he rode off in the mass male exodus. His behavior thrilled and irritated her at the same time. If he didn't want her, then why did he tease her?

On the same thought, she realized ten days without him was almost more than she wanted to contemplate. And so, the first day passed under a depressing cloud.

A second dreary day came and went.

Her feelings for Matt were more serious than apparently even she was aware. And what had he said to her? He'd always been fond as hell of her. Wasn't that romantic.

But when did she decide she needed romance?

On the third day, after helping Rosita in the kitchen and Susanna with general cleaning in the house, Molly headed out to the stable to spend time with Pecos. She didn't think her mood could possible get any worse, but one glance at the rider approaching and she knew she was wrong.

Against the glow of a bright orange sunset and the chilled air of dusk, the horse slowed. Molly knew instantly it was Davis Walker. She stood rooted in place, morbidly curious to see the man who was her birth father.

Dismounting, Davis guided his horse behind him and moved towards her. When they stood a few feet apart, he removed his hat. Blue eyes viewed her from an angular and weathered face, and gray stubble covered his cheeks and chin. Molly wondered if she looked like him.

"Molly, isn't it?" he asked hesitantly.

Nodding, she wasn't certain what to say. She wasn't certain if she even wanted to speak to him at all.

"I've been thinking since Jonathan came to see me a few days back. I've been thinking about when I saw you with Matthew. I was hoping you might be here."

Molly remained unresponsive.

"You know me, don't you?" Davis asked speculatively.

She finally found her voice. "Why do you say that?"

"You're a Hart, aren't you?" Davis' gaze was intent, concerned, almost worried. "You're the middle girl, Molly Hart."

There was no point in denying it, but neither would she confirm it. She watched him, her impassive gaze masking the pain threatening to bubble to the surface.

"Sweet Jesus," Davis muttered to himself. "It is you. I couldn't believe it, but then Jonathan came to see me and started rehashing all that business about the night the Hart ranch was attacked. And then I remembered seeing you with Matthew. There *was* something about you. Now I know why. Where the hell have you been all this time?"

"I don't see how it's any business of yours." Molly's flat voice carefully hid her emotions.

"I'm thinkin' it is my business." His expression seemed crestfallen, almost sad.

But that couldn't be, Molly decided. This man was responsible for the attack on her family. He was a ruthless, mean, and immoral man. But he was also her father. God, she felt ill.

"Your mother was very important in my life, and so were you. It really rattles me you're alive." He almost seemed sincere. "You can't imagine how devastated I was when Rosemary was killed, and then thinking you were also dead. I figured my sins had come back to haunt me, and maybe they still are. But I'm an old man now; maybe it's time for me to repent."

"I've no interest in hearing your confession."

"I think you must." He shifted from foot to foot, moving his hat from hand to hand. He was uneasy. Molly didn't like seeing Davis Walker as a man who could be vulnerable. It made it harder to hate him.

"I loved your mother," he said gruffly. "We went way back, before she ever married Robert Hart. It's a long story." Clearing his throat, he continued, "She broke my heart, a thousand times over, and still I could never hate her. She came to me for a time—I fear it was out of pity—but it made no difference to me."

"You don't have to tell me this." Why on earth was he confiding in her now? Why should he care that she know his side of the story?

"But I have to," he replied. "You're alive — you're here for a reason. There isn't a day goes by I don't think of Rosemary. That I haven't thought of you."

Molly finally understood. Davis knew he was her father.

"What is it exactly you want from me?" She couldn't keep the anger out of her voice any longer. "Do you want me to call you Pa and welcome you with open arms?"

"You know?" he asked, startled.

"Believe me, I wish I didn't."

"Rosemary told you? She vowed you were Robert's daughter, but I knew you weren't. She refused to let me near you."

"Is that why you killed him?" Her fury could no longer be contained. "Is that why you killed Robert Hart and my mama? Do you think you can get away with it, even after all this time?"

Davis stood very still, a stunned expression on his face. "I didn't kill Robert, and I sure as hell didn't kill Rosemary. Is that what you think?" His hands shook. Once again, she wished she hadn't noticed.

"It doesn't matter what I think. All that matters is the truth. You'll be held responsible for all you've done. In the meantime, I don't want to see you, or be around you, or be reminded of what you are to me."

"Molly, I didn't kill your mother, and though I'll agree I had my differences with Robert, I never wanted him dead. Sure, there were times I wished he would go away, but not like that. I haven't always been the man I hoped to be, I know I've hurt others with my actions, but I'm not a murderer."

"If you're looking for forgiveness, you won't get it from me." Molly fought back a threatening tide of tears. "I'm ashamed to have any relation to you!"

"Well," he said more forcefully, "I'm not ashamed. You're a part of Rosemary and me. I'll never believe that was a mistake."

Mounting his horse, he paused to watch her. Then, he turned the animal and rode away into the night. When Molly was quite sure he was gone, she willed her trembling legs to take her to Pecos' stall. It was a long time before she returned to the house.

The next morning Nathan Blackmore arrived and joined Molly and Susanna for breakfast.

"I know Matthew will be sorry he missed you," Susanna said, buttering a piece of toast. "You're welcome to stay until the men return."

Nathan smiled, the scar on his face pinching his cheek. Sitting across from him, Molly thought him a very nice-looking man, despite the now-healed injury. Dark hair, warm brown eyes, a strong bearing. But whether he was nice-looking or not, she'd felt a sharp twinge of disappointment when he'd ridden up to the main house earlier. For a moment, she'd thought he was Matt.

"I'll hang around a few days and see if they turn up," he replied. "Then I should probably be moving on."

"To California?" Susanna asked.

He nodded, drinking the last of his coffee. Frowning, Molly noticed his entire plate—full of food minutes ago—was now completely empty. Men ate so fast in these parts. Using her fork, she moved her eggs from one pile to another.

"My sister had a baby recently. Thought it was time I paid her and her husband a visit."

"My sister Emma lives in San Francisco," Molly commented. "Maybe I should go with you."

Nathan looked surprised by the offer.

"Now Molly," Susanna interjected, "I really think we ought to wait until we hear from your Aunt Catherine before making such a long journey."

"And I doubt Matt would want me ridin' off to California with you," Nathan said.

"Why should he care?" Molly asked, wincing at her sarcastic tone. She really should be more careful when she spoke in front of Matt's mother.

"Yes, why should he indeed?" Susanna murmured.

Standing, Nathan pleaded, "I'd best keep my mouth shut until Matt's here to defend himself. Ladies, if you'll excuse me. I'll see if I can't do some chores around here to lighten your burden."

"That's very kind of you, Nathan, but certainly not necessary," Susanna replied.

"No trouble. It'll keep my hands busy and my mouth shut." He left the room and seconds later the sound of the front door opening and shutting filled the quietness of the dining room.

Susanna sat back in her chair. "Nathan's a good sort. I can see why he and Matthew are friends."

"If you'll excuse me—" Molly started to rise.

"Wait," Susanna put a hand on her arm. "Are you in a hurry to leave here?"

Molly settled back into her seat. "I don't know what I'm in a hurry for."

"Davis was here last night. What did he say?"

She shrugged. "I don't know how to feel about any of this. He knows who I am, he knows he's my father, and he claims he had nothing to do with my folks' deaths."

"I see. Is this why you want to leave Texas?"

"Susanna, where do I belong?" The longing in her voice startled her. "I can't stay here forever, no matter how much your kindness makes that possible."

"Well, of course you can. I can't think of anything I'd like more." Susanna hesitated. "Is it Matthew?"

Unsure how much of her heart to share, Molly conceded only part of it. "He does confuse me."

Susanna laughed. "Oh, dear. I feel in an awkward position here. If it were any other man, I'd ask you to tell me exactly what's happened, offering any advice I could, but because the one in question is my own son I'm afraid it would appear I was meddling. So I'll just offer this bit of advice. Be patient—a man's heart can take time to come around, much more than...other inclinations. But most important, follow your heart, Molly. And if it leads you to California, then we'll support you completely."

"Thank you."

Susanna leaned forward and kissed her on the cheek. "We'd best get out to the stables and help Nathan. It's never good to let a man think he can run from women that easily."

For the first time since Matt left, Molly laughed.

* * *

Later that night a storm blew in, the rumbling sounds waking Molly where she slept on the floor. Unable to go back to sleep, she listened to the forces of nature outside, worried that Matt was out there, somewhere. All of the ranch hands were out there, she reminded herself, but Matt occupied her thoughts, always.

The flashes of light and claps of thunder put her in mind of the first night she and Matt had been together, at the abandoned remains of her family home, a place she had lived in for only a few years. But, for whatever reason, it was the home of her heart, the one she remembered. The one she judged all others by.

Pushing the covers back, she rose from her bed on the floor and walked to the window. Shivering from the cool night air, she wished for the longer gown Susanna had given her. For the past several nights she'd gone back to wearing one of Matt's borrowed shirts, her reasons rooted entirely in comfort. It certainly had nothing to do with the man whose broad shoulders had once filled it.

She heard a tapping sound. Thinking it was nothing, she folded her arms tightly in front of her.

There it was again.

Looking back to the door, she frowned. It sounded like a knock. Thinking it must be Susanna, Molly moved across the room and opened the door.

Her breath caught at the sight of a man, dripping wet and looming over her.

Matt.

Her heart leapt into her throat. Dazed, Molly didn't know what to do. The urge to throw herself into his arms warred with simply asking him why was here.

"I heard about Davis," he said. "I was worried about you. I came as soon as I could."

Unable to speak, Molly stared. They were alone in the middle of the night at the threshold of her bedroom. Surely, she wasn't misreading his signals.

"I can't stay away anymore," he said, his voice low, resolute, single-minded. "I don't want to."

She could hardly believe he was here; she'd missed him so much in the last few days.

"Then stop trying." In the intimate darkness, relief poured through her. Latching a hand onto his belt buckle, she pulled him into the room and shut the door.

Chapter Twenty-Three

Matt brought Molly's barely clad body against his and kissed her with all the pent-up passion and frustration he'd been fighting these past weeks. He wanted her, he needed her, and he could no longer deny it.

She met him just as forcefully. Knowing how inexperienced she was, he was both humbled and excited at her response. Ruthlessly discarding every reason why he shouldn't do this, he wondered how he'd had the willpower to stay away from her for so long. His body was close to the breaking point already, and he'd hardly touched her at all.

He would have her tonight, completely, without any barriers. The thought of that completion made him shudder, but he willed himself to slow down.

Holding her face in his hands, he whispered against her mouth, "Please tell me you want this."

"Yes." No hesitation, no fear in her voice. Her openness and trust amazed him.

"We have all night. There's no hurry." But he didn't know if he was trying to convince her or himself.

"It's taken me ten years to find you," she said, insistent. "I don't want to wait any longer."

Her mouth came to his and he consumed her, tasted her, memorizing the feel of her lips, the softness of her face, and the graceful curve of her neck. She was a dream to him, beautiful and perfect.

Her fingers worked at the buttons of his shirt. He stripped it off then ran his hands under the hem of her garment, cupping her buttocks. He tugged the bloomers down her legs, then slid his palms to her breasts, smiling at her sharp intake of breath. In one fluid movement he removed the last of her clothing, leaving her bared to him.

A flash of lightning illuminated her glistening skin and high round breasts responded to his touch. Kneeling, he kissed just below one, grasping her hips, then moved his mouth across her ribcage and to the enticing curve of her abdomen. Resting his forehead against her, he drank in the sight of the dark cleft of hair between her legs.

"You're beautiful," he whispered.

Taking a steadying breath, he stood and crushed her mouth to his. Her breasts grazed his chest and he knew he wouldn't last much longer with her completely unadorned like this. Putting his hands under her arms, he lifted her to the edge of the bed, entranced by the intense need written on her face. She wasn't afraid of him and for that he was mighty grateful.

He removed each boot, careful not to strain his almost-healed foot, then unbuckled his gun belt and shed his pants. Facing Molly once again, he waited to see if she was concerned by his nakedness, but she merely twined a hand into the mat of hair on his chest while tentatively running the other along his left thigh. He didn't need more of an enticement than that. Kissing her, he swept his tongue deep into her mouth, his hand grasping the back of her head. Nudging her legs apart, he stepped between them.

Hard and ready, he fought for one last shred of patience, laying her back onto the bed, her legs still hooked over the edge. Bracing himself with one hand on the soft mattress, he used a finger to penetrate her, her eyes widening in shock as her hips rose. Slick and wet, she was more than ready for him. He entered her with two fingers.

"I want to make sure I don't hurt you," he said, straining.

Withdrawing his fingers, he knew he couldn't wait any longer. With one thrust he pushed completely into her and a gasp caught in her throat. Pulling her hips to the edge of the bed, he used the angle to press as deep into her as he could get. Hardly moving, he leaned over and kissed her neck and collarbone. Her hands clasped his back as her body trembled beneath him.

He kissed her deeply, their tongues mating and mingling, and still he didn't move. The pleasure was excruciating and a part of him didn't want it to end, but Molly quickly lost patience with his slowness.

"Matt," she breathed, "please."

He reached down and brought her legs around him, then slid his hands to cup her backside. Only then did he move, driving into her. Within seconds his climax came, intense, consuming, obliterating his sense of time and place. Obliterating his sense of self.

As he poured the last of himself into her, he felt the convulsions deep within her own body, her own completion as she clung to him. Encircling his arms more fully around her, he held her tightly, holding her close as she lost herself in a passion uniquely theirs. Slowly, he came back to the present.

"Damn," he murmured against her neck. "I'm never gonna be able to stay away from you now."

"I don't think I have the energy to move," she whispered.

"Just give me five minutes, then we can go again."

"Really?" she asked breathlessly.

He laughed softly. "Actually, I think I'm ready now." He tested that statement with a short in-and-out movement. Yep, he was ready. Pushing onto his forearms, he gazed down at her. "There're other ways we can do this. If you're sore, that is."

"You have the advantage, since I have no idea what you're talking about."

He was about to tell her she had the advantage, and always had he suspected, but being here with her, like this, literally took words and breath from his mouth. Leaning down, he nibbled at her lips. "We'll take it slow." And that was the last coherent thought he had that night.

* * *

Just before dawn Molly awoke, lying on her stomach as Matt's fingertips ran lightly down her back. His lips soon followed, and he didn't stop until he ran the length of her legs. Need stirred deep within her again, shocking her with its intensity. She hadn't expected that she would enjoy making love so much, that she would give herself so freely in this way. Matt made her feel she was the most adored woman he had ever been with. Later, she would worry whether that was true or not.

With a happy groan she rolled onto her back, and Matt's mouth quickly set to work exploring the front of her body. She had no idea her breasts were so sensitive, no idea that his touch between her legs could pull from her a desire so fierce she would tremble and claw at him to satisfy it.

But come together they did, as profoundly as the first time they had just hours ago, leaving them sweating and heaving from their exertions.

Matt lay between her legs, his cheek itching against the skin just above her left breast. Molly ignored it, running her fingers through his hair.

"It's almost dawn," he said into the silence of the room, his breath warming her bare skin. The storm had finally stopped. "I need to leave."

She knew that was true, but a part of her didn't want the night to end.

"Why did you come back?" she asked, running a hand along the well-defined muscles of his shoulder. Looking down at their bodies, she liked the differences between his hard planes and her flowing curves. She had never thought of her body in such a way. It left her feeling feminine, almost delicate. The revelation was so new it was as if seeing herself for the first time.

"I heard Davis had been here. I didn't want you to be alone, dealing with whatever happened." Turning his head, he kissed the nipple just below his cheek.

"He knows everything," she said, "but he denied planning the attack."

"You don't have to face him alone. I'll be right there beside you, if that's what you want."

"What I want," she breathed, "is for this night not to end."

He lightly nipped at her breast. "I think I've made pretty good use of our time." He climbed the length of her until their faces met. "There was also another reason I came back. I heard Nathan had returned, and I was jealous."

"You were?" she asked, surprised. "He's very nice, in a rugged sort of way, but I've never had any interest in him, or anyone else for that matter. After last night, you can't doubt that."

"After last night, everything has changed."

Molly knew he was right and felt a little sad at the idea. Once Matt left this room, she feared they might never have the closeness of this time again.

"I have to go." He kissed her, but it quickly went beyond sweet and tender. Before it got out of hand, Matt pulled away. "I never thought leaving you would be this hard." He moved to the side of the bed and searched for his clothing.

When he had trousers on and a shirt hanging open across his torso, he leaned over her and dropped a quick kiss between her breasts. "Meet me downstairs later for breakfast."

"If I can walk," she teased, touching his face one last time.

Grinning, he quietly left her, limping only slightly as he carried his boots in one hand.

* * *

As Matt left Molly's room, light from the approaching sunrise began to creep through the lace-covered window at the top of the stairs. A door opened in the next room and Nathan appeared, dressed and ready for the day. He laughed when he saw Matt.

"Nathan." Matt shook his hand. "It's good to see you." He knew his brief pang of jealousy concerning Nathan and Molly was misguided, but it had been there nonetheless.

When his ma had sent word to his pa about Davis' visit and Nathan's sudden reappearance, Matt's overwhelming desire to get to Molly finally broke his resolve. Even an endless ride in the rain wasn't going to keep him from her.

"You've always had great timing," Matt said.

"You've never complained about my timing before." Nathan casually leaned one shoulder on the doorframe, folding his arms across his chest. "I doubt your sudden return during the night had much to do with me anyhow."

Matt glanced back at Molly's closed door. "Don't say anything yet," he said quietly. "I've got some things to work out first."

"I'll be damned," Nathan murmured, "you're gonna make it legal."

"Don't look so surprised." But Matt was astonished. Last night had blown him away, and while he had come to Molly fully intending to do the right thing, being without her simply wasn't an option anymore. "A man's gotta settle down sometime, even you."

Grinning, Nathan shook his head. "Haven't met a woman to tempt me yet. Does Molly have a sister?"

Matt ignored the question and started walking toward the stairs. "I need to get changed. See you at breakfast."

"If you don't fall asleep first."

Chapter Twenty-Four

Molly entered the dining room and froze when Matt and Nathan abruptly stopped their conversation and stared at her.

"Mornin'," Matt said, smiling. She thought it wasn't fair he should look so alert after the very sleepless night they'd had. And, of course, he also appeared devastatingly handsome. She tried to remain unresponsive, which proved impossibly difficult. Already her heartbeat had quickened to the pace of a stampede.

Taking a seat at the end of the table, she said a bit self-consciously, "Good morning. Where's Susanna?"

"She takes it upon herself to run the ranch when the old man's not around," Matt replied. "So she's been here and gone already."

"Oh." Molly rested her hands in her lap. Her gaze drifted from the tablecloth to the ceiling. When she chanced a look at Nathan and he winked at her, she realized she'd had enough. "Well, I'll just go to the kitchen and fetch something to eat. I hate to be a bother to Rosita." In a rush, she left the room.

She nearly pushed the old Mexican woman to the floor in her hurry to get breakfast. "Oh, Rosita! I'm so sorry." She helped to steady the woman.

"Why you in such a hurry?" Rosita asked, catching her breath.

"I was just coming to get something to eat."

The Mexican woman held out the plate of food. "Well, here you go. I was just bringing it to you."

Taking the plate, Molly paused. "Thank you." Thinking hard, she glanced at the long wooden table that frequently fed the ranch hands. "Maybe I'll just eat in here." Sitting down, she started to spoon the scrambled eggs into her mouth.

"I get you some coffee." Rosita returned to the table and poured the hot liquid into a ceramic cup decorated with flowers and swirly things. Molly stared at the design for a time.

"Why you in here?" the older woman asked finally.

"I've always enjoyed your company, Rosita."

She waved that off, smiling. "You lie so bad."

"I'm not lying," Molly replied, a little indignant.

"*Señor* Matt return last night." Rosita watched her, then nodded. "That's it. *Sí*, that's it."

"That's what?"

"He say his foot bother him, but he come back to see *you*."

Molly stuffed a biscuit into her mouth. "Possibly," she mumbled around the food.

Rosita laughed, returning to the dishes she had been washing. "I like you." She waved a soapy finger at her. "You are good for him."

Sighing, Molly gave up on her breakfast. She'd had her fill anyway. Did everyone in this house know about her and Matt? That Susanna might be aware left her feeling acutely embarrassed. Good Lord, the things Matt had done to her. Her face warmed and her body hummed with the inevitable reaction. She wondered if she would ever be able to occupy the same room as him again without imagining every naked inch of his trim and muscular frame. She doubted that was what Susanna had meant when she had told Molly to follow her heart.

"We have company," Susanna's voice beckoned from the front entryway.

Rosita peeked down the hallway before moving out of sight. "It is *Señora* McAllister," she uttered under her breath. "She got a pretty young woman with her." Then, more urgently, she added, "You better get out there and hook your claws into *Señor* Matt before that woman push her way where she no belong."

Molly's heart sank. The day was fast losing its luster, she thought dourly. With longing she looked at the back door, an image of Pecos and the vast prairies beckoning her. But then, that would leave Matt with the pretty young woman, undoubtedly Mrs. McAllister's daughter. The very woman handpicked to be Matt's wife.

With very little enthusiasm, Molly walked to the parlor. Matt and Nathan stood to her left, casually leaning a hand on a chair or a hip on the edge of a table. They didn't appear inclined to linger around for much conversation, giving Molly a tiny sliver of hope that this visit wouldn't last long.

Mrs. McAllister sat on the couch with her daughter, a lovely young woman with blonde hair pinned in ringlets atop her head. She wore what looked to be an expensive satin gown in a dark green shade. Susanna sat across from them, her back to Matt and Nathan.

"Molly," Susanna held a hand out to her, "please come and join us."

Molly sat in a chair next to Matt's mother.

"Why, Molly Hart," Mrs. McAllister commented, "I had no idea you were still here." Her tone bordered on snide.

Molly decided then and there she disliked the woman immensely.

"Let me introduce my daughter, Lizzie."

Molly nodded, forcing a half-smile on her lips.

"I'm pleased to meet you," Lizzie replied, her smooth skin free of freckles. She sat very rigid, her back so straight Molly thought a slight nudge would surely tip her over. She was certainly very pretty, but appeared misplaced in this land of dust, rain and desolation.

Unbidden, an image of Lizzie living with the Comanche flashed through Molly's mind, making her smile. The smell alone would have killed her.

"You've been away for a while, Lizzie," Susanna said. "It must be hard to readjust to life here. I would imagine things are much slower here than in Richmond."

"Yes, it has been an adjustment. Mama just couldn't wait to bring me here for a visit, however, so I hope you don't mind us stopping in."

"Not at all," Susanna replied warmly.

"I'm glad to see your foot is healing, Matthew," Mrs. McAllister commented.

"Almost good as new," Matt said.

"And Mr. Blackmore," Mrs. McAllister continued, "are you a Ranger as well?"

"Yes, ma'am. Although I'm takin' a leave at the moment to visit my sister in California."

"My, that's a long way from here. Where does your family hail from?"

"Missouri."

"How nice."

"If you'll excuse us, ladies," Matt said, "we really ought to see to some chores."

"Of course," Mrs. McAllister replied.

Out of the corner of her eye, Molly watched Matt and Nathan depart. She had to restrain herself from following, so strong was the desire to accompany them.

"Well, Molly, we've heard talk about you," Mrs. McAllister said, lifting her cup off the saucer to sip her coffee. "How dreadful what happened to your family all those years ago."

"Thank you," Molly said reflexively, wondering who had been talking about her.

"You're lucky to be alive. How long do you plan to stay here with the Ryans?"

"Molly is like family to us," Susanna interjected. "We've contacted her sisters and are awaiting a reply. Then she'll decide what to do."

"Yes, it's important to be with one's family, isn't it?" Mrs. McAllister said. "I'm so happy to have Lizzie back with me." She smiled at her daughter. "Perhaps you'd like to see the men working, dear. It will remind you of what it's like to live on a ranch."

"Some fresh air certainly would be nice," Susanna said. "Elizabeth, why don't you and I have coffee on the porch? I'm sure Molly won't mind taking Lizzie around."

"Splendid," the older woman replied.

Molly's spirit sagged. Her day had just been plucked clean by a swarm of vultures. She could only hope she wouldn't be stuck with Lizzie McAllister for long.

* * *

"It's so quiet out here," Lizzie commented, opening a parasol that matched her gown as they walked to the stables.

Molly looked to the sky. No rain in sight, but apparently Lizzie thought otherwise. Molly bundled her dark hair at the base of her neck and tied it with a rawhide cord, then pushed a hat on her head. "Do you ride?" she asked.

"Of course," Lizzie replied. "Although it's been a while since I've ridden the wild, mangy horses back here. In the east, women ride side-saddle."

"Hmm." Molly couldn't envision any practical reason for that. "Would you like to ride one of the Ryans' wild, mangy horses?"

"Maybe later." She wrinkled her nose as she stepped around a pile of horse droppings. "I suppose it was obvious but my mama has this crazy notion to marry me off to Matthew Ryan, so I suppose I ought to seek him out and tempt him with my womanly attributes. You understand, don't you?"

Not one bit, Molly fumed.

Lizzie put an arm out to stop their progress. "Tell me. My mama says you've known the Ryan family a long time. What's Matthew like? What kind of man is he?"

Molly stared at this gussied-up society lady and had no idea what to say. She could lie and say Matt was a lazy, immoral, two-timing scoundrel, but he didn't deserve such blemishes on his character, no matter what her motive. On the other hand, if she told the truth, that he was tender and caring, responsible, just and hard-working, and made love with a focus that stole her breath, then Lizzie would probably fall in love with him right then and there.

The same way Molly had.

She loved him.

Well, of course she did. After last night, how could she not?

"He's a good man," she finally said. "A finer man you'll never meet."

"Well, that's a relief," Lizzie said, a giddy laugh escaping her. "And what about Logan?"

"What about him?" Molly asked, confused.

"What's he like?"

"The same. Are you planning to pursue them both?"

"One or the other, my mama doesn't care."

"Well, don't *you* care?"

"Of course I do," Lizzie replied. "But I'll never survive out here on my own. Mama can't run our ranch much longer, and I honestly have no idea what to do. The sooner I marry, the better."

The sooner, the better. Would Matt really marry a woman like this? Or even Logan?

Matt had come to her last night and loved her relentlessly till the first light of day, but Molly had no idea what to think about it. She certainly didn't want to *hook her claws* into him, obligating him to be with her. If that were the case, then she was no better than Miss McAllister.

The two of them walked around the stables to a holding pen. Matt sat on the fence while Nathan worked with a beautiful snowy white mare, leading her around with a rope.

Distracted by the sight of the horse, Molly stepped onto the bottom rung of the fence to bring her closer to Matt's level. "She's magnificent," she said, mesmerized by the animal.

Matt grinned down at her, nodding also to Lizzie. "She's Nathan's. A mate for Black, if she ever shows any interest."

"He's put them together?"

"Yeah." Matt pushed his hat back, balancing easily where he sat. "But so far she's playin' hard to get. So now Nate's trying to saddle break her."

"What's her name?"

"Winter."

"Has anyone ridden her yet?" Molly asked.

Matt shook his head, then he glared at her. "Please don't tell me you've a mind to."

"Well, I handled some ornery horses during my time with—." She suddenly remembered Lizzie. "During the last few years," she finished.

Matt watched her closely, his eyes glittering with intensity and she knew exactly what he was thinking.

Smiling back, certain she blushed, she wished they could be alone.

Knowing he and Nathan could easily spend all day with the horse, Molly reluctantly hopped down. "Let me know if he needs some help." Hands on hips, she asked Lizzie, "You want a tour of the barn or something?"

"No, thank you. I believe I'll just stay here and watch Mr. Blackmore for a while."

Molly tried not to roll her eyes. Lizzie clearly had no desire to stand in the hot sun and watch the taming of a feisty animal, but she obviously felt she should spend time with Matt.

"Watch out for barn snakes," Matt yelled. Her eyes met his as she walked away and smirked.

"Snakes?" Lizzie asked.

Matt's laughter faded away as Molly went to the stables to fetch Pecos.

She had just finished brushing her horse's brown hide when she heard Matt shouting. "Get out of the way, she's gonna jump the fence!"

Quickly opening Pecos' stall, Molly hopped onto her, bareback, and rode out of the stable just as Matt and Nathan were running for their horses.

"What the hell are you doing?" Matt demanded when he saw her.

"I can get her." Kicking Pecos into a dead run, she was gone before Matt could finish his colorful response.

* * *

Cursing loudly, Matt saddled his horse while Nathan did the same. Molly had too much of a head start.

Lizzie came running after them. "Can I help? What can I do?"

Matt hardly glanced at her as he swung onto his mount.

"Thanks, Miss McAllister," Nathan offered, looking down at her. "We'll be fine. I'm sure we'll be back before supper."

Not if Molly breaks her neck, we won't, Matt thought angrily. He and Nathan set a fast pace, following the still-lingering trail of dust left in Pecos' wake. But, after several minutes of quickly covering a flat expanse of prairie land, they reined in at the edge of a short bluff leading down to a weather-worn arroyo.

Matt scanned the area, wondering where the hell one woman and two horses could disappear to, when Nathan pointed to the southeast. "There."

Pecos was traversing an incline sideways while Molly leaned back, attempting to balance them down the hill. Nathan's white mare continued to run farther ahead, the leather reins dangling to the ground as the animal moved with amazing speed through the bottom of the ravine. Stout junipers and jagged-looking mesquite didn't slow her much, if at all.

Matt turned his horse and urged it toward the edge Molly had just occupied, all the while keeping his eyes on her. As she reached the bottom of the valley, he watched in disbelief as she unhooked her skirt and pulled it over her head, tossing it to the ground. Next came her blouse. She now wore nothing but the long, thin chemise, bunched up at the waist and revealing slender legs barely covered by knickers.

That alone would have pissed him off, but it was what he suspected she planned to do that sparked his anger into a rage.

The damn woman.

Ducking branches, Molly quickly overtook the mare.

Thinking quickly, Matt stopped short of following her trail down the hill, instead moving east in an effort to cut them off. Nathan was right behind him.

After a quarter-mile, they stopped to determine the best angle to approach the group. Matt watched as Molly pushed Pecos into a stride to match the other horse, the animals running side by side. Then, his heart stopped and he forgot to breathe as Molly jumped from one to the other.

"Sonofabitch," Nathan muttered. "She's got more balls than both of us."

"Let's cut her off," Matt said through clenched teeth. "Who knows how long that mare will hold her."

Riding parallel to Molly's path, they rode hard, skirting obstacles and jumping uneven terrain. The sun shone from the west, thankfully at their backs, casting a golden glow on the land. Jackrabbits scattered before them and the distant flight of a pair of hawks caught Matt's eye.

As the bluff leveled out and their path met with Molly's, Matt had a better view of her. The flimsy chemise she wore blended with the mare's coloring, making it impossible to tell where one ended and the other began. Or perhaps it was simply her skill with the animal. She rode the horse with nothing to aid her, not even a bridle. Leaning low, she grasped the mane for balance, but exhibited a natural ease as she shifted constantly with the sporadic moves of the horse.

Woman and horse became one.

She spied him and waved, her dark hair swirling in the wind.

"Don't let go!" he yelled.

Nathan's horse moved forward on one side while Matt flanked Molly and the white mare on the left. He pushed ahead, trying to slow Winter. He noticed Molly pulling back on the horse's head, slowing her considerably. As they came to a gallop, Winter began resisting the pressure, shaking her head back and forth. Just as the animal began to buck, Matt moved his horse to the rear and grabbed Molly before she hit the ground.

Guiding his mount a short distance away, Molly shifted immediately so she could view the snorting female over his shoulder. Her face lit with the biggest grin he'd ever seen on her.

"What the hell were you thinking?" he demanded.

She laughed. "That was one hell of a ride."

"You could've been killed."

Molly looked at him, the smile faltering. "Are you angry that I tried to catch her? She was getting away. Every second counted."

Glancing down, he viewed the dark outline of a breast under her sleeveless top. Jesus, he hadn't realized how naked she was.

"We would've caught her eventually," he said sternly, unbuttoning his shirt.

As he pulled it off, she stared at his bare chest with concern.

"Matt, we can't...well, you know." Deliberately, she moved her eyes over his shoulder then back to him. "Nathan is here," she whispered.

Yanking his shirt around her, he covered as much of her as he could. Nathan had already seen too damn much. "I don't plan on making love to you. What you need is a swift kick in the butt."

"Well, you're welcome," she said sarcastically. "And just so you know, I've done that before, or else I wouldn't have attempted it now."

"Why doesn't that make me feel any better?" he said, more harshly than intended.

Nathan approached, leading the mare with a rope behind him. "Are you both done arguing?"

"We're not arguing," Matt replied.

"Of course not. Molly, thanks for the help. I appreciate it. You ride like you were born to it. The Kwahadi must have prized your horse skills."

"I was only average among the best of them. The women didn't ride as much as the men."

"You want her to ride with me, Ryan?"

"Like hell," Matt muttered under his breath.

"That's what I thought," Nathan said, laughing. "Let's go." He took off at a good clip.

Molly stuck her arms through the shirtsleeves draped around her, then with some effort climbed over his shoulders to sit behind him. He set a steady pace for their return, Pecos trailing them at a distance.

When Molly wouldn't hang onto him, he finally pulled her arms around his middle. "Hold tight."

He didn't like the feeling that she might not need him as much as he needed her.

Chapter Twenty-Five

Matt dropped her at the back of the house without a word. Molly entered the kitchen and Rosita glanced up with a start. The woman did a quick scan of her from head to toe, but Molly was simply too tired to explain any of it. With the sound of her boots filling the silence, she went to her bedroom without crossing paths with anyone else.

She unbuttoned Matt's shirt and removed it, but didn't set it down. Instead, she held it close to her face and inhaled the scent of him as she moved to look out the window, the last light of the day illuminating the stables. She saw Matt walking his horse and Pecos down below. Stripped to the waist, he looked tall, rugged, and utterly compelling. Lizzie darted from nowhere to join him, and Molly couldn't bear to watch as the woman flirted with the man she loved.

Crawling into the large bed, she smelled the still lingering scent of her and Matt from the previous night. Had it only been last night? It was fast becoming a distant memory, just what she feared would happen.

Maybe she had been wrong to go after the horse. Lizzie never would have done such a thing. Ladies didn't behave that way. Was that why Matt was so angry with her?

Molly's eyes drifted shut as she worried that she might not be the kind of woman Matt wanted.

* * *

When Molly didn't come down for dinner, Matt offered to check on her. When his soft knocks on her bedroom door went unanswered, he quietly opened it.

Molly was sound asleep in the center of her bed. For a moment he watched her, wishing he could lie down beside her and rest, only to awaken to her sleepy, seductive voice and enticing body. His anger with her had waned, and now all he wanted to do was be with her. But she was clearly exhausted, and his mother and their guests waited for him downstairs. Maybe later he could sneak back, but that was easier said than done—he and Nathan had been relegated to the bunkhouse to make room for Mrs. McAllister and Lizzie tonight.

Regretfully, he closed her door and returned downstairs.

* * *

Much later, Matt and Nathan crashed in the bunkhouse. He was dead tired, having had little sleep the night before. On the heels of that thought came a strong desire to go straightaway to Molly's room. Deciding he would doze for a short while then go to her, he lay down.

The evening had been fairly dull as he'd tried to shake Lizzie's company for most of it. The girl was trying her damnedest to catch his eye. He really ought to set her straight and save her the effort.

Removing his boots, he vowed he would talk to his pa as soon as possible. When he worked out the details of making Molly his wife, then it would be obvious to one and all where his intentions and his heart lay.

* * *

Molly rolled over in bed, wondering what all the ruckus was about. It was still dark outside, but she definitely could hear men shouting. A fleeting memory of the night her family's ranch was attacked came to her. Jumping from the bed, she grabbed a bathrobe and ran from her room.

Coming onto the front porch, she ran right into Logan. "Molly, pardon me."

"What're you doing here?" she asked in a hurry. "What's happened?"

Moving aside, she saw Matt materialize from the darkness, fully dressed and wearing his gun holster. The whinny of horses sounded from behind him.

"Where are you going?" she asked.

Men from the ranch moved past her.

Ushering her off to the side, he grasped her shoulders. "We've gotten word Davis Walker's been shot."

"What?" Shocked, she stared at him.

"No one's exactly sure what happened, but Logan rode in an hour ago with the news. We're gonna ride over to the Walker ranch and see what's goin' on. I want you to stay here, do you understand?"

"You think this has something to do with me?"

"I don't know. But I'm not taking any chances. Nathan's gonna stay here. Do what he says." He gazed at her intently. "Promise me."

She nodded numbly, reeling from the sudden turn of events. What if Davis died? What if *her father* died?

Matt moved away to talk to Nathan. Mrs. McAllister and Lizzie appeared in the front entryway, wrapped in robes, and began chattering nervously with Susanna.

"I'll send word as soon as we know something," Matt said to his mother, interrupting them.

"Be careful," she replied. "And for God's sake, tell your father to be careful."

"Where is Jonathan?" Molly asked, glancing around.

"He's gone ahead of us," Matt replied.

Logan moved past Molly. "C'mon, let's go."

Matt's eyes met Molly's and she saw an odd determination in them. He walked to her, took her face in his hands and kissed her, firmly, completely and with no doubt as to his intentions toward her.

"I'll be back as soon as I can," he said against her lips. "Wait for me." Then he, Logan and the rest of the men were gone.

Molly stared into the darkness, the pounding of the horses' hooves fading quickly with each passing moment. She could still feel the lingering effects of Matt's lips on her as her fingers brushed across her mouth. Memories of the past inundated her, shifting her focus. There had been much love in her childhood, but also tremendous loss. And so many lies hiding within the cracks of truth. And now, what of the future? What of *her* future?

Lizzie moved beside her. "You might have told me."

"Pardon?"

"That you and Matt were together. My mama will hate it, of course, but there's always Logan."

Molly wasn't in the mood for Lizzie's frivolousness regarding the man she planned to spend the rest of her life with.

Mrs. McAllister joined them. "Lizzie dear, please go inside. I'd like to speak with Molly alone."

"Yes, Mama." She left them.

Now, only Molly and Mrs. McAllister remained on the porch.

The stooped, gaunt woman faced Molly. "Shame on you."

"I beg your pardon?"

"Carrying on with Matthew like that, and under his family's roof, no less." Any semblance of friendliness had disappeared, making Molly realize how hard the woman must have worked to keep it up in the first place. "I've heard about you. I said as much earlier."

"I don't think this is any of your business," Molly shot back.

"Oh, it definitely is my business, especially if you plan to ruin Jonathan and Susanna's eldest son, seducing him with your body only to contaminate their blood with that of a woman raised with Indians."

Molly was speechless. Matt had warned her such people existed, people who hated and despised the Indians they worked so hard to displace, but she had never imagined such venom would be directed at her in such a vengeful way. She'd handled rattlesnakes with better dispositions than Elizabeth McAllister.

"You lived with the Comanche," the woman continued, her wrinkled face contorting itself like a wicked spirit from the deepest reaches of the night. "Do you deny this?"

Molly remained silent, gazing into the darkness that had just swallowed Matt and Logan.

"You slept with them, you ate their food, you behaved like them. And surely you opened your legs to the men. You're disgusting, coming back here, trying to live like a white woman again. You can't possibly believe Matthew would *marry* you. Your presence will ruin his family. Perhaps the Ryans have been too kind to tell you the truth, but I'm not. It's for the best you know your place, Molly Hart."

Mrs. McAllister clenched her bony hands into the velvet yellow robe she wore, then returned to the house. When Molly was certain she was good and gone, only then did she allow the tears she'd been holding back to roll down her cheeks.

* * *

Molly spent the remainder of the night in her room, awake, staring out the window as she thought of the path of her life. Knowing Mrs. McAllister was a bitter old woman still didn't take the sting from her words, because buried somewhere among them was a shred of truth.

She could never be what Matt deserved, a wife with an unblemished past, a wife who knew how to be a woman, how to behave like a woman. Despite his desire for her, even he was frustrated by her actions with the horse earlier. Whatever lay between them was destined to end. Perhaps it was better to curtail it now, rather than later, when leaving him would only be that much harder.

Maybe a life with Lizzie McAllister was best for him. Together they would have land, wealth, and social standing. They would offer their children only the finest in all things.

The thought saddened her. In her heart, Molly had hoped she and Matt might one day have a child. God help her, what if she was with child already? It was possible, she knew. They had done nothing to prevent it, despite Claire's warnings and memories of the Kwahadi women speaking of such things.

If she were pregnant, then she definitely couldn't stay here. She could never shame Jonathan and Susanna in such a way. And what would Matt do? Would he cast her aside? Would he marry her out of pity?

She didn't know what to think anymore, except that she suspected she had overstayed her welcome. Mrs. McAllister hadn't even mentioned that Davis Walker was, in fact, her father. She must not have known, but surely would in time. Such gossip would only hurt the Ryan family further.

Hastily, Molly packed a few things, changed into a pair of trousers and an oversized shirt, and stuffed her hair into a hat. As the first rays of light broke across the land, Molly put the SR, and Matt, behind her.

Chapter Twenty-Six

Molly rode Pecos to the northwest, across flat prairies and small ravines, the landscape familiar but hardly soothing. Too many memories existed for her in this place, both in the past and the present. By sundown her destination became clear — what was left of the Hart ranch.

Darkness descended as Pecos trotted into the protected valley where the long-empty ranch house stood. The structure was still as it had been several weeks ago, when she had spent a rainy night inside with Matt. It all seemed a lifetime ago. So much had changed in such a short time.

A wave of grief hit her. She missed her mama profoundly, with a sharp and twisting pain. So many questions unanswered, and a future now uncertain again. If she could see her mama once more, what would she say about Davis Walker? Did Walker even live at this moment? Molly would probably never know. Perhaps it would be best to leave Texas altogether, leave the past behind once and for all, and never look back.

She glanced at the tombstones on the hill, the final resting place for her mama, Robert Hart and a little girl named Adelaide. The wind blew hard, whistling around Molly's ears. The spirits were restless tonight. With a shiver, she wondered if her mama was among them.

As darkness descended, the decision to ride farther was made for her. She would spend the night here, then move on in the morning.

Taking Pecos to the dilapidated barn, she attempted to get her settled from the piercing tempest outside. As soon as she latched the stall, the sound of another horse startled her so much she jumped.

Molly couldn't understand where the other animal had come from, but she noticed tack resting nearby.

Someone else is here.

Instinctively, she started saddling Pecos again, but a man's voice stopped her cold.

"It's the snake lady," he said from behind her.

Stunned, Molly recognized the voice. It was the man with Walker that night by the creek. What was his name? Sawyer? As she glanced over her shoulder, the rifle he pointed left no doubt in Molly's mind the man was dangerous.

"But you're not just a snake lady, are you?" He smelled of heavy liquor. "You're a Hart. Come home to visit, did you?"

Releasing the saddle, she turned toward him. "What are you doing here?"

"Came back for old time's sake." Sawyer shrugged. "You don't remember me, do you?"

Staring at him, a flicker of something swirled in her head, but it wouldn't stick.

"Well, *I* remember *you*," he continued. "You're Molly, the middle girl. What a load of trouble you were back then. Who would've thought you'd rise from the dead? I really thought Davis was full of shit when he told me, but I guess you showing up here just proves it."

In a rush, it all came back. George Sawyer had worked for her family, here at the ranch, ten years ago.

It was midday and all the men were out working, doing whatever they did around the ranch. Molly was never quite sure, was never really that interested anyhow. But today, Matt, Cale and Logan were repairing a portion of the corral, so it was the perfect opportunity to pester them. Usually, they didn't hang about so close to the house during daylight hours.

Molly was using the Wren to practice her aim by shooting rocks off the far side of the enclosure, small splinters of wood flying in all directions each time she hit her target. The three young men were swearing at her, threatening her with a dunking in the horse trough if she didn't stop.

Molly just laughed, and threatened to tell her mama and papa about their coarse language. Then, the sound of fabric tearing could be heard as Cale dropped one of the horizontal posts and it caught on Matt's shirt.

"That's just great," Matt said, shaking his head.

Cale laughed.

Molly saw her opportunity. "I'll go to the bunkhouse and get you another one, Matt." She smiled sweetly as she trotted off to the building a few hundred yards away. Cale's voice trailed behind her.

"What do you want to bet she hides some sort of rodent in it?"

She smiled again over her shoulder, causing Logan to laugh and Matt to look worried. She'd show them. She just needed to figure out where to hide her pet. It was a harmless brown snake, but she was certain it would still give one of them a good scare. Under Cale's pillow seemed the most appealing spot, but the reptile probably wouldn't stay put.

Pushing open the door to the bunkhouse, she started reconsidering her plan since Cale would probably shoot the darn thing.

It took a moment for Molly's eyes to adjust to the darkness of the large, empty room, bunks lined along the far wall. She stopped short; she wasn't alone.

George, a young, wiry ranch hand held her younger sister Emma at the far end of the room. At first, Molly didn't understand what she witnessed as the youth handled her little sister so roughly the girl was crying. But then comprehension hit her, along with a wave of fear and nausea. Without thinking, she reached into the pocket of her dress and grasped one of the larger rocks she had collected earlier in the day. Using her slingshot, she shot George Sawyer in the back of the head.

Using words she'd picked up from Matt and Cale, she yelled, "You son-of-a-bitch! You let her go!"

Rubbing the back of his head, George spun around. "What the hell?" His pants hung open from his hips.

Molly couldn't believe what this sickening man was trying to do to her eight-year-old little sister. She loaded another rock and shot it into his face.

"You little piece of shit," he cried, covering his face with his right hand while trying to pull his pants up with his left. Blood oozed between his fingers.

"Emma," Molly said urgently. "Come here, quickly."

Her little sister ran to her side.

"You'll be sorry about this mister," Molly said, her voice shaking. She put an arm around Emma and held her close.

"I'll be sorry?" George cackled. "You little witch! You'll regret this."

"No," Molly said calmly. "You'll regret this. I'll make sure of it."

George made a move to lunge for her but stopped when Matt's voice could be heard outside.

"Molly? You better be behaving yourself in there."

George hesitated, then turned and went out the door at the back of the building.

When Matt entered, Molly still rigidly held Emma to her side.

"What's wrong?" he asked immediately.

She almost told him, but a sob from Emma stopped her. Although unsure as to exactly what had happened, she did know it was bad. She also knew she would do anything to protect her sister.

"Nothing's wrong. But I need to see my papa immediately."

Matt seemed ready to argue, but she quickly moved past him, pulling Emma with her.

After calming her sister down, Molly found her father and without flinching lied to him, slowly and carefully. Instinctively, she knew how she told the story would determine George Sawyer's fate. So, she told her papa how Sawyer cornered and attacked her in the bunkhouse. She also included several other incidences, untrue of course, but Molly suspected maybe that hadn't been the case for Emma.

At all costs, she would protect her sister. Any shame on the victim would be shouldered by Molly. She and Emma agreed later that night not to speak of it again, to anyone. And the next day, George Sawyer was gone.

Chapter Twenty-Seven

"Where the hell is she?" Matt demanded.

As he looked from Nathan to his mother, Matt experienced a surge of alarm he hadn't felt since that day ten years ago when a nine-year-old Molly had gone missing.

"Settle down, son," his father said from behind him.

"Maybe she went to see Davis," Nathan said.

"Now, why on earth would she do that?" Mrs. McAllister asked. "I think it's clear her gypsy ways finally got the best of her, and she simply moved on."

Matt stared at the elderly woman. Lizzie stood nearby, as did Logan. He thought he glimpsed Rosita lurking somewhere in the hallway; breakfast had been laid out and quickly forgotten.

"And what would you know of Molly's gypsy ways?" Matt asked slowly, knowing he needed to tread carefully, but his gut told him somehow the old bat was involved.

"Well, I won't deny the rumors I've heard about Miss Hart," the old woman said in her defense.

"And what rumors would those be?" he asked lethally.

"She lived with the Comanche, the most ill-bred and contemptible of all savages."

Lizzie gasped. "Is that true?"

"Yes, it's true," Mrs. McAllister continued. "I'd hoped to spare you the grisly details, Lizzie, but it's probably for the best it's come out into the open."

"Best for who?" Matt barely kept his anger contained. "You have no idea what you're talking about. What exactly did you say to her?"

Glaring back at him, Elizabeth McAllister pursed her lips and coolly assessed him. "I explained to her what she was, and how her presence would do nothing but hurt the Ryan family. You've all been far too kind to the girl. You couldn't possibly hope for her to become one of us again."

Matt moved toward the old woman but his mother intercepted him, grasping his shoulders. "Matthew."

Logan shifted to stand beside him, as did Nathan.

Susanna turned around to face the woman. "I'm afraid there's been a grave misunderstanding, Elizabeth. Molly is a part of our family, and your interference — however well-intentioned you believe it to be — is most unwelcome."

"But your own son is carrying on with her," Elizabeth shrieked. "You would allow this in your own home? You would allow a bastard child contaminated by the filth of *those people*?"

"That's enough!" Jonathan roared. A heavily charged silence engulfed the room. After a moment, he continued, his voice lowered but just as decisive. "Susanna and I trust our son. Anything beyond that is none of your business. I must ask you and Lizzie to get your things and leave immediately."

Elizabeth McAllister clamped her mouth shut, but her nostrils flared obscenely with every ragged breath she took. "So be it." She walked stiffly from the parlor.

Lizzie stayed back, her face pale and stunned. "Mr. and Mrs. Ryan, I had no idea," she said in a rush of breathless words. "Please accept my sincerest apologies. I like Molly and don't agree with any of what my mama just said."

"Thank you," Susanna replied.

"Run along now and help your mother," Jonathan said gruffly. "I'll see the both of you home."

"Yes, sir." She left the parlor.

"I hadn't realized Elizabeth's malice ran so deep," Susanna said.

"Why do you say that?" Logan asked.

"Maybe you can have pity on her if you knew what her husband did to her years ago," his father replied. "Charles McAllister became involved with an Indian woman, and Elizabeth eventually learned of his betrayal. It would seem she's laying the blame at the feet of all Indians rather than face the very real marital problems she and Charles had during the time we knew them."

"That's no excuse to attack Molly," Matt said furiously.

"No, but that's behind us for the moment," Jonathan said. "What we need to do now is find her. Then I'll sit down with you, Matthew, and you can explain your intentions to me. And they'd better be damn good!"

Matt stared at his old man. "Yes, sir."

"How is Davis?" his mother asked.

"He'll live," his pa answered.

"Did you find out who did it?" Nathan asked.

"A man named George Sawyer, who worked for Walker," Logan answered. "We tried to find him, but lost his trail about thirty miles northwest of here."

"Sawyer?" Susanna repeated softly. "Was he the same George Sawyer who worked at the Harts' years ago?"

"Yeah," Matt answered. "Do you remember him?"

"No, but I do remember Rosemary telling me about an incident with him and Molly. She was just a child." She paused. "It was terrible really. He tried to…force himself on her."

"What?" Matt couldn't hide his outrage.

"Molly finally told Robert what happened, so of course he let the man go immediately. I believe that was the end of it."

Matt swore under his breath. It certainly wasn't the end of it as far as he was concerned.

"Logan, go with Matt and track Molly down," Jonathan commanded. "She can't have gotten far."

"I'll go too," Nathan offered.

"Make haste, boys." The old man hesitated, then clapped Matt on the shoulders. "I've always been proud of you, and I trust your judgment, but when you find her, keep your damn hands to yourself. You hear me?"

"We'll chaperone them, Mr. Ryan," Nathan added, departing with Logan to get horses and supplies ready.

"Don't know how good a chaperone that Blackmore fella would be, so I'll just trust you to do the right thing." His father grabbed his hat then left the house, the screen door banging behind him.

Matt looked at his mother.

"Do you love her?" she asked.

He hadn't thought of his feelings for Molly along those lines, but his answer came quickly. "Yes." It all fell into place then, the rightness so obvious he wondered why he'd fought it for so long. The future only mattered if Molly was a part of it. All these years, she was the missing piece. All these years, a part of him had waited for her. He'd been given another chance, and this time he was determined not to fail.

"Then tell her."

* * *

Matt, Nathan and Logan tracked Molly to the remains of the Hart ranch. It wasn't difficult. Pecos' distinctive gait was easy to follow and fortunately it hadn't rained during the night. A search of the premises, however, showed it to be deserted.

Nathan came out of the stables. "It was definitely occupied. There are fresh droppings."

Logan came out of the homestead holding an empty whiskey bottle, a somber expression on his face. Matt didn't like any of this. Someone else had been here with Molly.

"There's somethin' else you should see," Logan said, gesturing for the other two to follow him back into the house.

He led them into the main bedroom, the one Matt had shared with Molly several weeks ago. The memory of that night made his stomach muscles tense. He wouldn't lose her now, not after finding her again. Not after finding her *here*. The chance of their paths crossing in the middle of nowhere was too much of a coincidence.

He had been drawn to this place, drawn to *her*. There was no plausible explanation for it because nothing was reasonable or logical about loving her.

Logan pointed to a pillar near the fireplace. A rope was tied around it, the ends ragged, as if quickly cut.

"Someone tied her up," Nathan said flatly.

"Who the hell would take her hostage?" Logan asked.

Matt turned it over in his mind, knowing he had the answer. "We lost Sawyer's trail near here."

"You think he's the one who's got her?" Logan shook his head in disbelief. "Why would he go to the trouble of hauling her with him? He'd move much faster alone."

"Not if he has a vendetta against her." Matt suppressed a rising swell of panic. He needed to think clearly or else he'd never find her.

"You mean about what he did to her when she was a little girl?" Logan considered the possibility. "How would he even know it was her?"

"I don't know. Maybe he simply took her as a bargaining tool, in case the law caught up with him for shooting Walker."

"Why *did* he shoot Walker?" Nathan asked.

"No one was quite sure," Logan responded. "Davis still hadn't come to when we were there so he couldn't tell us, but knowing Davis, I'm sure it was a deal gone bad."

"Logan, do you remember when Robert Hart sent Sawyer packing?" Matt concentrated on the memory.

"Not really," his brother replied.

"I have to admit, I didn't give it much thought at the time either, but I do remember Hart looked a little roughed up afterwards, like he'd been in a fight. I know if I were in his position, I would've beat Sawyer until he couldn't breathe anymore."

"Perfect motive to come back later with a posse, kill the man responsible, and steal the child who turned you in." Nathan's words hung heavy in the room.

It all made sense to Matt now. And every nerve in his body told him Sawyer knew exactly who Molly was. He had to find her.

"Let's go."

The three of them were in the saddle and riding hard in the space of a heartbeat.

Chapter Twenty-Eight

Molly felt like vomiting. Sawyer made her ride Pecos on her stomach, draped over the saddle sideways, her hands tied behind her back, her feet bound at the ankles. All day she'd endured this. As nightfall approached, he finally stopped and pulled her to the ground. She immediately fell to her knees. With effort, she steadied herself until the world stopped spinning.

Sawyer laughed. "Feeling sick?" He grabbed the back of her shirt and shoved her away from the horses. Tripping, she fell on her face.

Desperately she tried to focus her thoughts. If she didn't escape, Sawyer would almost certainly kill her, but not before he had fun with her, something he'd crudely commented on all day.

Bile rose in her throat. She thought of Matt and tears burned her eyes. It was hard to imagine this might be the end for her, and that she had stupidly left without saying goodbye to him. She owed him that, at least; owed Susanna and Jonathan a thank you for all they had done for her. But she had run away, and now she might never have the chance.

Sawyer hobbled the horses, then made a fire. Molly lay on the ground and watched him. He was really a very shortsighted man, she decided — smoke from the fire would easily be spotted by a search party. She knew, however, such a hope was small, if it existed at all. No one would know where she'd gone, if they even noticed she *was* gone in the first place. Regretfully, she realized she should've left a note.

No, a rescue was most likely not a possibility, even with the help of Sawyer's smoke signals. She would need to get away on her own.

Sawyer finally approached and pushed her up to a sitting position, grabbing her breasts roughly at the same time.

"Keep your hands off me!" she yelled, struggling to get away from him.

He contemplated her for a moment and a blank expression crossed his face. With a peculiar demeanor he walked off, abruptly leaving her alone.

Molly glanced around the clearing where they had stopped for the night. The sound of running water could be heard in the distance. She scanned the area again, noticing the large cluster of cottonwoods off to the right and a gradual uphill slope to the left. She knew this place, this particular pattern of vegetation, and the hill especially.

Had she dreamt of it? Taking a deep breath, she tried to remember why this area seemed so familiar to her. *The Kwahadi.* They had camped here one summer when she was with them. The teepees were placed closer to the water, but Molly could remember scouting this area many times with her Comanche sisters.

There was a cave located on the hill. It was the very place Running Water had almost been attacked by the rattler, the very place the snake had bitten Molly instead. She wondered if she could still locate it. All she needed was a chance to run.

"Could you untie my feet?" she asked, her voice hoarse. "They've gone numb."

"Too bad." Sawyer rifled through his saddlebag, undoubtedly searching for something to eat.

"I need to relieve myself."

He glanced at her, and his greasy hair and dirty face turned her stomach. She could hardly bring herself to hold his gaze.

"So shit all over yourself," he said loudly, waving his arms and leering at her. "I don't care."

"Why are you even bothering with me?" She attempted to swallow past the dryness in her throat.

Sawyer had spoken very little to her the previous night, managing to tie her to a post inside the house before passing out, obviously from too much whiskey as evidenced by an empty bottle nearby. Molly spent several hours trying to free herself, but to no avail. Despite being drunk, he had still been able to bind her hands and feet much too tightly.

"When I think back on it," Sawyer sneered, "you really were the start of all my bad luck. Finding you yesterday was the first bit of good luck I've had in a while. You and that goddamn slingshot."

Molly watched him, cautious of where this was headed.

"You told your pa such filthy lies about me," he continued. "He not only sent me walking—he whipped me good before he did. I didn't deserve that. It was all your fault, you know. You're due payback. Thought I was done with you when Cale brought back that wonderfully burned body."

She flinched at his words.

"I took care of your pa and you in one very productive night," he added.

"What did you say?" A chill overtook her.

"I told you, you'd regret ever messin' with me."

As understanding dawned, her heart broke anew. "*You* attacked the ranch that night," she whispered. "*You* killed my folks."

"Killed a few more people than I intended, but you can't arrange for everything. I had some nice plans for you, but then those damned Indians snatched you. I had to dispose of the bodies they left behind myself, not an easy job that one. Those Comanche must've liked you after all, to let you live. But now here you are, back in my arms again. Must be fate." Sawyer grinned, his teeth rimmed with black. Revolted, she looked away, devastated by what he'd just told her.

It hadn't been Davis Walker who'd sent a group of men to murder her parents. It had been George Sawyer, and all because she lied to Robert Hart about Sawyer forcing himself on her.

Molly couldn't regret the untruth because it had protected Emma, but the chain of events that followed had been in some way her own fault. If she had found some other way to deal with Sawyer all those years ago then maybe Robert and Rosemary Hart would be alive today.

The knowledge shattered her. Shaking, she tried to conceal it from the man sitting across from her. No, not a man, an animal.

She hung her head down in defeat. Perhaps Sawyer was right. Perhaps fate had brought her back to him.

* * *

Matt rode hard until nightfall, Nathan and Logan on his heels. He wanted to make as much progress as possible before it became too dark to see the trail left by Sawyer and Molly. Sawyer must have felt confident he wasn't being followed because it was almost impossible not to track him. Even when he crossed water, he didn't go very far downstream before hitting dry ground on the other side. Matt was hopeful they'd overtake them by dusk.

The complete darkness now encompassing them, however, forced Matt to stop. They couldn't risk getting too far from the trail. Reluctantly, he reined his horse in, swearing silently to himself and praying Molly would be safe tonight.

In silence, Nathan and Logan made camp, tending to the horses first then offering Matt hardtack and dried beef since they would have no fire. The routine was a familiar one.

Often when tracking a man or group of men, Matt and the other Rangers would stop to eat an hour or two before nightfall then ride beyond the evidence of the campfire to settle in for the night. But doing so now would cost precious time, and he was unwilling to do that.

Not hungry, he forced himself nevertheless to eat and drink, knowing instinctively he wouldn't be any help to Molly if he was weakened from hunger or dehydration. He knew his body needed sleep as well, but his restlessness made that difficult. He felt helpless, and he didn't like it.

"You should try getting some rest, Matt," Nathan said as he positioned a bedroll onto a grassy patch of ground. "I'll take the first watch."

"No, I'll take first watch," Matt replied. "I won't be able to sleep anyway."

"Then I'll take second," Nathan said. "You're last, Logan."

Logan nodded from where he lay, then positioned his hat across his face and promptly went to sleep.

Matt moved away from the two sleeping men and sat on a log. It had obviously been there for some time, for a thick mat of moss blanketed the wood. The sounds of the night filled the brisk air and the stars flashed in the cloudless sky.

Matt wondered where Molly was, if she was scared, if she was hungry, if she was hurt. He took his hat off and scratched his fingers through his hair. He was frustrated, angry, and terrified like he'd never been in his life. If anything happened to her, he wasn't sure he could bear it.

Not doing anything was torture. Who knew what the hell Sawyer had done to her, what he'd do to her tonight. Grimly, Matt knew he would kill the man. There was no doubt in his mind. He just hoped when the deed was done, it would be in time to save Molly. He refused to even consider a second funeral for the girl who had become as much a part of him as breathing.

* * *

Sawyer gave Molly no food or water. After a while, he checked the ropes around her ankles and wrists. He then proceeded to vent his anger on her. She'd expected this, but it still didn't prepare her any better for it.

Repeatedly he kicked and slapped her, beating her to a point beyond pain. Torres had done this to her. She'd survived then, she could survive now. She wondered if he would force himself on her. He would have to untie her legs, and for the first time she felt hope. It might be the only opportunity she'd have to fight back and escape.

Something warm ran down her face and she realized her nose bled. Every inhalation she took hurt. Closing her eyes, she waited for him to continue, but he stopped and walked to the opposite side of the fire.

From her position on the ground, blood pooled in a puddle near the tip of her nose. She watched him pace back and forth, his contorted face wavering before her. Finally, he lay down on a smelly, dirty piece of cloth she suspected at one time had been a bedroll. After several long minutes, he began to snore.

It was too much of an effort to get herself to a sitting position, so she remained where she was, watching the crackling of the fire as her breath came in painful, jagged gasps. At least she had warmth against the chill in the air. As Sawyer began to snore more loudly, Molly wondered why he hadn't attacked her sexually. He'd certainly spoken of it enough throughout the day.

But when he'd grabbed her breasts earlier it was almost as if the contact disgusted him. Although grateful he'd stopped, she wondered why he hadn't followed through.

Then it occurred to her. Perhaps he couldn't stand to touch women. Maybe all he wanted were children. With a disgusted feeling, Molly realized Emma probably wasn't the first, or the last, child he'd gone after.

Continuing to gaze into the fire, she contemplated how she might get loose. She had a knife inside her right boot, but there was no way she could reach it since the ropes were bound too tightly.

She hadn't seen Sawyer carrying a knife, so even if she could scoot herself over to him, the awkwardness from her secured limbs would surely awaken him if she tried to search his body for something sharp.

The fire continued to lick the few pieces of wood remaining, the flames swaying back and forth, hypnotizing her.

That was it.

She could burn the ropes off.

Moving as quickly as possible, she struggled closer to the fire. The pain from her ribs was excruciating and she tried desperately to keep from crying out, always watching Sawyer for any signs of awakening.

She would have to burn the ropes around her feet first since she knew it was impossible to get herself to a standing position otherwise. Breathing heavily, her body shaking from the pain and the effort, she swung her legs over the fire while lying on her back. Immediately the smell of scorched rope, cloth, and leather filled the air. She gritted her teeth and hoped it wouldn't rouse Sawyer.

Her feet became hot inside her boots, but luckily they protected her flesh from being scorched directly. Her weakened state caused her legs to fall twice into the fire. The bottom of her pants burned. Rolling to the side, she smothered the flames in the dirt, but she wasn't fast enough. The back of her legs began to sting.

For what seemed an eternity, she kept alternating between holding her feet over the fire and pulling them to the side to extinguish her trousers catching fire.

Tears and sweat ran down her face. She bit her lower lip to keep from screaming. Finally, the ropes started to loosen. Molly twisted her feet against each other, working the bindings off. One strand snapped apart, and after more ankle-twisting her feet were finally free.

Exhaustion threatened to consume her, but she knew she couldn't give in. Fighting to a standing position, her hands still tied tightly behind her, she stumbled into the night in search of the cave.

Chapter Twenty-Nine

Matt was certain now. He smelled smoke. And it wasn't just from firewood. Something else burned.

Moving quickly, he awoke Nathan and Logan. Jerking his head slightly, he motioned for them to follow. Without a sound they swiftly shook off the remnants of sleep, gathered up their gear, removed the ropes from the horses, and trailed Matt into the darkness.

They didn't ride but guided their animals to a large cottonwood and tied them off. Quietly, each man pulled extra ammunition from his saddlebag. Matt and Nathan checked the cylinders of their six-shooters. Logan strapped on a second gun, then all three pulled Sharps rifles from their scabbards. They left their hats with the horses.

By now the smell of smoke was strong. The three of them fanned out, approaching the encampment from several directions.

Moving through a wooded area, Matt slowed only when he saw the glow from a fire. Taking cover behind a tree, he crawled on his belly until he could view the camp clearly. Although a low flame still burned brightly, there was no one in sight, only an old worn bedroll visible.

Matt stood, still taking cover from the large tree. Off to the right, he caught a glimpse of Nathan.

Following his friend's line of sight, he saw the two horses grazing beyond the firelight. Even in the black of night, he recognized Pecos.

Where the hell are Sawyer and Molly?

Off to the left, Logan gave him a hand signal. The perimeter was clear. Matt left his cover and approached the fire.

He froze.

The blood on the ground was unmistakable.

Panic and fear gripped him, but he pushed it aside, replacing it instead with a rage that consumed him.

Molly! Don't leave me! Tell me where you are!

He motioned to Nathan and Logan to spread out and search. Sawyer and Molly couldn't be far.

* * *

Molly ran toward the hill, faltering when the ground shifted upward, and a sob escaped from deep inside her chest. She needed to be quieter, but terror and pain rang in her ears, and she wasn't sure if what she heard was real or in her mind. The climb became steeper. She found it extremely difficult trying to clamber up with her hands tied behind her. At the same time, the familiar terrain unleashed memories from the past.

"Cactus Bird," Running Water yelled. "Wait for me!"

Molly turned and smiled as her young Comanche sister ran after her. Running Water moved quickly, hence her name. The girl was often just a blur of motion.

"Sits on Ground is coming," the young girl squealed. "Let's hide."

Molly laughed and waited for Running Water to reach her, then they both climbed the hill and searched for a good hiding place. They were practically upon the cave before they realized what it was.

"In here," Running Water exclaimed, running past Molly into the darkened interior.

The girl's sudden shriek jolted Molly. She rushed inside and stopped, hearing the rattling noise before she could see the snake. As her eyes adjusted, a very large, coiled rattlesnake was but an arm's length from them, poised to strike at any moment.

Molly gripped Running Water's shoulders to hold the girl still. "Don't move," she whispered, her heart beating at a frantic pace.

The girl trembled. Molly knew she didn't have much time. Slowly, she began to inch backward, guiding her Indian sister with her. "Careful," Molly murmured.

Watching the snake, she fixated her gaze on its large head, its tongue flicking in and out. They were almost to the threshold of the cave. It was just a little bit farther.

Then Molly saw the snake coil tighter, and she knew it would strike. There was just enough time to turn around and push Running Water out of the cave, but it wasn't quick enough for her. The snake bit the heel of her right foot.

She and Running Water ran and ran, not stopping until they reached the Kwahadi camp. It was then she realized she'd lost all feeling in her leg. As she comprehended what had happened, she fell forward to the ground and into blackness.

As Molly approached the opening of the cave, she paused. Breathing loudly, she contemplated the memory of the rattlesnake. She'd been very ill after being bitten, and there was talk among the elders that she might lose her leg.

Closing her eyes, she braced herself. She couldn't go inside that cave, not helpless as she was without the use of her hands. The damn snake was probably still there. She imagined he was even bigger and meaner than he'd been all those years ago.

Molly struggled to push her rear end through the space between her arms. With clenched screams, she strained her arms downward in frustration, feeling as if they were coming out of the shoulder sockets. Heaving and sweating, she fell backward but managed to drag her legs through the opening created by her bound wrists. Shaking, she fumbled for the knife in her boot. As she attempted to position it between her hands, she dropped it twice, the tears in her eyes blurring her vision. Finally, she gripped the blade between her boots and for several long minutes worked the rope against the sharp end.

When enough of it frayed, she yanked her wrists from the bondage entirely.

She was free.

Rubbing her wrists, she felt the weight of her aching arms and the lack of feeling in her fingers. Her ribs throbbed and her face stung. As she stood, raw pain shot through her feet and calves. She picked up the knife, carefully, and staggered toward the cave.

A dark mass rushed her and knocked her hard to the ground. Dazed, she struggled to breathe. No air.

"Just where the hell do you think you're going?" Sawyer hissed.

Shoving her onto her back, he sat astride her as she labored to fill her lungs. Suddenly, the pain was too much. Screaming, she let all of the fury and helplessness she'd felt since encountering him—since the last ten years—pour out of her. Sawyer might kill her, but she'd be damned if it happened without a fight.

In a burst of energy and frenzied anger, Molly raised the knife above her head with both hands and drove it deeply into his chest.

A stunned silence engulfed them. Time slowed until only the ebb and flow of life could be heard, one heartbeat after another. And within the stillness, the end came to George Sawyer.

What have I done?

He slumped onto her, and Molly wailed as she tried to push him from her like an unwanted attack of red ants. Coughing and choking, her body tried to expel the contents of her stomach but it was empty.

Crying, she slammed her hands into his shoulders and pushed at his dead weight. He wouldn't move, and she had no strength left to fight him, even in death. She closed her eyes. Her mind whirled chaotically, pulling her away from the wretchedness, extracting her from this place. The voices of the past greeted her, and in gratitude she went toward them.

* * *

Matt raced up the hill at the sound of a woman's scream. When he saw Molly lying on the ground, he immediately dragged Sawyer's body from her. Nathan and Logan arrived. Matt was only half-aware of them moving the bastard's body even farther away.

Matt's entire life became sharply focused to this one instant in time. He knew nothing would ever be the same after this, that *he* would never be the same. He was afraid to touch Molly's lifeless body, for a part of him simply couldn't handle knowing if she truly was gone, but compelling need pushed him forward.

He sank to his knees and reached out to touch her. Her skin felt warm. Thank God. He sucked in a ragged breath.

"Molly," he whispered, his voice rough, uneven. "Open your eyes. I'm here. You're safe now."

No response. Carefully, he placed a hand on her stomach and felt a faint, shallow breath. She was alive.

Open your eyes.

In the distance, the staccato of pounding hooves filled the silence.

"Rider," Nathan said matter-of-factly. "I'll go." He slipped away into the darkness.

Matt hardly noticed.

A faint movement, however, brought his finely-honed fighting reflexes back in a flash. He jerked his gaze to Logan, who immediately leveled his rifle in response.

"It's all right," Nathan said, reappearing. "It's Cale."

"How'd you find us?" Logan asked.

"Long story," Cale replied. "What happened?" He stopped short when he saw Molly.

"It looks like Sawyer beat her up pretty bad," Nathan said, his voice empty. "We just found her."

Panic shot through Matt, and with it an agonizing glance into the future if he lost her. He couldn't imagine having to live through that again. He'd endured so much misery and destruction in the last ten years, including a crushing imprisonment that had nearly destroyed him, but the madness skirting the edges of his mind would certainly take him this time if Molly slipped beyond him for good.

A muscle in Cale's jaw twitched. "Sawyer?"

"Dead," Logan responded quietly. "Molly stabbed him in the chest."

Cale swore under his breath. "Let me have a look at her, Ryan." Kneeling beside her, he examined her face.

"Careful!" Matt shot back.

"I need some light," Cale said.

Nathan and Logan retreated, then quickly returned with two hastily made torches. In the flickering firelight, Cale examined Molly.

Matt noticed the many cuts and bruises on her face and a swollen lower lip, caked with dirt and blood. Cale lifted her shirt from the bottom and inspected her abdomen.

"He must've kicked her several times," he said tightly. When he applied slight pressure to her ribs, she moaned and stirred briefly.

Hope flared in Matt.

"Some of the ribs might be broken," Cale stated. He moved to her feet. "Help me pull her boots off."

Matt held each of her legs as Cale removed Molly's footwear. Cale shook his head when he saw the blistering flesh on the back of her calves. "She's been burned. I don't think we can move her tonight, except maybe off this hill to lower ground. I'll need to clean these."

In the orange haze of the torchlight, Matt glimpsed Cale's grim expression, not unlike the look on the man's face when he'd returned with the burned body of a girl everyone had assumed was Molly. Angry, Matt refused to accept the same horrific fate for the girl he had once adored and the woman he now couldn't live without.

"Damn you!" Matt said through clenched teeth. "She *will* survive."

Cale fixed him with a stony gaze, revealing nothing in the shadowed contours of his face. In silence, he nodded. "We Walkers are a tough lot."

Matt saw the acceptance in the other man's face, the knowledge that Molly was his sister. With quiet resolve, he knew Cale would protect one of his own.

Chapter Thirty

Matt helped Cale move Molly to a grassy area near the fire Sawyer had built. Using what blankets and bedrolls they had between them, they fashioned as comfortable a bed as they could for her. Nathan and Logan took care of Sawyer's body, wrapping and stashing it until they could ride it to Fort Richardson. They also took care of food and water needs.

Cale cleaned Molly's feet, legs, and face, applying a juice brewed from dried purple coneflower to prevent infection. He wrapped the back of her legs in strips torn from each man's shirt and also had Matt bind her ribs.

While a batch of coneflower tea brewed, Cale took a small buckskin bag from inside his saddlebag and sprinkled a yellow powder over her body.

"*Ha-dintin*," he told them. "A pollen the Apache hold sacred."

He formed a yellow cross on Molly's head, chest, arms, and legs. Matt watched as Cale's actions electrified the atmosphere. The air became charged with life and death, something Matt had experienced countless times, but never in this way. It was as if the four of them stood on the threshold of the land of the living and the realm of the dead, and Molly had to decide which one to inhabit. One glance at Nathan and Logan—their somber expressions transfixed on the scene—told him they weren't immune to the reverence of the moment either.

They held vigil over Molly's body as the night slipped away, Cale repeatedly stoking the fire. "Sweat cleanses the body," he said.

"I would've never pegged you for a healer, Walker," Nathan said quietly from across the fire.

Cale leaned back against a nearby tree, rubbing his eyes. "One of my best kept secrets. Might ruin my reputation as a bounty hunter if word got out I was a *di-yin*."

Nathan laughed, though his expression was tired and haggard. "Yeah, I suppose it would."

"How did you find us?" Logan stretched out on the ground several feet away.

"When my pa came to, I had a long talk with him." Cale paused. "It seems he and Sawyer had a long history together, one that began when Sawyer came to him after Robert Hart kicked him off his ranch. Apparently, Sawyer filled him with stories about Hart stealing cattle and changing the brand. As it turned out, Sawyer was stealing from my pa as well as Molly's family. He probably took Ryan beeves as well."

"He was behind the attack on the Harts, wasn't he?" Nathan said.

"That's why Pa and Sawyer argued the other night," Cale said. "Pa finally realized what Sawyer had done, that he'd organized the attack, and Pa let slip Molly was alive. That seemed to set Sawyer off. He unloaded a few shots from a pistol and ran, I guess because he thought my pa would turn him in.

"Once I learned this, I decided to track him, not stopping until the little shit was dead. I rode to the

SR to see if any of you'd give me a hand, and that's when Jonathan told me y'all went in search of Molly." Cale contemplated the fire a moment. "What I don't understand is why Sawyer grabbed her."

"He blamed her, I think," Matt said quietly from his spot beside Molly. "She turned him in."

"For what?" Cale asked.

"According to my ma, the reason Sawyer was let go from the Harts' was because he tried to force himself on Molly."

Cale stared at him. "But she was just a child."

"If he weren't dead already, I'd give you a shot at him," Matt said coldly. "But only after I was finished with him."

Cale put another log on the fire, then sat back. "Somehow I doubt there'd be anything left after you got through with him."

On that point, Matt agreed.

* * *

By mid-morning, Molly was feverish, thrashing about, crying, and talking incoherently. Matt felt encouraged—at least she was responding in some way—but Cale's flat expression made him feel immediately defeated. Cale brewed a tea from prickly ash bark, and he and Matt tried to get as much into Molly as they could.

Nathan and Logan set out to scout the area while Matt remained near Molly's restless body. Cale suggested he sleep, but Matt couldn't. Looking weary, Cale reclined on the ground and tried to doze but Molly's voice startled him awake a short while later.

"*Pasinugia*," she cried.

Cale sat up.

"She's not awake," Matt said, concerned.

269

"*Niatz! Uehquétzutzu!*"

"What's she saying?" Cale asked.

"I'm not sure, but it sounds Comanche. Something about a snake, I think."

Cale felt her forehead. "I'll make more tea, then we should check her legs again. I have some acorn oil that might help with the dryness."

The two men ministered to Molly for the rest of the day. Nathan and Logan returned at dusk with two rabbits and three wild turkeys. The food helped revive their dwindling spirits.

As they sat around the fire, Matt forced himself to eat but even swallowing was a hardship. Nothing seemed important to him anymore as long as there was a chance he might lose Molly.

"I'm hungry." Her voice startled all of them.

Matt moved swiftly to her side.

"Molly." His heart pounded as she looked into his eyes.

She tried to smile, but winced from the effort. "I'm so glad you're here." Her voice was scratchy and hoarse.

"Try not to move," Matt said gently. "Cale thinks some of your ribs are broken."

"I can believe it," she whispered. "My chest hurts like a son-of-a-bitch."

"You always did swear too much as a child," Cale said from beside her.

Molly glanced up at him. "I learned it from you and Matt." Her eyes moved to Nathan and Logan, standing nearby. "What are all of you doing here?"

"Watching over you," Matt said. "Cale's been taking care of you."

She tried smiling again, only half getting there. "Thank you."

"Matt's the one you should thank," Cale replied. "He hasn't left your side since we found you."

Standing, Cale gestured for Nathan and Logan to follow. They disappeared toward the creek so Matt could be alone with the woman of his heart.

Relief and gratitude consumed him like nothing he'd ever experienced in all his twenty-eight years. Drinking in the sight of Molly alive—her blue eyes still vibrant despite pain, fatigue, and exhaustion—he was reminded of her strength and the sheer determination she'd possessed during her long ordeal over the last ten years. He should've known her spirit wouldn't be so easily tempted by the escape of death. Her right cheek was covered with black and blue bruises and her lower lip remained swollen, but she had never looked more beautiful to him.

She would survive. A warm wind blew the darkness of the night from Matt's bones, and he inhaled life as he never had before.

Stroking hair from her face, he smiled, knowing his eyes watered. "You had me scared," he said.

"How did you find me?"

"We've been tracking you since you left the SR. Why did you leave?"

Trying to lick her dry lips, she looked away from him. "Mrs. McAllister—"

"Isn't worth another thought," Matt finished for her. "Whatever she said, it's not true. My folks insisted I bring you back. You belong with us."

"But you don't deserve the talk, what people are saying, and your family...I couldn't do that to them."

"I couldn't care less what people think, and neither could my folks. If it's any consolation, my pa

271

kicked Elizabeth McAllister out of the house on her bony, spiteful ass."

She tried to laugh, but instead groaned. Then, she started to cry.

Matt took her hand and leaned close. "Sweetheart, your home is at the SR now. Your home is with *me.*"

Nerves gripped him. It hadn't occurred to him until now that Molly might not want to stay with him, might not agree to be his wife. She'd welcomed him into her bed with an amazing openness, but maybe that was the extent of it.

"Matt, stop." Still weakened, she was barely able to put a hand to his chest. "Before you say anything else, you must know I can't change the last ten years. I spent half my life with the Kwahadi and I'll always carry that with me. I'm not ashamed by it—they were good people—but it would kill me to bring shame to you or your folks because of it."

"Well, then you don't have to worry. We've never held that against you, and never will." He clasped her hand with great care. "I always planned to do right by you. Maybe I'm not prime husband material, but since that night we were together I realized I could never watch you walk away from me. I could never watch you find another man to settle down with. I'm afraid you're stuck with me, a damaged Ranger without a roof to call his own. But if you'll let me, I'd like to try and give you a better life than the one you've known."

She sobbed convulsively, so Matt kissed her, gently wiping her tears with his thumbs.

"I love you," he whispered, brushing his nose against hers, "and I hope to God you feel the same."

"Of course I do," she said on another sob, followed by a hiccup.

His lips softly met hers and he savored the simple fact they were together. For the first time, he felt a sense of closure on the gaping loss her disappearance ten years ago had inflicted on his heart. He marveled that he'd found her at all. How easily he might never have known she lived, how easily the paths of their lives might never have crossed.

But he *had* found her, and he knew with a certainty deep in his heart and the very essence of himself that he was meant to love Molly Hart. She was the missing part of himself he had never understood was gone until she had filled his life with her presence, touching his heart and healing his soul.

"Since I have no experience in asking a woman to marry me, I hope you realize that there's a marriage proposal in there, too."

"It's all right." She smiled as much as her bruised lip would allow, sniffing and wiping her nose. "I'm nowhere near a gussied-up society lady. I hope you realize what you're getting."

"I wouldn't want you any other way."

Lying down beside her, he held his future wife close.

Chapter Thirty-One

Cale, Nathan, and Logan returned well after dark, having snared a rabbit for Molly. Nathan quickly skinned and roasted the animal, and she was able to eat a small amount. Cale prepared another batch of tea for her.

Molly made a face after her first sip. "Do you make this for all the girls?" she asked. "It's awful."

"Quit complaining." Cale sat across the fire from her. "And I only make it for certain girls."

When Molly glanced at him, he grinned. Tears filled her eyes as she returned the smile, accepting the fact she and Cale shared the same father. There were so many things to acknowledge and at the top of the list was her ordeal with Sawyer. Still shaky, she had avoided thinking about any of it. The constant pain in her chest and the raw fire-burns on her legs certainly helped keep her mind from the details.

Wiping her eyes with the back of her hand, she took another sip of tea as she sat on the bed they had fashioned for her. Matt gently stroked her back, the touch reminding her of the one good outcome of all of this.

She and Matt would have a life together — an amazing, almost unreal, possibility considering all that had happened. He wanted everything with her. Until he'd said he loved her, she hadn't realized just how much she'd ached for such a life, or just how strongly she had come to love him in return. For so long, she'd been alone. And now, she wasn't. It would take some getting used to.

"How did you come to spend time with the Apache?" she asked Cale, not sure what kind of relationship she could have with her new brother, but thought they should start somewhere.

"I was attacked by a mountain lion." As he spoke, he shrugged one shoulder out of his shirt to reveal a jagged and knotted scar. Chunks of flesh were missing.

"Jesus, Cale." Logan's voice held a combination of concern and disbelief. "You're lucky to be alive."

"Yeah." Cale slid his shirt back into place. "That's what the local shaman thought, too. After they nursed me back to health, they insisted I consider the path of a *di-yin*. The mountain lion marked me. They believed it was a part of my spirit."

"So a medicine man taught you?" Molly asked.

Cale nodded. "And also a medicine woman."

"Apache women can do that?" she asked in surprise.

"Not usually, as near as I could tell, but this woman had been struck by lightning, and became greatly revered in the tribe because of it. The Apache can be very superstitious." He threw another log on the fire.

"The Kwahadi were superstitious about snakes. Did you know I almost put one under your pillow, when you worked at our ranch years ago?"

The four men watched her in silence.

"It was just a harmless little thing," she continued, staring into the fire. Pausing, she considered her next words. "That same day I also did something terrible after I caught George Sawyer in the bunkhouse with Emma." Her voice was just a whisper now as she remembered, overwhelmed by the need to confess.

"It wasn't you he attacked?" Matt asked her.

"No. It was Emma, but she was frightened and I wanted to protect her. And I wanted to make sure Sawyer was punished for it, so I lied to my father." She glanced at Cale, shaking her head in resignation. "I lied to *Robert Hart*. I told him it was me, and I heaped a bunch of falsehoods on it to make sure Sawyer didn't get away with anything."

"If it's any consolation," Matt said, resting his hand against her neck, "I'm fairly certain Robert gave Sawyer quite a beating that day."

"No," she said forcefully, "you don't understand. Sawyer came back and killed my folks because of *me*, because of the lies *I* told. It was my fault. If I'd just handled it differently, none of this would've happened."

"You were nine years old, Molly," Logan said. "You could hardly have known how things would play out."

"Don't play this game with yourself," Nathan said. "It won't help. Sawyer set certain things in motion. I doubt anything would've stopped him."

"From what my old man said, Sawyer was into a lot of illegal activity," Cale said. "He was a conniving piece of shit, playing all angles. He also slithered around as the lowest form of life because he preferred little girls to women." With more compassion in his voice, he continued, "You shouldn't think for a minute any of it was your fault. Everyone in your family paid a high price the night Sawyer attacked your ranch, maybe you most of all.

He got exactly what he deserved when you killed him."

The thought sickened her all over again. She had ended a man's life. It hardly made her happy, or left her feeling proud over what she'd done. It had been necessary, she told herself. But was that really true? She had no idea.

"Molly," Matt said. "Sawyer was a dead man."

Looking over her shoulder at him, she saw the certainty and resolution in his eyes. Matt had had every intention of killing George Sawyer before this ordeal was through.

"Bad luck put you there instead of me," he continued, "but don't for one minute regret what you did. After what he'd done to you, do you think Sawyer was going to let you live?"

Molly considered his words, and more tears filled her eyes. She knew he was right, that what all of them said held merit. The past was gone, only full of memories, betrayals and, most of all, regrets. Her own regrets. Could she live with them? She had no choice but to try.

As if reading her thoughts, Matt said, "We'll face the demons of the past together. It'll get easier in time."

One part of the circle was finally closed.

Maybe now, her mama, Robert Hart and Adelaide could rest in peace. And maybe, in time, peace would find Molly as well.

She slept soundly that night, with no dreams. Matt never left her. The fire warmed her on one side while Matt's body warmed her on the other.

The next morning, Nathan and Logan rode ahead of them with Sawyer's body. Logan planned to ride home and inform his folks that Molly had been found. Nathan would ride to Fort Richardson to drop the body and file a report.

Molly could only ride Pecos at a slow gait, so Matt and Cale flanked her as they rode slowly through what had once been Comanche territory. She couldn't help but reflect on what had happened to her in the last ten years.

Her time spent with the Kwahadi had been bittersweet. Just when she had begun to forge a bond with her Comanche family, they'd abruptly traded her. Were they still alive? Did they ever think of her? She hoped they'd found at least some measure of happiness on the reservation. Staying in one place permanently would have been a huge adjustment for them, she knew. Was it an adjustment for her, too? Could she reside in one place with Matt from this point forward?

They hadn't really discussed any details of how or where they would live once they married. Glancing at him on her right, his face shadowed from his hat as well as the makings of a beard, she knew without hesitation it really didn't matter. She loved him. More than she would ever have thought possible. To be without him would reduce her life to merely an existence.

Anticipation for the future filled her, something she hadn't had in a very long time. Reflexively, her hand covered her abdomen, bringing a smile to her lips. With the blessings of the Great Spirit, she and Matt might even have children one day.

By nightfall, they were still at least thirty miles from Ryan land, so Matt and Cale made camp, pestered Molly until they both felt she'd eaten enough, then insisted she rest. As soon as she lay down, she was asleep.

* * *

When Matt arrived at his family's ranch house, he felt a great sense of relief. He'd worried constantly about Molly during the long ride back from the high plains territory. His mother and Rosita came outside immediately to greet them.

"Molly," Susanna said, reaching up to help her from her horse, "let's get you inside right away. Rosita, help me."

Matt dismounted quickly and reached Molly's side before his ma took charge, easing her gently down from Pecos. Molly smiled up at him, the bruises on her face a harsh reminder of all she'd been through.

"I'm fine, really," she said, but she leaned much too heavily on him.

"Promise me you'll sleep for at least three days," he said.

"Only if Cale doesn't make me any more tea," she responded.

"I didn't realize he had any domestic qualities," Susanna remarked.

"I don't," Cale said from atop his horse.

"Come down from there, Caleb," Susanna demanded. "You look like you need a rest as well."

"I appreciate the offer, Mrs. Ryan, but I think I'll ride on back to Walker land and see how my pa's doing. Molly, promise me you'll get some rest. I'll be back for the wedding." He turned his horse and was gone.

Molly smiled, and Matt wondered how much time should pass before he made her his wife. She would need several days to recover. He debated how long he could wait. He needed to have that talk with his pa as soon as possible.

279

"I'll check on you later," he said.

Molly nodded.

"Rosita, please take Molly into the house," Susanna insisted. "Put her in Matthew's bedroom— she can't possibly make it upstairs after everything that's happened."

"It is good to see you, *señorita*," Rosita declared. "You not look bad at all. I take good care of you, and I have a stew with hot peppers that will fix anything that ails you...," her voice faded away as they stepped onto the porch and into the house.

"I'm glad you found her," his ma said, her concern evident. "Is she really well?"

"I think so," Matt said. "Cale took good care of her."

"Logan told me. Cale never fails to surprise me." With hands on hips her gaze became thoughtful. "So, when should this wedding take place?"

"One week," Matt said without hesitation, refusing to let his mother intimidate him.

Raising an eyebrow, she shook her head. "That's hardly enough time to make plans. And Molly might need more time to recover."

Matt heard what his mother was saying, knew she was right, but the patience that had become an integral part of his personality abandoned him now.

"Two weeks," he conceded.

"Four."

"Three, and that's my final offer."

Nodding, his ma agreed. "All right, three. I think I can pull it together by then." She smiled, her eyes filling with tears, then she hugged him.

"What's that for?" he asked.

"Because I'm your mother, and I'm proud of the man you've become. And sometimes you remind me so much of the man I married." She released him, then went into the house.

Matt didn't waste any time locating his pa, in the barn packing supplies onto a mule as he prepared to head back to the roundup.

"You need me to come and help?" Matt asked.

Startled, his old man turned, then pulled him into a rough embrace. "Logan said you were comin' in. How's Molly?"

"She's well." Matt stepped back and smiled. It dawned on him he was a very happy man.

"Don't bother with the roundup—they'll be finishin' up soon anyhow. You stay here and get some rest, then we can talk about Molly's future."

"That's why I'm here." Matt adjusted his hat. "I mean to marry her pa, and I'd like to ask if the offer for Ryan land and a stake in this ranch still stands."

His pa laughed loudly. "You're damn right it does." He slapped Matt on the back. "Never thought I'd live to hear those words. It's about time, son."

"Yes, sir, it is." And under the bright Texas sun, Matt's future with Molly was sealed.

Chapter Thirty-Two

Three weeks later Molly sat on the edge of Matt's bed and wondered what she should do with her hair. Having never fussed much with it, she was a little baffled. Since today *was* her wedding day, she knew she better figure something out, and quickly.

Rosita burst into the room carrying the beautiful ivory gown Susanna had purchased in Dallas two weeks ago. Molly loved every lacy loop and soft contour of the silky material. She'd worn it several times over the last few days for last minute fittings.

"Why you sit there, looking lost?" Rosita asked.

"Well..." Molly chewed on her lower lip. Thankfully, it was no longer swollen. All that remained of her ordeal with Sawyer was faint bruising on her ribcage and several red scars on her legs, but both would be covered by the beautiful gown. Matt had made it clear that after the ceremony, when the gown was gone, the scars wouldn't bother him in the least. That thought made her blush.

She and Matt hadn't been intimate since the one and only time when he'd come to her during the storm. It had been frustrating, but he was determined to respect the wishes of his folks, as well as pay honor to the woman he intended to make his wife. Or, so he told her during a few heated kisses.

"You have second thoughts?" Rosita said.

"No," Molly replied immediately. "Of course not. But what should I do with my hair?"

"Ah, I help you." The elderly woman hurried over to her and started humming then frowned, muttered to herself in Spanish then shook her head as she scooped Molly's hair into different configurations with her fingers. "This a big decision."

"What is?" Susanna asked, entering the room.

"*Señorita* Molly's hair."

"I think it would look lovely down," Susanna replied, moving to smooth out the gown draped on the bed.

The two women took several minutes to arrange Molly's curls around her face. Her hair was now long enough to brush the top of her shoulders.

"And now," Susanna said, surveying their handiwork once they were done, "we really need to get you into that dress."

With much buttoning and primping, Molly soon stood adorned in her wedding gown. The dress, with elbow-length sleeves and a lace design sewn into the torso, fit snugly around her. The off-white material hugged her waist and outlined her bosom, as it had done in the fittings. But Molly suddenly worried that perhaps it was a bit too much.

"Should I cover myself more?" she asked, her hand skimming the flesh just below her collarbone.

"Nonsense." Susanna examined the dress thoroughly for any problems. "You're a beautiful young woman and this is your wedding day. All eyes will be on you. It never hurts to keep a man on his toes."

"Pardon?"

Susanna stopped and gazed warmly at her. "Your own mother can't be here, but I'm certain she's watching from somewhere. And I'm sure she's just as proud as I am of you and Matthew, and the happiness so long overdue you both. If Rosemary were here, she would cry and hug you and dawdle over you until you looked just perfect." Pausing, she grasped Molly's hands. "If there's anything you need to know, if there's anything troubling you, I hope you know you can always come to me."

"Thank you," Molly whispered, tears flowing.

"Do you have any concerns about the wedding night?"

Molly coughed then started to laugh, embarrassed as she wiped her eyes with the back of a hand.

Susanna shook her head, pursing her lips. "Men." She smiled. "They've no patience. But then, we wouldn't want them any other way, would we?"

"No, ma'am."

"I've never told Matthew," Susanna said, "but I was pregnant with him before my wedding day."

"You were?" Molly asked, eyes widening.

Susanna nodded, taking a handkerchief out of her apron pocket and dabbing at Molly's tears. "Everything will be made right today. And I couldn't be more pleased to finally call you daughter. Oh my, I almost forgot!" Reaching into her other apron pocket, she pulled out a letter. "This just came for you from Mary."

With a rush of excitement Molly took the communication, savoring the chance to finally connect with her family.

"You sit and read," Susanna said. "Rosita and I will return in a bit."

The two women left the room while Molly sat down in the chair by the window. She carefully unfolded the letter.

Dearest Molly,

I was never more shocked than when I received Mrs. Ryan's letter telling me you're alive. I can't believe it. It's such a miracle. I can hardly wait to see you! Have you written to Emma? She is still with Aunt Catherine in San Francisco.

I guess you know the truth about Mama and Papa. It was such a difficult time for Emmy and me. I can't begin to describe it, but I realize it must have been so much harder for you. You were always the strong one, though. I guess I shouldn't be surprised you're still alive.

I wish I could come to see you right away, but I'm very heavy with child. The baby should come any day now. I was married five years ago to a man named Tom Simms. He's wonderful, and I'm very happy. We have two other children, Robert Thomas is five and Molly Rose is three. My daughter is very much like you and well named. She hardly sits still!

We have a ranch in the Arizona Territory, east of Tucson, and Tom is doing well. I haven't seen Emma since Molly Rose was born. We really should attempt to meet — so many years have been lost. Once the baby is born, Tom said he might be able to bring me to Texas to see you.

I would like to ask a favor. I have a very dear friend named Tess Carlisle who is looking for Cale Walker. Do you remember Cale? Tess thinks he might have information regarding the whereabouts of her father. It's a long story, but I was hoping you could ask Mr. or Mrs. Ryan if they might know how to get in touch with him.

Please write at your earliest convenience. I look forward to seeing you as soon as possible. With love and fondness, Your Sister Mary

Molly wiped at the tears that appeared to be never-ending on this day. Mary was well and happy. For a desperate moment, Molly wished she could see her sister now, at this very instant, to hug her and forget the last ten years, to remember the brief childhood they'd shared, to remember the good times.

Mary had named her daughter Molly. It warmed her heart and left her speechless. Hopefully, one day soon, she'd be able to meet her namesake.

Mary's casual mention of Cale made her realize, however, that she would have the distasteful task of telling her sister about their mother's betrayal. How would Mary take the news that Cale was Molly's half-brother?

Susanna peeked into the room. "Is it a good letter?"

Molly nodded, tears spilling down her cheeks. "She's due to have her baby any time, but she wants to come visit afterwards. I feel a little guilty getting married today without either of my sisters present."

"Would you like to postpone until we can get them here?"

Molly shook her head. "Who knows how long that could take. By then, Matt and I would probably have three children."

"And I'd be a happy grandmama." Susanna entered the room wearing a beautiful white and blue dress. "Everything's set. Are you ready?"

"Yes." Molly stood, trying to quiet the fluttering of her stomach. Putting the letter safely on Matt's dresser, she walked out of the room and toward her future.

* * *

Molly waited in the front entryway for Matt's father to escort her outside. The ceremony was to be underneath a beautiful mid-summer day. Fiddling with the lace on her dress in an attempt to calm her nerves, she heard the door open and looked up.

Davis Walker's large frame filled the doorway. Stunned, Molly froze.

"May I speak with you?" Davis asked, his hand hesitating on the doorknob.

Molly gave a curt nod.

Entering, he favored his right side. He shut the door, then faced her.

"Are you on the mend from your wound?" Molly asked, finally recovered from the initial shock at seeing him.

"Yes." Davis' eyes watched her with a haunted expression. "I know I deserved worse. I didn't know if you'd see me, but I couldn't stay away, not today. I suppose it's too much to ask your forgiveness now, but I hoped that maybe…well, I'd like to get to know you. Be a part of your life, if you'll let me."

Molly heard the sadness in his voice. This man was her father. For a short time, or maybe a long time, her mama had cared for him, in some way.

Molly knew she couldn't turn her back on him, but she also didn't know how much she could give him. He had become the enemy in her mind. While she no longer felt such a strong animosity toward him, she wasn't sure she could open her arms and forget everything that had occurred.

"I'm not certain," she said. "We can try, but I'll be honest with you — it'll take time for me to get past all of it."

Davis nodded. "I understand. I won't pressure you."

It startled Molly to see tears in his eyes.

"You look beautiful today," he said, his voice catching. "You look like your mother."

"I wish she were here."

"So do I."

Chapter Thirty-Three

In the late afternoon sunlight of a brilliant Texas day, Molly became Matt's wife in a simple ceremony that was over all too soon. Hiding her trembling hands beneath a bouquet of red and yellow wildflowers, she gazed into Matt's blue-green eyes as he watched her intently throughout the exchange of vows. He had never appeared more handsome, dressed as he was in a black jacket, vest and trousers, a crisp white shirt and black tie.

Logan—almost as striking as Matt in similar attire—and Rosita were the witnesses, the Mexican woman whooping for joy when Molly asked her several days ago.

"*Sí*, I witness you," she had answered. "I wait a long time to see a Ryan boy get a good woman. *Señor* Matt, he get the best."

Molly sincerely hoped so. She would hate to disappoint him.

About forty people attended the ceremony, neighbors and ranch hands, most unknown to Molly but all interested in the woman who had caught Matthew Ryan. Apparently, she was known not only as the girl who had risen from the dead, but from the shadows of the mighty Comanche as well. No one seemed to harbor the deep-rooted prejudice practiced by Mrs. McAllister, who was conspicuously absent.

Instead, Molly learned she had a bit of a reputation, for tales of her childhood were told with much enthusiasm. Matt also had high regard of his own across Texas, or so many of them told her. A tough army scout, a shrewd Indian negotiator, and a Texas Ranger who never hesitated to put his life on the line for his men or the Texans he was bound to protect.

But Molly knew such a life came with a price. She had seen the damage inflicted by Cerillo to Matt's leg. Only once did he speak of it to her, briefly describing how the man had broken it repeatedly with an iron rod.

Molly sensed what Matt didn't say — that the attack had been brutal and he'd barely survived. She knew he would never admit that his imprisonment and torture still affected him, but some things could never be erased from a person's mind.

But new memories could replace old ones, and Molly hoped she could fill Matt's life with enough happiness to put much of the last ten years to rest, for both of them.

* * *

In the aftermath of the ceremony, the crowd of people offering congratulations separated Matt from Molly, but his height allowed him to continue watching her.

She'd removed the flowers from her hair, and the early evening breeze blew the dark, unbound mass gently away from her face. Smiling, she greeted each person who spoke to her, listening closely to whatever they said.

The sight of her amazed him.

As a child, she'd been both endearing and exasperating at once, arousing in him a protectiveness he'd never felt for anyone. As a woman, she captivated him on so many levels he was unsure he would ever be able to completely explain the spell of Molly Hart in his life. One thing he knew for certain, though — he couldn't imagine it without her.

Moved by emotions that always caught him by surprise when it came to Molly — when it came to *his wife*, he amended, a thought both strange and exciting — he loosened his black tie.

"Already feeling tied down?" Nathan asked, brandishing a bottle of whiskey. He handed Matt a glass filled with the amber liquid. Cale and Logan appeared from the throng of guests, shot glasses in hand also.

Matt laughed at Nathan's question. "Someday you'll go willingly, too. I look forward to meeting the woman who brings you to your knees."

"Molly brought you to your knees?" Nathan asked. "Sounds interesting."

"We must be desperate if we're at all compelled to dig into my brother's love life," Logan said.

"There isn't much to pick from in these parts," Nathan remarked.

"There never was," Cale cut in. "Now, if you want to discuss quilting next, I might be forced to make a scene. Don't tell me your wife has already pestered you into not drinking anymore?"

Matt grinned at his new brother-in-law. The four men saluted each other briefly, then consumed the contents of their glasses in one swallow. Nathan refilled them.

"Here's to a long life with Molly," Cale said. "She's a keeper, but if she ain't, make no mistake. You'll answer to me."

Matt accepted Cale's threat in the spirit it was given.

"Here's to a quiet life as a rancher," Nathan said.

They downed another shot.

"Here's to you and Molly having a whole passel of babies to make your life anything but quiet," Logan said.

"You'll get yours," Matt replied.

"Maybe, but you're gettin' it first." Logan grinned. "I knew when you tried to marry her off, you were in piles of it too deep to get out of."

They laughed, finishing the liquor in their glasses. But that was it for Matt, for he planned to be wide-eyed and bushy-tailed for his wedding night. Molly appeared, her face glowing as she smiled up at him. He settled his arm around her waist.

He drank in the swell of her breasts, outlined by the lacy fringe of her dress. She was enticing without ever meaning to be, and he began to contemplate getting her alone soon. But then he remembered the other men, and Molly's dress was suddenly too revealing for his peace of mind.

"You look cold," Matt said. "Why don't you take my jacket?"

"I'm all right." Molly looked somewhat confused by the offer.

Nathan laughed, and Logan swore under his breath.

"She married you," his brother said. "Ain't that enough?"

Matt glared at his brother. "Yeah, but pickin's are slim around here, so y'all can go get your own."

"Cale," Molly said, "I wanted to talk to you before you left. I received a letter from my sister Mary today. She said a woman named Tess Carlisle is looking for you. Mary hoped you could get in touch with her."

"Carlisle...," Cale muttered to himself.

"Do you know her?" Nathan asked.

"No," Cale said, "but I know the name. Did Mary say why she's looking for me?"

"She's searching for her father and thought you could help."

"I'll be damned," Cale said. "She must be Hank's girl."

"Hank Carlisle?" Nathan asked. "The name sounds familiar."

"J. Howard Carlisle."

"The infamous bounty hunter?"

"Yeah. I rode with him years ago, but I haven't been in touch with him in a while. I doubt I'd be much help in locating him."

"Mary's living somewhere near Tucson, in the event you'd like to help this woman out," Molly said.

"I'll look into it," Cale said thoughtfully. "I owe Hank, several times over. And his daughter couldn't be much older than you."

"Meaning?" she asked.

"A young woman chasing after a bounty hunter like Hank could likely end up in some dangerous situations."

"You don't even know this woman," Molly said matter-of-factly. "Maybe she's tougher than you think."

"You're right. If I'm lucky, maybe she'll be like you." Then, he added, "Or maybe that wouldn't be so lucky."

Molly laughed. "I hope she proves to be a thorn in your side."

"Spoken like a true Walker." Cale smiled at Matt's annoyed expression as he put an arm around her. "C'mon." Guiding her from Matt's possessive embrace, he added, "It's time to break the news to T.J. and Joey about their new sister."

* * *

Molly leaned against the corral fence and watched Winter prancing around. In the near darkness, two things stood out—the horse's beautiful hide and her own wedding gown. She would have climbed up to have a better look, but didn't want to ruin her dress.

"She's all yours," Nathan said.

"You're not serious." Molly stared in awe that Nathan would ever part with such a magnificent animal.

"Yeah, you're not serious." Matt stood beside her, an arm hitched on the fence.

Nathan laughed. "You can rest easy. I've been working with her these past few weeks. I think Molly can handle her now."

"I could handle her before," Molly murmured.

"I heard that." Matt's breath was hot on her neck as he leaned over her. She shivered from his nearness. The noise and chatter of the party could still be heard from inside the house, but soon it would be over, and then she and Matt would have their wedding night. Her stomach fluttered with anticipation.

Logan and Susanna approached from the house. "There you are," Susanna said, her tone immediately catching Molly's attention.

"What's wrong?" Molly asked.

"We just received word that Lester Williams is at Fort Sumner and he's very ill."

"How bad?" Matt asked.

"It sounds bad enough," Logan answered. "I'm gonna ride out at first light."

"You want me to come?"

"Nah. Cale's gonna keep me company."

"What about Claire?" Molly asked. "Is she sick, too?"

"We're not certain," Susanna said. "She's not mentioned in the telegram."

"I'll try to find her," Logan said.

Molly nodded, concerned about the welfare of her friend.

"There's more," Susanna said, clearly reluctant.

Molly waited. Perhaps it had been too much to hope that her wedding day would go off without a mishap.

"I just found this letter." Susanna indicated the parchment in her hand. "It was buried under paperwork on Jonathan's desk. It's from your Aunt Catherine, dated two weeks ago. I opened it since it was addressed to me, but I think it's really meant more for you."

"Is it bad news?" Molly asked.

"Yes, and no. Your aunt is thrilled you're alive and hopes to see you soon, but apparently Emma ran off before receiving my letter."

"She ran away?"

"It seems she planned on coming to Texas anyway, before she knew you were alive. She left a note for your aunt, but with an odd side-trip along the way. She decided to visit a large canyon in the Arizona Territory, but your aunt is concerned because Emma asked there be no mention of her whereabouts to anyone. Catherine says some men came looking for Emma shortly after she left. She didn't tell them anything, but now she feels Emma may be in trouble and she's unsure what to do."

"We should go and find her," Molly said. "Do any of you know where this canyon is?"

"I do," Nathan replied. "It's called Grand Canyon. I've been there although not down inside — it's larger than anything you could ever imagine." A look of disbelief crossed his face. "Quite amazing, really. She probably just wanted to see it for herself. Maybe I can track her down on my way to California."

"You're certain?"

"Consider it a wedding present," he said.

"You were about to give me Winter as a gift," she reminded him. "I think your offer is too generous. I can go and look for her."

"No," Matt and Nathan said at the same time, although Nathan's denial didn't have as much heat as her husband's.

"Send word if you need backup," Matt said over her shoulder.

Nathan nodded.

Molly put a hand on her hip, knowing this was probably the best solution but she worried nonetheless. "And if you do need help," she glanced back at Matt, "then we'll both come."

"Would you happen to have a picture of Emma?" Nathan asked Matt's mother.

"Yes, I might. Let's go back to the house and have a look."

They all moved past the many guests still drinking, eating and socializing on the porch and in the parlor, then entered Jonathan's study.

Susanna retrieved a box from a wall shelf and rummaged through the many letters until she found what she searched for—a small black and white photograph of a young woman. "Catherine sent this to me a few years back. I believe Emma was about sixteen at the time."

Nathan took the picture, and Molly peeked around his broad shoulders to have a glimpse at the sister she hadn't seen for ten years. The girl looking back wasn't smiling, but she definitely had a glint in her eye, a twinkle that leapt from the photograph. Dark hair framed her face with curls, and her eyes stared straight into the camera with a forthrightness and assurance that was at odds with her youthful appearance.

"She looks almost the same as when she was a child," Molly said. "She's very lovely."

Nathan stared at the picture a moment longer. "Yes, she's very lovely."

Before Molly could ask what was wrong, he placed the picture in a pocket inside his dark jacket.

"I'll head out in the morning with you and Cale," he said to Logan, who nodded.

"Thank you," Molly said to him. "This means a lot to me."

"Just take good care of Matt. I'm glad I won't have to rescue him anymore."

"I will," she said. "And I'll take care of Winter until you return, but then you can have her back." She shook her head when he began to protest.

"You might as well stop now," Matt said to Nathan, placing a hand on her shoulder. "You can always tell Emma that Molly was prepared to trade her for a horse."

"I don't know," Nathan considered. "Winter's a damn fine animal."

Looking from Matt's straight face to Nathan's serious expression, Molly became irritated until she realized they teased her.

"Well, you're right," she replied. "Winter is a fine horse. Maybe I should have you retrieve both of my sisters in exchange."

"I call a truce," Nathan said, throwing his hands up in defeat. "I can't spend all my days tracking down wayward women."

"Sounds better than chasing outlaws," Logan said. "Less likely to get you killed."

Susanna grimaced. "All right, enough of this talk. You boys are going to keep me tossing and turning all night with worry." She grabbed Logan's hand. "Promise me you'll be careful. Bring Lester home, and make sure Claire is well." Then, she settled on Nathan. "With luck on your side, you'll find Emma quickly. Be...considerate when you tell her about Molly."

"Yes, ma'am," Nathan agreed. "But maybe I shouldn't be breaking that news to her."

"No, tell her." Molly looked into Nathan's brown-eyed gaze. He was a man much like Matt— honest, reliable, and caring—although his exterior was more hardness and grit, traits carefully honed in a land that demanded nothing less of a person. She hoped that someday love might blow through his heart. "And tell her I've missed her."

Nathan nodded. "I will."

"We'd best return to our guests," Susanna commanded. "This wedding day is still far from over."

But Molly hoped she and Matt wouldn't have to entertain for much longer.

Chapter Thirty-Four

In the darkness, Matt rode away from his folks' ranch house with Molly snug in his arms. It was the first step in their future together.

"Look at all the stars." She craned her head back. "Where are we going?"

"It's a surprise." He kissed her neck. She smelled of sweet wildflowers, desert wind, and infinite possibilities.

After a short ride, he brought them to the abandoned building his family had occupied years ago, the same one he'd brought Molly to after she learned Davis was her father. It was here he realized that he'd been fighting a losing battle. He wanted Molly, needed her, and he'd been a fool to keep railing against it.

They dismounted. "Stay here," he said. He went inside to light an oil lamp, then came back to retrieve his wife. Just before entering, he scooped her into his arms and carried her into their new home.

"Is this where you've been all those days when you disappeared?" she asked as he set her down.

He nodded, glancing at the fruits of his labor. Windows had been installed and curtains hung. A large wooden bed had been brought in from Dallas and adorned with a quilt made by his mother as a wedding gift. He'd cleaned the cast-iron stove,

300

added a table and chairs, hung shelves and a cupboard, and stocked it with food, plates, cups, and utensils.

"It's small," he said quickly, "but it's private. And I promise to build you a big ol' house soon. We'll need more room when the children arrive."

Molly faced him. "I love it. This is more than I ever thought I'd have. Thank you."

He smiled at her, knowing he was a lucky man. Molly still wore her wedding dress. Dark curls hugged her neck and led to curves that called to him on more than just a physical level. She looked feminine and vulnerable, and he knew Molly Hart had lived in his heart from the beginning of time, or at least the beginning of his time. His life was clear and focused now, his path obvious. As a wren leaves a path of markers to its home, so was there such a path for him. And at the end was Molly.

* * *

Moved by all the effort Matt had gone to for her, Molly could hardly believe she finally had a real home.

"I have something for you." He reached into his pocket and carefully pulled out a white cloth then opened it.

"You kept them?" she asked in surprise when she saw the contents.

He handed her the golden cross still hanging on the same chain that had carried it around her neck ten years ago. He also gave her an old, tattered yellow ribbon, the one she had worn the night she disappeared.

"I've kept them with me every day since I lost you. But now, I don't need them anymore, because I have you instead."

Reaching into his trouser pocket, he pulled one last thing out to give her — a silver badge with a star at the center and the words TEXAS RANGERS in the surrounding circle. "You can have this, too. I'll not be needing it anymore."

She began to cry but he kissed away her tears, stripping away the barriers of the past between them while stripping away their clothing. They came together, blazing as hot as the Texas sun, loving each other with tenderness, with need, and finally with desperation.

Molly felt at peace as she lay in Matt's arms, as the darkness surrounded them. Silence was no longer an enemy and her unyielding journey had finally come to an end. She'd been lost, but Matt found her.

At dawn, Molly left her husband sleeping soundly in their new bed. She lingered over his slumbering form, his nakedness barely covered by the thin sheet. They hadn't rested much, instead feeding their unending hunger for one another until sleep could no longer be ignored.

She noticed that her clothes and personal items had been brought to their new home, and Matt's thoughtfulness filled her heart once again. She quickly threw on a chemise and her boots.

She spied the rusty metal box that had been her survival kit. Opening it, she removed the well-worn slingshot from her childhood, the Wren's rawhide strap cracked and broken. Then, she gathered the gold cross, the yellow ribbon, and the Ranger badge from the table and headed outside as a light blue haze began to fill the sky.

Tying the ribbon at the base of the slingshot, she positioned it in a resting place within the trunk of the cottonwood tree that protected the house. Then, she hung the necklace from it, the cross dangling back and forth before it settled into position. Finally, she placed Matt's badge at the base of the slingshot. A sliver of sunlight shot across the land and the metal shone brilliantly. Molly squinted against the brightness.

She remembered the child she had been — wild and spirited, bound to the land in ways even she hadn't understood. She imagined Molly Hart would forever run across the prairies, slipping through gullies, catching snakes, and collecting rocks for the Wren.

Deliberately, slowly, she turned away and walked into the dawning of a new day, a new future as Molly Ryan.

Matt appeared behind her, shirtless and sleepy, looking untamed and dangerous, his own rugged strength drawn from the same land. He wrapped his arms around her and they stood strong against a new wind blowing.

As one, they welcomed the sunrise.

THE END

I'm so pleased you chose to read *The Wren*, and it's my sincere hope that you enjoyed the story. I would appreciate if you'd consider posting a review. This can help an author tremendously in obtaining a readership. My many thanks. ~ Kristy

Bonus Scene

December 24th, 1877

Matt shifted the two gifts to one hand as he opened the door to the bedroom he and Molly shared. He'd brought her to his folks' house for the holidays so she could be closer to her family as well as his ma, since her growing belly did little for his peace of mind. While the impending birth of their child filled him with joy and pride, he also worried like a mother hen. His days as a Texas Ranger seemed tame by comparison to this next stage of life.

Molly sat on the bed, her back against a pile of pillows. Balancing a plate atop her ballooning stomach, she spooned a large bite of food into her mouth.

"Is that Rosita's caramel cake?" he asked. "I thought it was all gone." The Ryan's cook had baked her delicious concoction for the large family gathering this evening. It was based on a recipe his ma had long used, however Matt was certain Rosita had added a few peppers to spice it up.

Molly nodded, unable to speak around the sweet dessert. Her auburn hair, having finally grown longer, tumbled out of the bun from earlier and she still wore the emerald gown his ma had given her as a gift a few days prior.

He approached the bed, sat beside her, and reached for a morsel of cake. Molly shifted the plate away from him.

He laughed. "I can't have any?"

She glared at him. "It's the last piece. And I'm eating for two."

Matt knew not to come between his wife and food. He was glad she could keep something down at long last, having recently recovered her appetite after a long bout of morning sickness. But now that her hunger had returned, it was like the force of a passel of nursing piglets.

"I wanted to give you these tonight." He placed the boxes beside her.

She beamed and quickly consumed the remainder of the cake, then set the dish aside. She opened the first gift and went still.

"Where did you get this?" she whispered.

The portrait featured Molly with her mama, papa, and sisters, Mary and Emma. It was likely taken around 1866 since Molly looked to be about eight years old. While everyone stared straight ahead with a stony countenance, young Molly had a mischievous smirk on her cherubic face. Matt smiled every time he looked at it. This was the Molly he remembered — wild, tenacious, and curious. She'd crawled into his heart, becoming a part of his blood and bones, the very spirit that breathed life into him.

He gave silent thanks that she was in his life, as he had every day since he'd found her again.

"My ma had it," he said. "After your folks were killed, and your sisters were sent away, she went through the Hart homestead and collected whatever mementos she could find. I had a new frame sent from Dallas. I thought you might like to have it."

Molly's eyes welled with tears. Matt reached out to snag a crumb from her cheek. She kissed him, tasting of Rosita's cake, both sweet and spicy.

"We can put it on the mantle of the Rocking Wren when the house is complete," she said against his lips, referring to the ranch he was building just for her. She resumed staring at her gift. "I can't wait to show Mary and Emma tomorrow."

Matt knew this was a special Christmas for Molly. After having lived with the Comanche for years, she hadn't celebrated the holiday since she was a little girl. And now, both of her sisters were with her. Emma had returned weeks ago and promptly married Nathan Blackmore; Mary had arrived a month ago with her husband and three children, having traveled from the Arizona Territory with Cale Walker—Molly's new-found half-brother—and his wife, Tess. Matt's folks had a full house at the moment, including his brother Logan, his wife Claire and her younger brother Jimmy.

He handed Molly the second gift. She swiftly discarded the paper and retrieved the item inside the box. Once again, she froze. Delight quickly transformed her face as she clasped the brand new slingshot, admiring the smooth design. Raising an eyebrow, she asked, "Am I allowed to use it in the house?"

"No."

She pulled on the rubber sling. "I'll call it 'Wren the Second'." Watching him with a glittering gaze, she smiled. "These are very thoughtful gifts, Matt." Molly took his hand and brought it to her belly. He felt the babe move, and he marveled at the good fortune in his life since encountering, many months ago, a woman he'd thought long dead.

"I have a gift for *you*," she added. "And I know what you're thinking, but that will come later, once the cake settles." She gave him a sly look as a blush spilled onto her cheeks and, unable to resist the love of his life, he nuzzled her neck.

Pushing back, she admonished him with a mock grimace. "I have something else to give you." She brought his hand back to her taut belly. "Emma told me we're to have a son."

Molly's younger sister had a knack for the *knowing* of things. Matt never put much stock in such nonsense, but when Nathan had told him the wild tale of his adventure with Emma in the Grand Canyon, Matt found it difficult to discount Emma's abilities.

A son.

He lowered his head and gently kissed the boy through the fabric of Molly's gown.

Matt had everything he wanted.

"If Rosita makes more cake tomorrow," he murmured, "I'll swipe it just for you."

"Promise?"

He sat up and gathered her into his arms. "I promise."

About The Author

As a child, Kristy McCaffrey frequently narrated to herself. It soon became apparent that she had an affinity for this writing thing. Raised on a steady diet of sci-fi/fantasy and tales of King Arthur, she transferred this love of mythic storytelling to penning western romances once she decided, at long last, to pay attention to her natural inclinations. Educated as an engineer, she swiftly gave that up to be a stay-at-home mom and aspiring author. She and her husband live in the Arizona desert, where their four children are in varying stages of flying the nest. A great love of travel frequently ends up on her blog, along with attempts at humor. This is often at the expense of her kids, which has led them to proclaim, "We will no longer read your blog, Mom." They also refuse to follow her on Twitter. Kristy believes life should be lived with curiosity, compassion, and gratitude, and one should never be far from the enthusiasm of a dog. She also likes sleeping-in, eating Mexican food, and doing yoga at home in her pajamas.

Connect with Kristy
Website – kristymccaffrey.com
Newsletter
    kristymccaffrey.com/Newsletter.html
Blog – *Pathways* – kristymccaffrey.blogspot.com
Facebook
    Facebook.com/AuthorKristyMcCaffrey/
Twitter – Twitter.com/McCaffreyKristy/
Pinterest – Pinterest.com/kristymccaffrey/

Amazon Author Page – Amazon.com/Kristy-McCaffrey/e/B004NXSCNC/

If you'd love to connect with readers and authors in the western historical romance genre, please consider joining the Pioneer Hearts Facebook Group – Facebook.com/groups/pioneerhearts/. Lively discussions, author interactions, and members-only giveaways are guaranteed.

The Dove
Wings of the West: Book Two

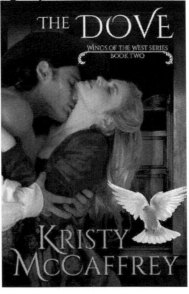

Disappointment hits ex-deputy Logan Ryan hard when he finds Claire Waters in the midst of a bustling Santa Fe Trail town. The woman he remembers is gone—in her place is a working girl with enticing curves and a load of trouble. As a web of deceit entangles them with men both desperate and dangerous, Logan tries to protect Claire, unaware his own past poses the greatest threat.

Plagued by shame all her life, Claire is stunned when Logan catches her on the doorstep of The White Dove Saloon dressed as a prostitute. She lets him believe the worst, but with her mama missing and the fancy girls deserting the place, she's hard-pressed to refuse his offer of help. As she embarks on a journey that will unravel the fabric of her life, one thing becomes clear — opening her heart may be the most dangerous proposition of all.

The Sparrow
Wings of the West: Book Three

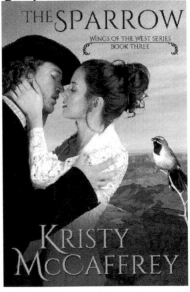

In 1877, Emma Hart comes to Grand Canyon — a wild, rugged, and, until recently, undiscovered area. Plagued by visions and gifted with a second sight, she searches for answers about the tragedy of her past, the betrayal of her present, and an elusive future that echoes through her very soul. Joined by her power animal Sparrow, she ventures into the depths of Hopi folklore, forced to confront an evil that has lived through the ages.

Texas Ranger Nathan Blackmore tracks Emma Hart to the Colorado River, stunned by her determination to ride a wooden dory along its course. But in a place where the ripples of time run deep, he'll be faced with a choice. He must accept the unseen realm, *the world beside this world*, that he turned away from years ago, or risk losing the woman he has come to love more than life itself.

The Blackbird
Wings of the West: Book Four

Bounty hunter Cale Walker arrives in Tucson to search for J. Howard "Hank" Carlisle at the request of his daughter, Tess. Hank mentored Cale before a falling out divided them and a mountain lion attack left Cale nearly dead. Rescued by a band of Nednai Apache, his wounds were considered a powerful omen and he was taught the ways of a *di-yin*, or a medicine man. To locate Hank, Cale must enter the Dragoon Mountains, straddling two worlds that no longer fit. But he has an even bigger problem — finding a way into the heart of a young woman determined to live life as a bystander.

For two years, Tess Carlisle has tried to heal the mental and physical wounds of a deadly assault by one of her *papá's* men. Continuing the traditions of her Mexican heritage, she has honed her skills as a *cuentista*, a storyteller and a Keeper of the Old Ways. But with no contact from her father since the attack, she fears the worst. Tess knows that to reenter Hank Carlisle's world is a dangerous endeavor, and her only hope is Cale Walker, a man unlike any she has ever known. Determined to make a journey that could lead straight into the path of her attacker, she hardens her resolve along with her heart. But Cale makes her yearn for something she vowed she never would—love.

The Bluebird
Wings of the West: Book Five

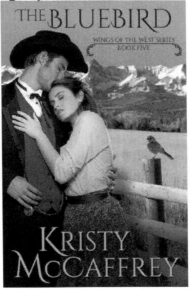

Molly Rose Simms departs the Arizona Territory, eager for adventure, and travels to Colorado to visit her brother. Robert left two years ago to make his fortune in the booming silver town of Creede, and now Molly Rose hopes to convince him to accompany her to San Francisco, New York City, or even Europe. But Robert is nowhere to be found. All Molly Rose finds is his partner, a mysterious man known as The Jackal.

Jake McKenna has traveled the bustling streets of Istanbul, exotic ports in China, and the deserts of Morocco. His restless desire to explore has been the only constant in his life. When his search for the elusive and mythical Bluebird mining claim lands him a new partner, he must decide how far he'll go to protect the stunning young woman who's clearly in over her head. A home and hearth has never been on The Jackal's agenda, but Molly Rose Simms is about to change his world in every conceivable way.

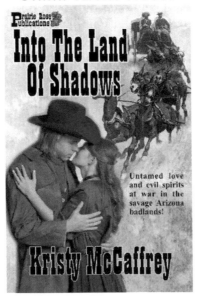

Kate Kinsella has no choice but to go after Charley Barstow and talk some sense into him. After all, he's skipped town, leaving a string of broken hearts and his pregnant fiancée, Agnes McPherson. But Kate didn't count on being kidnapped by a band of criminals along the way.

Ethan Barstow is hot on his younger brother's trail, too. He rescues Kate, believing her to be Charley's fiancée, and suggests they try to find him together. Kate's reluctance has him baffled.

All hell breaks loose when they discover Charley in search of a copper mine—not wishing to be found by anyone; certainly not Kate! But, then, Kate was always trouble — and now she's brought it to his doorstep, with tales of a pregnant fiancée and his brother Ethan, who he hasn't seen in five years.

Can Ethan and Kate ever find their own love and happiness with one another through the dark deception and hurt? Or will they both return INTO THE LAND OF SHADOWS...